THE
JILTED
COUNTESS

ALSO BY LORETTA ELLSWORTH

The French Winemaker's Daughter

Tangle-Knot

Stars over Clear Lake

Unforgettable

In a Heartbeat

In Search of Mockingbird

The Shrouding Woman

THE
JILTED
COUNTESS

A Novel

❧❧

LORETTA ELLSWORTH

HARPER ● PERENNIAL

NEW YORK ● LONDON ● TORONTO ● SYDNEY ● NEW DELHI ● AUCKLAND

FIRST EDITION

Library of Congress Cataloging-in-Publication Data

Names: Ellsworth, Loretta author
Title: The jilted countess : a novel / Loretta Ellsworth.
Description: First edition. | New York, NY : HarperPerennial, 2026.
Identifiers: LCCN 2025036289 | ISBN 9780063457140 trade paperback | ISBN 9780063473614 hardcover | ISBN 9780063457058 ebook
Subjects: LCSH: World War, 1939-1945—Fiction | LCGFT: Historical fiction | Romance fiction | Novels | Fiction
Classification: LCC PS3605.L476 J55 2026
LC record available at https://lccn.loc.gov/2025036289

ISBN 978-0-06-345714-0 (pbk.)
ISBN 978-0-06-347361-4 (simultaneous hardcover edition)

Printed in the United States of America

25 26 27 28 29 LBC 5 4 3 2 1

To Janet, who told me to write this story. So glad I listened to you!

THE
JILTED
COUNTESS

CHAPTER ONE

⚜

ST. PAUL, MINNESOTA, 1948

THE STARTLED SCREAM IN MY THROAT CAME OUT AS A squeak, causing the prim-faced woman seated across from me to arch her eyebrows. I looked away, my cheeks warm, not wanting to explain that I had accidentally fallen asleep. That sleep often gave way to remembering, and to nightmares prancing through my mind. At least I hadn't cried out loud this time.

The train made a wide turn, and I clutched my handbag to my chest and steadied my posture so I wouldn't slide across the slippery bench.

I had no control when I was sleeping; my mind slipped back of its own accord. I mustn't allow myself to doze on the train again. I mustn't remember.

"Are you all right, dear?" the woman asked.

"I am fine, thank you," I replied.

"Sorry I didn't introduce myself earlier. You fell asleep so quickly. My name is Thelma. I'm a schoolteacher traveling to North Dakota."

"North Dakota? I am not familiar with that place."

"It's a state west of Minnesota. Not nearly as progressive. I'll be in the small town of New Salem, where my sister and her husband live."

She made it sound like an untamed wilderness. She looked well fed, like all the Americans I had seen, instead of the half-starved, suffering victims I was used to, aristocrats and commoners alike. Her plaid button-up dress looked too tight.

"My name is Roza Mészáros," I offered.

"Where are you from, Roza?"

"I am Hungarian, but have been living in Vienna. I am traveling to St. Paul, Minnesota."

"And what brings you all the way to Minnesota?"

"I am coming to marry my fiancé. We met when he was stationed in Vienna."

Thelma clucked her tongue. "How lucky that you're pretty."

"Thank you," I replied cautiously, hearing anger in her voice. She was plain-looking, with a thick nose and slightly graying brownish hair tied back in a tight bun under a green pillbox hat. She had thin lips, the kind that rarely smiled.

The woman looked down at me through her glasses, her dull, gray eyes holding judgment. "You must feel grateful to our American soldiers. They defeated the Germans, and one soldier even took pity on you and offered to marry you."

I swallowed back a bitter reply. I would have snubbed this priggish woman only a few years ago as unfit to sit in the same compartment with me.

"Well, I must continue with my reading," Thelma said, her face filled with smug satisfaction, as though she'd just put me in my place. She opened a book and adjusted her cat's-eye glasses.

I picked at the fabric of my coat, wondering if its shabbiness or my Hungarian accent had put the woman off. I regretted telling her that I was coming to marry my soldier sweetheart. I took off my coat and set it on the seat. My navy-blue dress and matching hat made me feel less poor. I'd bought them in the fashionable Kärntner Strasse district before the war. To think that Mama would buy a new hat for every occasion, and at one time I had so many dresses that I didn't even wear them all.

That was before the Nazis, of course, before we lost everything, including the mansion near Budapest and the apartment in Vienna. Before Papa disappeared.

The long train ride was tiring. I pointed my foot out, then flexed my toes, feeling the tightness in my ankles and calves. Even though I'd given up dancing, the importance of maintaining strong, limber feet had been ingrained in me. Point and flex, point and flex . . .

The schoolteacher pushed the glasses up on her face and arched her eyebrows again. I ignored her. Instead, I turned my gaze to the brightness outside the window.

So, this was the Midwest that Joe had spoken so fondly of? The smooth, tedious landscape reminded me of Hungarian fried *lángo*s. The river bluffs of the Mississippi River had been a nice distraction, but after that it had been more of the same; prairie and farmland. It could never match my Hungarian birthplace. When I closed my eyes, I could still see the mist hanging over the forest near our country estate.

The Midwest seemed so plain in comparison. I had to admit the earth had a richness about it, though, a deep fertile color. And it looked so pristine, unlike the bombed landscape I'd left behind. In Chicago, where my plane had landed, I'd seen no streets full of rubble or starving refugees lining the roadways.

Even the sun shined brighter in America. There were patches of fertile land beneath the March melting snow, and fattened cows and pigs standing near brightly painted red barns. I started to open the window, but Thelma sniffed and held a handkerchief to her nose. "Please leave it closed. I don't want to get chilled."

I slumped back in my seat. I wanted to take in the fresh country air and imagine myself at Joe's farm, where I could finally forget the last few years. A place where there were no physical reminders of a war.

"You will love Minnesota," Joe had said as he embraced me that last morning in Vienna before he left.

I opened my handbag and took out the photo of us in front of the Belvedere Gardens and kissed it as I thought of our three-month whirlwind courtship set among the ruins of war-torn Vienna, where Joe was stationed. He looked beguiling in his uniform, the little cap perched on the front of his head, the adorable dimple in his left cheek.

Thelma cleared her throat; she'd seen me kiss the photo. But I did not care.

Our unusual love story could have been lifted from the books my French governess read to me. But hers often had unhappy endings, such as the legend of Princess Wanda of Krakow, who fell in love with a kind prince, but then a cruel knight demanded her hand in marriage. If she denied his request, his army would destroy the land and slay all her subjects. Rather than marry a man she didn't love, Wanda threw herself from a cliff into the Wisla River.

"The prince should have rescued her," I had complained.

"Princes don't rescue women, and love stories don't have happy endings. You must learn that so that you do not grow up to be a ninny," Mademoiselle had responded. "One day you may become a duchess or queen. Love will have nothing to do with it."

What had become of Mademoiselle Petit? Had she survived the war? I doubted that anyone who didn't believe in love could find happiness.

Thelma bit into an apple as she read a book and my stomach responded with a growl. Tucked in my handbag was the last half of a sandwich I had bought in Chicago. I took out the sandwich and nibbled on it.

As the train blew its whistle and slowed down, I could barely sit still. The St. Paul depot came into view, and I scanned the faces outside the window, a quiver of panic settling in my stomach.

I put the photo back into my handbag filled with Joe's letters, my visa, and some American money he'd sent. And something that bulged at the bottom.

Finally, the train came to a complete stop.

"Good luck with your marriage, Miss Mészáros," the schoolteacher said in a condescending voice, and now that I thought of it, the woman had the same sour smile as Mademoiselle Petit.

I turned to look at the prudish woman across from me. "I am *Countess* Mészáros."

I jumped up, a satisfied smile on my face, and followed the line of passengers departing the train, where I was met with brisk air and a cacophony of sounds: a train whistle blowing, people shouting, babies crying. I was jostled along the bustling platform. I searched through the billowing steam that filled the air for the dark, handsome face of my fiancé. I stared into the gaze of countless strangers, but Joe's familiar grin didn't appear.

Random pieces of conversation broke around me, some in accents hard to understand.

"Hello, darling," a man said, and I instinctively spun around to hug him, then pulled back awkwardly as he embraced a woman and hoisted a little boy up onto his shoulders. Another man in uniform presented a bouquet of flowers to a white-haired woman, and she hugged him tight. He was U.S. Army, just like Joe. "My son, you've come home," she sobbed.

I moved out of the way, bumping into a man who barely noticed me as he hurried through the crowd.

"Excuse," I repeated, as I tried to glimpse over heads and between bodies for a sign of my beloved, hoping he would be also be holding a bouquet of flowers as he'd promised. As the crowd slowly thinned, I gave up any pretense of that perfect meeting. My feet ached and my hat perched lopsided on my head. I no longer cared about the flowers. I only wanted to see Joe. The smile I'd plastered on my face had long vanished.

"All aboard!" People hurried onto the train while others claimed their luggage and left. The lingering smell of steam and oil, combined with cigar smoke, made me nauseous. I walked one end of the platform to the other, holding my stomach and swallowing back the anxiety that built with each step. When the porter brought out my trunk, I stood near it as though anchored to the spot. The platform was almost empty and still no sight of Joe. I walked circles around the luggage, looking in every direction. Had I somehow missed him?

"Excuse, what time is it?" I asked a porter.

"Three fifteen," he responded, then hurried off.

Forty minutes had passed.

The train whistle blew, announcing its departure, and I stood guard over my small trunk, my heart beating faster with each passing minute. White steam filled the platform as the large wheels turned, leaving me alone but for a few stragglers. Where was Joe?

I'd received his last letter three months ago, wishing me safe travel. I had written to tell him when I'd be arriving. Had my letter gotten lost? How would I contact him? I had no idea how to get to his farmhouse. His address was a post office box number in a small town that Joe said was an hour away.

I leaned against the trunk, my stomach reeling and my legs wobbly as I clutched the picture of Joe tightly, my knuckles white, my eyes now fixed on the wood beneath me to hide the tears that were streaming down my face.

Was my fairy tale doomed like the ones Mademoiselle Petit read to me? I was all alone, a solitary figure on the now empty platform.

CHAPTER TWO

AMA'S WARNING CAME BACK. WHEN I'D WRITTEN TO
tell her of my engagement, Mama had dismissed it. She'd
written:

> Soldiers make promises to women they meet. They never
> come true. You've always been a hopeless romantic. You
> need to return to your Hungarian home.

Poor Mama. She was raised for idle luxury. She missed her lavish gardens and sunlit rooms, the majestic ballroom and grand piano. Before the war she'd employed dozens of servants to tend the house and gardens and had rented out much of the ten thousand acres of farmland. Now Mama and my younger brother, János, were no better off than the servants.

The war had kept us apart; I hadn't been able to leave Vienna once the Germans invaded. But Hungary was not the same country now that the Russians were in control. Mama and János lived in a small apartment in Budapest, our home and land taken over, first by the Nazis, then by the Communists. I knew that dear Papa was dead, even if Mama refused to believe her husband was gone. Like the majority of Hungarian nobility, he was anti-Nazi, but Papa was not one to keep his opinion to himself, and he was arrested during the occupation, and disappeared.

What was there back in Hungary? The Communists were no better than the Nazis. I would never dance for the Communists.

And who would I marry there? Mama had been in an arranged marriage and would have attempted to arrange one for me if all the aristocrats weren't dead or hadn't fled the country. Mama couldn't understand. Joe was honest and compassionate, and I wanted to choose my own suitor. Mama didn't know what true love was like.

Now my head filled with doubts. Had Joe had an accident? Had he changed his mind? Was I at the wrong place? I had no way to contact him. And here I was, in a foreign country with little money left. What could I do?

I put a hand on my chest, barely able to breathe. I was shaking, overcome with the panicky feeling of being utterly helpless. Not even my ballet training could help me now, as I was so out of my realm.

Had I brought this on myself because I was, as Mama had put it, "a hopeless romantic"? A "ninny" who believed in fairy-tale endings? To be left here at the station would be a bitter pill to swallow.

"Are you look for Joe Harbeck?"

I turned, grateful to hear the sound of my beloved's name, even if it did come from the lips of a stranger. A man and a woman stood in front of me. They were both short and round. The woman wore a simple rayon dress with a plaid scarf covering her head. The man's ill-fitting wool suit and bowler hat were like those worn by peasants in Hungary.

"Yes, I am," I replied in my best English, feeling strength return to my legs. I touched a handkerchief to my eyes, trying to still my shaking hand.

"*Grófnő Mészáros*," he said and bowed.

"Countess Mészáros," his wife corrected him, using the English translation as she curtsied. "And prima ballerina."

"No." I quickly shook my head. "Those titles have long been abolished. Please call me Roza."

"We are Jakab and Mariska Katz," the short man said. "Mr. Harbeck arrange for you stay with us tonight. He come tomorrow."

"Why isn't Joe here?" He expected me to stay with strangers?

Mariska gave her husband a sideways glance. "We do not know. Perhaps he busy with work," she said.

"How long have you known Joe?"

"Not long. He come to our church, where is mostly Hungarian people, and asked for someone to meet you today because he is unable. We agreed to help."

I shook my head, trying to understand. My eyes grew misty once again. "I was expecting that Joe would meet me."

"And he will," Mariska said encouragingly. "After you have chance to rest and freshen up."

I didn't want to be a ninny. I'd waited this long. What was one more day? I couldn't stay here at the station. I tried not to look disappointed. "Thank you. You are kind to help. You're right. Joe must be terribly busy."

Mariska nodded. "We are delighted, Roza. You have only this one piece of luggage?"

"Yes. It is all I have."

"But you are an aristocrat."

"I prefer to travel light." How could I admit that I'd sold all my clothing on the black market to buy food and stay alive? I blinked back tears. ". . . But I am sure Joe will buy me new clothing in America."

Jakab took my luggage and led me through the cavernous depot. I looked up at the vaulted ceiling and high skylights, which were still blackened over from the war like blackout curtains. Benches were occupied by weary travelers, and long queues stood in front of ticket windows. I gaped at the food vendors, the same as I'd done in Chicago. The food looked plentiful and fresh. My heels clicked on the marble floor, and I noticed men with dark skin and red caps who shined shoes and carried luggage.

The aroma of pasta and garlic caught me off guard and made my stomach growl. There were still shortages in Vienna and all of Europe. And here was a fine Italian restaurant right in the depot! It was all so much to take in, this abundance of food and, yes, even laughter. How long had it been since I'd heard that?

"Is it like this in all of America?" I asked, gesturing toward the restaurant. "Food in every window?"

Mariska nodded. "If you can afford the prices."

"My fiancé can afford them," I said with confidence.

We left the depot and walked a long block in the bright sun, Jakab carrying the brown trunk. The paved streets were smooth and white, and so much wider than those in Europe. Jakab placed my trunk in the rear of a rusted-out car with fading blue paint. Mariska insisted on sitting in the back.

"This is not what you are used to. We are humble people," Jakab apologized.

"I am overwhelmed by your graciousness," I replied, surprised he owned a vehicle and was able to obtain gasoline rations. "As is Joe, I'm sure."

"How did you meet Mr. Harbeck?" Mariska asked.

"We met at a victory party that celebrated the four Allied forces in Vienna. Joe asked me to dance," I said, remembering the blue satin evening gown I'd worn, the only formal gown I hadn't sold on the black market. I'd sat with a British woman who worked for the Auxiliary Territorial Service. It was the first formal meal I'd eaten in years, with salmon, Wiener schnitzel, roasted potatoes, warm rolls, and pastries made from real sugar. I remembered every morsel of the meal, and when no one was looking I wrapped a pastry in my napkin and put it in my bag. That's when I caught a young American man watching me from across the room, his gaze subtle, as though he were trying hard not to stare. My face had warmed when our eyes met. Had he seen me put the pastry in my clutch?

"It sounds very romantic," Mariska said from the back seat as she wiped her sweaty face with a handkerchief.

"It was," I agreed. "Joe swept me off my feet."

He had a firm chin and an easy manner, and his American accent exuded a certain warmth. His olive-colored uniform was impeccably pressed and his trousers had sharp creases. A little hat was cocked to the front of his head. He was healthy looking, well fed.

"I want to apologize for staring at you all night," he said when he finally approached me. "I'm Lieutenant Joe Harbeck and I've never seen anyone so beautiful. I've been wondering if you're a famous actress."

"Actress? No. I am a ballerina," I replied, although I hadn't danced professionally since the Vienna State Opera had been accidentally bombed by the Americans in March 1945.

"Now I really feel like a knucklehead. I was going to ask you to dance and impress you with my two-step. Clearly, I'm outflanked."

His humility impressed me. I flashed him a warm smile. "Not at all, lieutenant. A man who has conquered the battlefield will easily master the waltz."

"I don't know about that," he said, "but I'll give it my best."

He took my hand and kissed it, then led me onto the floor, displaying a confidence I didn't expect. And even though he wasn't as proficient a dancer as Count Kinsky, his charming smile more than made up for it. We danced the entire night.

So caught up in my memories that I didn't notice the passing landscape, the gritty reality now hit me. I focused on the dirt road in front of us, lined with decrepit buildings occupied by poorly clad women sitting on rocking chairs while dirty-faced children hung on to them.

I pinched my mouth shut to keep from saying anything when

Jakab stopped in front of an older wood-framed two-story apartment building. It had balconies on both levels, which looked dangerously lopsided.

This wasn't at all how I planned my first night in Minnesota. I was supposed to see Joe, to stay with his relatives and get to know them as family before the wedding. He'd shown me pictures of the two-story white house with a wide porch that wrapped around the sides. It had a charm about it, and its size reminded me of the estate our family had lost. I felt safe in the thought of that abundance of land.

"My bedroom is there," he'd said, pointing to a window at the top. "You can see the brook and almost all three hundred acres from up there."

I had dreamed of hearty family meals around a rugged kitchen table, of walking through fields of tall corn, with the breeze cooling my brow and my feet burrowing into fertile grass.

But instead, I stood outside this decrepit building like an impoverished immigrant. It had been almost two years and Joe couldn't be here to meet me? Or anyone from his family?

I felt my eyes tear up again and shook my head to stop the flow. "How long have you lived in America?"

"We came before war," Jakab said, nodding at his wife as he got out to open her door. "I have Jewish ancestry. We feared for our son."

"You were wise," I said.

"No, we were fortunate," Mariska said. "Jakab have friends here. Joe said your father—" She stopped and put a hand over her mouth.

I willed my voice to remain strong. "Too much horror. But now it is time to move forward."

I glanced around, noting the shady oak trees that cast shadows across the sides of the building. As I had done so many times in the past, I forced myself to look for the good in this situation. True, it was run-down, but there was no rubble here, no trace of a war that was a constant reminder of all I'd lost. Soon I would be at my new American home, the sturdy farmhouse I would share with my new husband and his family, where we would have many children and a yard full of chickens, and tall trees like the ones I saw now.

This place, the Midwest, as Joe called it, would be the perfect place to forget the horrors of the war, to start anew.

CHAPTER THREE

⊱✽⊰

M ARISKA HAD MADE *FŐZELÉK* STEW; THE SMELL OF PA-
prika and onions wafted through the three-room apartment.
They introduced their son, Péter, a ten-year-old with dark, curly hair
who spoke English with barely a trace of accent, better than all of us.

"Tell me," I asked them, "how is life in America?"

Jakab held out a chair for me. They all waited for me to sit. In
Hungary, everyone's class was imprinted on their well-tailored suits
and manicured hands; their manners, etiquette, and speech. I barely
remembered it except for the reminder now.

"We are safe here. Life is good but different. Harder in some
respects. In Hungary, our path was set for us. We followed the ways
of our ancestors. Here, we must make our own way."

I remembered Papa lecturing me on the Russian aristocracy
who had been overthrown in the revolution of 1917; how the Russian proverb "An empty stomach has no ears" led to most of them
being killed or having to flee the country. The path of our ancestors
was now defunct. I worried about János and Mama. What would
become of them?

"What have you done these past years since the war?" Mariska
asked. "You no longer dance with the ballet?"

"No," I said, not admitting that I'd had to sell everything to
keep from starving. "I danced for three years before the Opera
House was bombed. I've been working at an orphanage for children
born during the occupation."

I didn't say more as Péter was present, that many of the children were the result of rapes by Soviet soldiers when they defeated the Nazis in Vienna.

My mouth watered at the sight of the food, but as I sat at the small table, I couldn't eat but a bite. All this food in front of me and my stomach clenched at the mere thought of putting anything in my mouth. I was too exhausted.

"Please excuse me," I begged, my eyelids heavy. "It has been a long day."

The Katzes insisted on giving me their bed for the night. The room contained a small bed with an iron headboard, flanked by a white dresser. The bathroom to the left of their apartment was shared by another family.

The room was as small as the one I'd shared with my roommate, Greta, during the war, but this room smelled of mothballs and sweat. I was too tired to be disgusted.

As I undressed, I thought of the four-poster bed I'd slept in as a child, of the thick embroidered quilt and matching tapestry in my expansive bedroom. Despite the temporary hardships of the last few years, I couldn't forget the finery I'd become accustomed to. I had been a dancer and knew princes and dukes by their first names. I had dined with Richard Strauss!

I remembered my first ball. I was just thirteen. My father thought I was too young, but Mama, who still resented Papa's decision to let me enter ballet school, had talked him into allowing it.

"She is as tall as me already. People need to see her as the daughter of Count Mészáros, not as some ballet dancer. In a few years she will be making her entrance into society."

I hadn't cared, as I had just learned I'd been accepted to the Vienna State Opera Ballet School. But I *had* cared about the dazzling green gown I'd worn, accompanied by an emerald necklace and matching earrings, my gloved hand on the arm of a nobleman dressed in white tie and tails.

The orchestra had played *The Blue Danube*, the polished floors sparkled beneath the chandeliers, and Mama's friends had gasped when they saw me and declared me the belle of the ball. It would be my only entrance into high society, as the war prevented my debutante ball.

Who was wearing my gown and jewels now? Some sow who bought it off the black market and who couldn't possibly look as good as I did in them. I instinctively rubbed the small ring on my finger that Joe had given me. It was useless to think of these things. My life had been stripped to the bare essentials, which now included this lumpy bed offered by kind strangers. The artifact in the false bottom of my handbag was worth many jewels, but it could also get me sent back to Hungary as a criminal.

I flinched and pushed the thought from my head. It was dangerous to own such an artifact. But wasn't everything dangerous that happened during the war? And hadn't our family lost enough? The Chopin score might one day buy freedom for my mother and brother.

The sound of clattering dishes in the kitchen brought back a memory of Vienna, where figures sifted through the gutters and rubble for usable junk to sell, with only the moonlight as their guide. They skittered among the debris like the rats who kept them company. There were more of them now, both rats and people.

I shivered. Thank God I was away from all that, although this room didn't seem much better. But it was clean, and this family had plenty to eat, even if Mama would consider it peasant food. I preferred another memory, one of clattering dishes, of eating lobster and Sacher torte while sipping champagne at Café Demel, where the crystal chandeliers sparkled above and where men wore white silk shirts. The memory was now as distant as the rats of Vienna.

As I climbed into bed, I flexed my toes again, my body's molded response from years of training. I thought of all I had given up.

What bothered me most was dancing; it had been my one true passion, and the war and Papa's death had taken it away. I no longer had the strength or the desire. But perhaps someday I would have a daughter who might take an interest in ballet. I fell asleep with the thought of my daughter, who would have Joe's dark eyes and my trim figure, and a future bright with possibility. I would name her Anna, after Mama.

CHAPTER FOUR

⌘

THE SUN WOKE ME THE NEXT MORNING, BLINDING ME AS IT hit my eyes through a slit in the curtains. I blocked the brightness with my hand, then smiled. Today I would see Joe. Finally!

I put on the navy-blue dress that accentuated my blue eyes and wore an heirloom diamond bracelet that had belonged to Nagymama and that I'd managed to keep during the war, although I'd been tempted many times since then to sell it. Grandmother had made me promise never to part with it.

"It was given to me by Count Zamoyski on my wedding day," she'd told me when I was eleven. "I give it to you with the promise that it will stay in our family for eternity."

Then Nagymama had put the bracelet on my small wrist and let me admire it before she put it away. She had died a year later, and I vowed never to part with this remembrance of the stately but tender woman.

"You must have been very tired. I have reheated food for you," Mariska said as she served hearty sausages and potatoes she had made. My stomach had recovered and I ambushed the food, barely touching the tepid coffee in front of me. Mariska's husband had already left for his job at a flour mill.

"Do you know what time Joe will arrive?"

Mariska looked away, studying the dish in the sink as though it held the answer. She still wore the scarf of a Hungarian villager. I couldn't help but think that, even though the pattern was colorful, it made her look common. Her thick sweater and long skirt didn't help either.

"I believe it later, perhaps in evening."

Another whole day of waiting! I felt the frustration build inside.

"I would think he would be more anxious to see me than his crops," I said.

"Tonight he be here," Mariska said.

I fidgeted with a leftover piece of sausage, feeling the gnaw of disappointment inside. And something more ominous. This wasn't like Joe. He'd never been late for a date. All the countless walks in the countryside, all the sites we'd visited together. He was always on time, always anxious to see me.

Those first few dates he'd held my hand as we walked, put his arm around me on the streetcar. He felt strong and secure. I'd been stubbornly going through the motions of life, just trying to survive, not letting myself give in to the fear. Now I had someone beside me, wanting to protect me. It was too much, and I almost broke down in tears.

"You know, most of the buildings here are older than the state I live in," he'd joked. "If you dropped a bomb on Minnesota, nine times out of ten you'd hit farmland."

"I am sure you eat well with all that farmland." Standing in ration lines all day had given me lots of time to think about food.

"You bet we do. My mom makes the best fried chicken and pot roast. And apple pie." He had a dreamy look in his eyes.

"When will you return home?"

"I'm supposed to go back in three months."

"Is there a special girl back home?"

He shook his head. "The only special girl I know is sitting right beside me."

I had shivered and squeezed his arm.

"I MUST BE GOING OUT TO WORK IN GARDEN," MARISKA SAID, interrupting my thoughts as she put on her coat. "You do not mind being alone?"

"No. I am fine."

I watched her leave and went to pack. As I looked around the small room with its simple furnishings I took in a deep breath and remembered the graciousness of my host. Things were different now. I was no longer an aristocrat with servants who catered to my every whim, or a ballerina with adoring fans. Mariska was my equal now, and she was an American, which I desperately wanted to become. How could I repay such kindness?

I changed into something more suitable for working in the dirt.

A small garden sat behind the apartment building, partitioned into segments for each occupant.

"This tiny plot is your garden?" I thought of our family's estate, of the large flower garden next to the sparkling pond, and beyond that the fruit and vegetable plots that I rarely entered.

"Yes. It is not much, but is good soil," Mariska said. "And is early spring, so we prepare ground for planting."

I had no gardening experience. Mariska seemed to know this because she showed me how to pull weeds; thick, dangly creatures that crowded the soil she was digging to plant cabbage and other early season plants like head lettuce and peppers. The tangled green mess made my hands itch and my back hurt from bending.

"Is this work that all farmer's wives are required to perform?" I asked. Mariska said it was warm for March, but my hands were cold.

"I do not know. I am certain you would not be expected to do such work," she said in an assuring voice.

I hoped not. Joe hadn't mentioned it.

This busyness kept me occupied. But I couldn't get the uneasiness out of my mind. Mariska revealed little despite my continued questioning. Surely she knew more than she was letting on. Joe hadn't even left a note! What possible reason could he have? Something was wrong. My thoughts grew more desperate until my hands shook.

I replayed our last day together over in my mind, how Joe had knelt down on the steps in front of the bombed-out shell that used to be St. Stephen's Church. He'd held out a ring with a small diamond on it, no doubt one he got from the black market.

"You know I love you, Roza, and I don't want to leave you behind. I can't offer you much and I know it's not the life you're used to. But it's beautiful country with good farmland and thousands of lakes. It's a simple life, but a rewarding one."

I had looked at the massive bell of St. Stephen's where it had crashed onto the cathedral floor. The whole city was in ruins. "This last year I spent more of my life in air-raid shelters than outside," I had said. "A simple life in the country is like heaven to me. Yes, I will marry you."

We'd celebrated at a bar that was full of American soldiers, where we had caviar sandwiches and cognac. Joe gave me money and cases of food. "I'll send money when I get back," he promised. "To tide you over until you come to the U.S."

We made love that night for the first and only time. Afterward, I worried Joe would forget me when he returned home, but he continued to send money and letters. Surely Joe loved me! So why was I here pulling weeds when I should be resting in his arms?

Joe had made me feel important. I had missed that since I was no longer dancing. My favorite role at the Vienna Opera House had been Giselle, who dies of a broken heart after finding out the man she loves is a nobleman in disguise and unable to be with her. It was the first time I was chosen to be a principal dancer. It was a difficult role, as Giselle dances herself to death, and I had to perform thirty-two fouettés. But the tumultuous applause afterward was like nothing I'd ever experienced; I remembered the curtain calls followed by standing ovations and bouquets thrown onto the stage. I'd never before felt so proud and important.

Joe had given that back to me. What would he say if he saw me kneeling on the ground bent over these plants?

Finally, I gave up and went inside to wash, scrubbing my nails hard to get the dirt out. I put my dress and bracelet back on and brushed my hair until it shone.

I couldn't eat. I could barely keep track of the endless chatter at the kitchen table, responding only when I had to. After dinner, Mariska and her husband and son left for an evening walk.

"To give you privacy," she said and squeezed my hands. I smiled, thankful we would have time alone together, but noticed that Mariska did not smile back. I searched her eyes, but she looked away.

Something was definitely wrong.

CHAPTER FIVE

I PACED BACK AND FORTH ACROSS THE SMALL APARTMENT, twisting my handkerchief until it looked like white twine. The lingering smell of Mariska's kolbasz sausage made my stomach lurch. The small trunk was packed, ready to make the journey to our new home. I pulled it into the front room, near the door.

All the while my mind raced. Was Joe having second thoughts? Was that why he hadn't met me at the station? If that was it, then perhaps seeing me again would assuage his doubts. I'd kiss him and then he'd remember how much he loved me, and it would erase the time apart.

When the knock on the door finally came, I ran to open it. Joe stood before me in a dark suit, his hat in his hand. His deep brown eyes and square chin made me catch my breath. He was as handsome as I remembered, more so.

"Joe!" I reached to embrace him, but he hugged me stiffly, then let his arms drop to his side.

I backed away, my joy replaced by panic. Where was the passionate man I'd known?

"May I come in?" Joe asked.

"Of course." Why was he asking permission?

"You're acting so shy," I said, thinking his stiffness was due to my long absence.

He closed the door and took a tentative step into the room. He still held his hat in both hands, and I noticed the hat quivering against his suit coat.

"How was your trip?" he asked.

"So formal, my fiancé! Have you forgotten how to embrace me?"

I put a hand on his arm and felt him stiffen again.

"Joe, what is wrong? Why did you not meet me at the train?"

"I didn't know how to tell you, Roza." His lips were tight, and he didn't look me in the eye.

"You can tell me anything, darling. It's me, the woman you made love to your last night in Vienna, after you asked for my hand in marriage." I reached out to stroke his hair. His hand caught my arm in midair. And that's when I saw it. The silver band on his finger.

"What is this?" My voice trembled.

He let go of my arm and reached into his pocket. He brought out a folded-up, faded letter. The handwriting was unfamiliar. "You remember the Dear John letter I got while I was overseas?"

"Yes. You said you no longer loved that woman. You said you hated her."

"I did . . . I mean I thought I did. I thought it was over between us. When I came back, she said she'd made a mistake. I told her I was engaged to someone else. To you. But it's been two years," he said softly. "That's such a long time, Roza."

Hearing him speak my name was like a punch in the gut. The last time we'd been together he'd whispered words of tenderness into my ear.

"But we have been writing. We have been planning our lives together. You sent money and letters." I wanted to open my trunk and get them out to show him all the letters I'd saved, ones that spoke of his love.

"I know. I wrote you another letter a month ago, but I guess that letter didn't reach you on time."

Another letter? I hadn't received any letters other than ones that spoke of romance and love.

"I'm sorry, Roza. We got married three months ago."

"You are married?" I asked, still not believing. "This must be a joke. You are teasing me, aren't you?"

"No joke, Roza. I'm really sorry."

Sorry?

It all made sense now. The way Mariska and Jakab looked at each other, the way they avoided any talk of Joe.

"Look, I didn't plan this. I meant to marry you. But I was going to marry her first. She was my childhood sweetheart. I only spent three months with you. And when I came back, over the last two years or so we just—"

"Enough!" I put my hand up. "I do not want to hear this. You do not have the courtesy to show up at the train station and you make me sick with worry. And now I am supposed to hear this wretched excuse?"

I willed myself not to break down in front of him, but already felt salty tears streaming down my face. "I had other suitors in Vienna. But we made a promise to each other. *I* made a promise to the man I love, and it was one I kept all this time. I have your ring!"

I took it off and held it out for him to see.

"I know. What can I say, Roza?" Joe took a step forward, but I backed away.

"American swine! You tricked me! You only wanted to get into my bed."

"It wasn't like that. You know I loved you."

"Love? You do not know what love is!"

He took out his wallet. "I'll pay for your travel home. I can't afford airfare, but you can take the train east and book passage on a ship in Boston."

I threw my arms in the air. "You think I would accept money from you now? Typical American, you think you can buy me off!"

"I didn't mean . . ."

I threw the ring at him. "*Gonosz gazember!*"

"I don't expect you to forgive me. But please understand."

"What is there to understand? Make me understand why I waited almost two years! Why I never cheated on you when I had opportunities, but you obviously did."

He looked down at the floor. "I can't."

"That is what you have to say after all this time? Leave now! I never want to see you again!" I struck him across the cheek.

He stood there, a hurt look in his eyes. I felt my blood rise. The audacity of that look! How dare he look that way after what he'd done! I pushed him. "I said leave!"

He turned. "I'm sor—"

I cut him off. "I do not want to listen to the words of a coward. No honorable man would do this."

He turned, his eyebrows narrowed as though my words against him were worse than his disgrace against me. Then he left. I slammed the door behind him and ran to the bedroom, where I collapsed on the bed in tears.

CHAPTER SIX

J OE'S WORDS REPLAYED IN MY HEAD. *SHE WAS MY CHILDHOOD sweetheart. I only spent three months with you.*

Had he only turned to me because he was heartbroken? I'd believed him when he said he no longer loved that woman. He'd barely talked about her and hadn't even mentioned her name.

I remembered the first time Joe said he loved *me*, as we sat on a bank near the snaking Danube, its emerald waters lapping against the shore below. I'd burst into tears.

"Roza, are you all right?" Joe had said.

I'd sniffed and stroked his cheek.

"I love you, too, Joe. It's just, I've felt so alone, and now I've met you and you're going to leave soon."

"It doesn't seem fair," he'd said. "I don't ever want to be apart from you."

I loved him so much! If I'd known then what would happen, that he would betray me now, I wished we'd never met. I tossed and turned, crying and muttering angry curses in Hungarian and English. When Mariska knocked on the door, I rejected her offer of food. How could I face her? She must have known the whole time.

I rolled over and moaned. I'd spent so much time dreaming of my wedding. It would be very American, but I would incorporate some Hungarian traditions, like the candlelight waltz, and perhaps a horse-drawn carriage. Those perfect images were now shattered. Both the wedding and the groom had vanished.

I was such a fool! Mama was right. She'd said nothing good

would come of this. I could hear Mademoiselle Petit's tinny voice in my head. *You're a ninny!*

What would become of me now?

AFTER THREE SLEEPLESS NIGHTS OF TEARS AND FEELING sorry for myself amid Mariska's constant prodding, of her leaving food at the door that I barely ate, of hearing the loud whispers between her and her husband, wondering what to do with me, I finally came out of the bedroom. I took a bath and tried to make myself look presentable. Mama had always said that it did no good to wear your emotions on your sleeves.

Then I took a breath and entered the kitchen and gratefully accepted a cup of tea from Mariska.

"Thank you," I murmured. It was as much as I could muster without breaking down.

Mariska sat across from me and put a hand on my arm. It was a strong, ruddy hand that came from hard work, but it had a soft quality that reminded me of Mama. Appearing stoic in the face of Joe's insult was so very hard. Tears stung my eyes. Mariska handed me a handkerchief.

I swallowed hard and accepted the gift, dabbing at the corners of my eyes.

"I don't know what to do," I said softly. "I cannot go back to Hungary. I have disgraced our family. And you know what it is like there now. One demon has been replaced by another. Mama said that there is strict rationing; she waits in line for hours for bread. And anyone speaking out is arrested. Communist leaders are keeping lists of people who fraternize with Americans. I could be sent to prison."

Mariska nodded and blinked back tears. "What about Vienna? You could return. Or somewhere else in Europe. You could dance again."

"No." I shook my head. "There is nothing for me in Europe but starvation. It will take many years to rebuild and the economy to stabilize once again. And I am not a dancer any longer. It has been too long. No company would want me."

"But you are a countess. That must mean something."

"Not anymore." I sniffed and my voice became sharp. "My GI visa will expire in just over two weeks. I will not have a choice but to return, and since my origin country is Hungary, I will be sent there. I want to stay in America. It is my dream."

"If only there was a way," Mariska said, patting my hand. "If my Péter was a man, he would be honored to have you for a wife."

"I wish Joe had felt the same." I couldn't help but let the tears fall again. "I did not think he would turn out to be so dishonorable."

When I'd regained control, Mariska set a piece of bread in front of me. "You are but skin and bones. You must eat and keep up your strength."

"I no longer care about food," I said, pushing it away. "But it is time I leave and give you back your bedroom. I have overstayed my welcome."

I stood to go pack.

"Do not go! You have nowhere to go. Both Jakab and I insist you stay."

I sat back down. "That is so kind of you both. I am sorry for all the hardship I have caused."

"Joe did not mean to dishonor you." Mariska pushed the bread back in front of me. "The horse has four legs and still stumbles," she said, quoting a Hungarian proverb. "And he did not see you for almost two years."

"And all that time I have thought of no one but him, of nothing but my future life as an American wife. And how did he repay me? He betrayed our love and married someone else."

"He send you money to come. It was not intention to betray you."

"And now I am supposed to forgive and forget?"

"What else can you do? Get married in two weeks?"

Two weeks. Who could get married in two weeks? But I'd fallen in love with Joe in only three months. And now love was gone. In its place was survival.

I had survived the war. I'd survived skimpy rations and brutish men. I'd sold most of my belongings on the black market. I'd been sick with fever and cold and had seen other people give up and die. But not me. If the brutal demands of ballet had taught me anything, it was that I was strong and could push through anything. I could endure this as well.

I set the handkerchief down on the table. "I will marry someone in two weeks. This is America, after all. Anything is possible."

"But how? And who?"

My mind was already turning. It would have to be someone who had military experience. Someone my age, no older. I was twenty-four years old. I'd had enough of young love; now I wanted someone who was mature. A man of good character, who liked to dance and was fond of children.

"I need to have more than one suitor to choose from," I said, thinking out loud now. "Otherwise my options are too limited. I will not take just anyone. How can I contact many men at once to make a plea for marriage?"

"What would I know of such things?" Mariska said, her voice aghast at the idea.

"Why do you act so shocked? Most of my ancestors had arranged marriages."

"And mine as well," Mariska replied. "But they were approved by parents."

"I don't have time for that. You and Jakab will have to give approval."

"And how will you find suitors?"

I glanced down at the table and noticed a wadded-up newspaper under Jakab's breakfast plate. I had read an American newspaper on the train, one that held human interest stories of people who needed help. I snatched the paper and held it triumphantly in the air. "This is how I will find a husband. I will tell my story to the press."

"No," Mariska insisted. "That is more disgrace. You are aristocracy!"

"Didn't Jakab say that we have to find our own way in America? Fine, I won't let them print my name. I will be, *névtelen*, what is the English word, anonymous?"

"Who will marry you without name or picture?"

I ran my fingers through my curly hair. "You are right. I will ask the press to publish my picture. Then they will know what they are getting."

Mariska put her head in her hands. "*Ez őrültség!*"

"I do not care if it is craziness. I have come this far and I have no intention of going back." My heart lifted. I had a plan and a purpose once again. Joe may have destroyed the fairy tale, but this countess was stronger than that.

CHAPTER SEVEN

T HE *MINNEAPOLIS STAR* BUILDING WAS A MODERN-LOOKING
five-story structure flanking downtown Minneapolis. In Europe
we didn't build such high buildings, and everything was old and
more compact. The black-and-white columns looked cold and un-
approachable as I stood near the entrance. Mariska may have been
right. This was certain madness.

I carried last night's edition of the newspaper under my arm,
which I'd read cover to cover. A name was circled in pencil. This
man was my only hope.

Taking a deep breath, I went inside the sprawling lobby. An
older woman with dark hair and glasses and a thick waist looked up
from some papers on her desk near the front door. "May I help you?"

I held my hands together so they wouldn't shake and betray my
nervousness. "I am here to see Cecil Anders, please."

"Do you have an appointment?"

An appointment? I hadn't thought to get one. "No, but it is important that I see him."

"Mr. Anders is a very busy man," she said in a snobbish voice. "I
can perhaps schedule you for a time next week."

It would be too late then. I stood tall and faced the woman,
summoning the look Mama used when dealing with unsavory commoners. Now it was my turn to sound snooty. "He will want to hear
my story. Let him know I am Roza Mészáros, a Hungarian countess
here to see him."

The woman's eyebrows rose above the rim of her glasses. She

stood to get a better look. I was glad I'd worn a conservative sweater and skirt, along with my diamond bracelet. I looked presentable, even if I wasn't dressed in the latest fashion.

"Just a moment," she said in a flat voice and picked up a phone.

"Mr. Anders, a woman who claims to be a Hungarian countess wants to speak with you. Yes. I understand. All right."

She hung up, then gave me a begrudging nod. "His office is on the third floor to the right of the elevators."

"Thank you." I flashed her a smile that said *Told you!*

I found his office and stopped in front of the open door, trying to calm the fluttering in my stomach. Mr. Anders sat at a messy desk, his jacket hung on the chair behind him. A typewriter occupied the center of the desk. He was bent over a typed paper with a pencil in his hand, scratching out words and scribbling in the margins. Framed pictures filled the walls; I recognized Eleanor Roosevelt and the Hollywood actor Bob Hope.

Suddenly Mr. Anders looked up and saw me standing in the hallway. He put down his pencil and stood up. "I expected some old dowager to walk into my office," he said, smiling in such a way that I immediately felt at ease. "Not a beautiful young lady. Please come in."

I paused. "Do you mind if I close the door?"

"Certainly," he responded with raised eyebrows. "Can I get you anything? A cup of coffee or a glass of water?"

I shook my head.

He pulled a chair up next to his. "Please, have a seat."

I sat down. "Thank you. My name is Roza Mészáros."

He took my hand in his and covered it with his other hand. "I'm Cecil Anders, and I insist you call me Cecil. What is it I can do for you today?"

I thought of all I had to tell him. I blurted out the words. "Help me find a husband."

His eyes widened. "A beautiful young woman such as yourself certainly doesn't need my help."

"But I do," I said in a pleading voice, feeling suddenly unsteady. "I have until March 23 before my GI visa expires."

His eyes widened. "I suspect there is a very interesting story here."

He took out pad of paper. "Okay, Roza. Why don't you start at the beginning?"

"Can you please not use my real name? It would be an embarrassment to my family."

"I understand completely. What should I call you?"

"How about Llona?" It was a common name in Hungarian, as well as the name of the queen of the fairies.

Cecil nodded. "Llona it is then. Tell me about yourself."

"I am Hungarian. I graduated from university, and I spent three years as a ballet dancer. My father was the Hungarian minister to Austria before the war. We lost everything during the war."

"And where is your family now?"

"My father was taken away by the Germans. He never returned. My mother and brother are in Budapest, waiting for him to come back." I shook my head. "She will not accept that he is dead."

"I'm sorry," Cecil said, pausing so that he could reach across and pat my hand.

"Thank you. Two years ago, after the war was over, I met a GI at a party in Vienna. We fell in love immediately. He was there for three months, and we saw each other almost every night. We danced, took long walks through the countryside. He told me about America, about his family, about his ambitions. We became engaged. 'As soon as I get home, I'll send for you,' he told me. 'You'll like my hometown. It's in what we call the Midwest.'"

"And did he?" Cecil leaned forward.

"Yes, but it took two years to obtain my visa and for Joe to send the five hundred dollars for the required bond. And for the money for travel. I studied English, increased my vocabulary. I didn't look at another man. And then when I finally arrived, I thought we would be reunited and live happily."

My eyes glistened and a handkerchief was momentarily thrust into my hand, as though Mr. Anders was used to young women crying in his office. I dabbed at my eyes.

"I take it that didn't happen," he said in a warm voice.

"No." My voice was almost a whisper. "He didn't meet me at the train, but a kind Hungarian couple offered accommodations until Joe could come for me."

I shook my head and let the sadness spill out. "The minute he walked in the door, I knew something was wrong. He was cold and distant. Then he said he'd married someone else three months ago. I screamed at him, told him to get out of my sight. That was four days ago. I have barely eaten or slept since then."

I kept dabbing at my eyes as the tears flowed once again. I'd wanted to be strong, but as the words came out, so did my feelings.

"I'm sorry," he said, shaking his head. "The war caused too many broken hearts."

"The worst part is, I cannot go back. Communist leaders are keeping lists of people who fraternized with Americans. And my GI visa is only good for a little more than two weeks."

I looked at him through tear-soaked lashes. "I want to stay in America."

"Miss Mészáros, are you asking me to be your marriage broker?"

I nodded. "Yes. If you are willing."

He stood up and walked around the desk. "You know, I search for stories for my column all the time. But I don't expect them to walk into my office. This has all the elements of a yarn that might easily become the best story of the decade."

"Does this mean you will help me?"

He clapped his hands together. "Countess, I'm your man."

I sat back, perplexed by what he said. "I do not mean that *you* should marry me."

Cecil let out a belly laugh. "That's good, because my wife and kids might object. Now you sit right here. I'm going to go grab a photographer."

He winked before he left. "That face will go a long way in courting any lonely soldiers back from the war."

MINNEAPOLIS STAR NEWSPAPER

March 7, 1948

IN THIS CORNER

CECIL ANDERS

SO FANTASTIC, SO BIZARRE is the tale that it will probably sound incredible to you. But I've checked every detail carefully and know whereof I speak. If the plan we're about to launch should happen to click, we'll have all of a yarn that might easily become the best short story of the decade. Through the years, for some curious reason, this little office of mine has become a sort of confessional for certain types of troubled humans. I have become a patient listener, and many times that's all a distressed soul needs. Last Friday I ran into an all-time high in wretchedness. She was probably the most woeful human being I have ever encountered. And there were reasons galore for her misery. I'm going to unfold the tale as she told it and then wind up with a plea. In summary, this is the story: A Hungarian countess wants a husband and she must meet, woo and win him in two short weeks...

WE'LL CALL HER Llona. That isn't her name but she wants some protection. She came into the office and said, "Do you mind if I close the door?" That is always a tip-off. She had something very intimate on her mind. Her voice was soft, her accent very pleasant. It soon became obvious that she was a cultured young woman. She's 24, a Hungarian, born in Vienna, is a college graduate, has spent three years in the ballet. Her father was the Hungarian minister to Austria before the war. Her family has lost everything since . . .

TWO YEARS AGO, after the war was over, she met a GI at a party. They fell in love immediately. He was there for three months, they saw each other almost every night, they danced together, took long walks through the countryside, he told her about America, about his family, about his ambitions. They became engaged. "As soon as I get home, I'll send for you," he told her. "You'll like America. You'll like my hometown. It's in what we call the Midwest." He told her of the opportunities that young men have here. They planned their home, their future together. It wasn't unlike thousands of other romances. His army hitch ended and he returned to America. For two years they wrote letters regularly, added to the attachment they had for each other. For two years she never went out with another man. She waited. She read his letters over and over again. She relived all the happiness they had had together in Vienna. She tried to picture America as he had described it. She studied English, she increased her vocabulary. She wondered how his family would accept her . . .

THEN ONE OF his letters contained the money for the plane passage to America. He had posted the $500 bond necessary to bring her over here. It took her seven months to get her visa and arrange all the details for her trip to America. She kept writing in the meantime. So did he. Their letters were filled with plans for their marriage. Her plane landed in Chicago. She came from there to Minneapolis. A young married Hungarian couple met her and brought her to their apartment. She and her GI fi-ancé were to meet at the home of this couple.

SHE'LL NEVER FORGET that day. She hadn't seen him for two years, remember. She wondered if he had changed. She wondered what he'd look like in civilian clothes. She thought of their first embrace, of what a joy it would be to have him in her arms once more, to ruffle his eyebrows and pinch his chin and tweak his ears and squeeze his hands and listen to his voice. She heard a knock at the door. "Here he is!" she shouted. Her heart danced, but not for long. She sensed something as he walked in the door. He was no longer the gay, spirited lover she had known in Vienna. They embraced, but it was a cold, depressed embrace. She spoke intuitively. "Tell me, dear, what is it?" The scene was short. Their arms dropped to their sides. Instinctively they braced themselves—he for the blow he was about to deliver, she for the blow she was about to receive . . .

"I'VE BEEN MARRIED for three months," he told her. "Get out of my sight," she screamed, "get out, get out!" He left. That was four days ago. She has hardly eaten since. Every night has been sleepless. She still looks dazed. "I will NOT go back to Hungary," she says emphatically. "I cannot go back. My people will not have me, my country will not have me. My family dis-approved of my contemplated marriage from the beginning. We are in the Russian zone. The Communists have lists of people who fraternized with the Americans. They have posted all who went to capitalistic America. I am now their enemy. I cannot go back. I am stateless . . .

SHE MUST GO, though. Her GI visa says that unless she has married a GI by March 23, in just a little over two weeks, she must return to her native Hungary. "I have come to love America even in my bitterness," she said. "Now I must marry a GI and I must do it within the next two weeks." If in that time, she can meet an ex-GI, an ex-officer, anybody who was in the war, she can stay here.

"WHAT KIND OF husband would you like?" I asked her. "I prefer a city man, somebody between 25 and 45. I do not like extremely young boys. Religion is not too important. I can cook. I love to dance. I am educated. I am fond of children. I would like a man of good character, a man who enjoys the nice things of life." . . .

THERE IS HER story. Llona is five feet four, weighs 120 pounds, dresses conservatively, has soft blue eyes, pretty teeth, a trim figure. Right now she's upset, but who wouldn't be? A Hungarian countess wants a husband and she must have him within two weeks. She is a charming young woman, and if I weren't an old married man I'd be first in line to court her.

NOW FOR THE PLEA: If this young woman without a country appeals to any ex-GI or anybody who was in the war, she would like to have the prospect get in touch with her. This Corner will serve as go-between. She would like to have you write her a letter, enclose a picture, suggest a meeting place. If you ex-GIs (a service connection is a must) will address your letters to "Llona, in care of This Corner" we'll forward them immediately, treat them all in confidence, guarantee you no embarrassment whatsoever. May I suggest, however, that you do not treat this as a lark. Please do not make a prank out of it. Here is a young woman in very desperate circumstances and a woman's distress should not be toyed with. If you are at all interested, get a letter off today with your picture. Time is a very important factor. Remember, there should be no embarrassment for anybody.

CHAPTER EIGHT

✣

THE GRAINY BLACK-AND-WHITE PHOTO STARED UP AT US from the newspaper splayed out on Mariska's kitchen table. A picture of me, an elbow resting on my knees, showing my legs from the knee down, with a hand tucked under my chin. My grandmother's bracelet glittered on my wrist and I had a half smile on my face.

"Try not to look too woeful," Mr. Anders had told me as the photographer took the picture.

Mariska covered her mouth when she saw the picture. I had to read the article to her as she didn't read English. "It says that Llona is twenty-four years old, five feet four inches, one hundred and twenty pounds, dresses conservatively, and has soft blue eyes, pretty teeth, and a trim figure."

"What will your mother say when she sees this?"

"I won't send it to her. And even if I did, the Russians censor mail from America and she may not even receive it."

"But she would not approve."

"Of course she wouldn't. She still expects me to marry an aristocrat. Never mind that many of them are as destitute as we are. Here is what it states I am looking for," I said, summarizing the column. "A man of good character, between ages twenty-five and forty-five. She wants a man who is mature. She prefers a city man. Military experience is required. She likes to cook and dance and is fond of children. She would like a man of good character, a man who enjoys the nice things of life. Religion is not important, but timing is. Her

GI visa says that unless she has married a GI by March 23, she must return to her native Hungary."

Mariska gasped. "Religion is the most important thing of all. How can you say that it is not important?"

I sighed. "I have just over two weeks. I must marry a military man for the GI visa. But I cannot limit myself too much or no one will respond to the column."

"But this is for the rest of your life. What if a Protestant responds?"

"I don't care. I just hope someone does."

It was the first time I'd said it out loud—my greatest fear, that no one would come to the rescue of a jilted countess who had no money and very little to offer. Even the picture might not help. I was attractive, but was that enough? I was twenty-four, ancient in Mama's opinion. I should have been married years ago, but the war made everything difficult, even romance.

Mr. Anders assured me that the column would reach a wide audience; that it would be picked up by many newspapers in the Midwest. But that didn't quell the anxiousness I felt.

And I still cried at night at the thought of Joe in another woman's arms. Would I be able to forget him enough so that I wouldn't get teary-eyed at the mention of his name? How would my new husband, if I was lucky enough to find one, feel about my former fiancé? Because, try as I might, I had spent two years in love with Joe. I would not have time to replace him in my heart.

"I do not approve," Mariska announced, folding her fleshy arms. "But that does not mean I will not share my judgment of a suitor."

"Thank you. It will mean a great deal to have your approval. You are my only friends in America."

Mariska cocked her head. "Very well. Regardless of what it says, if I am to give approval, you will not have to resort to marry a Protestant."

I nodded, thinking that I might not have a choice in the matter. At this point I would consider myself fortunate if anyone wanted to marry me.

I told Mariska that the column informed anyone interested to forward their letters to Llona in care of Mr. Anders's column at the newspaper, and that he'd added a caveat: "Please do not make a prank out of it. Here is a young woman in very desperate circumstances and a woman's distress should not be toyed with." I added that he encouraged them to write immediately, that time was a very important factor.

A flush of embarrassment swept across me as I read the word "desperate." Mama would disown me if she read this.

I was already an embarrassment to her because of ballet. She had attended only one of my performances, because as she said, "Public performing is déclassé." She thought I was too headstrong, and she told me often how that would bring disgrace to the family.

And now this.

I tried to keep busy that week, rearranging my small trunk, trying to stay cool in the stuffy apartment. I even ventured out to help Mariska in the garden, but my thoughts often returned to Joe. In my daydreams, he appeared at the door, hat in hand, repentant and ready to make me his wife.

I spat in the dirt when this happened. Such thoughts were useless. I needed to move on.

Although I was not as religious as Mariska, who kept images in her flat of St. Stephen, the patron saint of Hungary, I reverted to my childhood prayers during quiet moments, even though they hadn't saved Papa.

Lastly, I sent a telegram to Mama and gave her Mariska's temporary address. I told her I was staying with a friend. I didn't mention Joe or the wedding. I would explain it all later. And if no one wanted to marry me, I would show up on Mama's doorstep very soon.

On Friday evening Mariska walked with me arm in arm to a nearby park as Péter ran ahead, stopping when his mother reprimanded him to slow down.

"You walk different," Mariska told me. "You move lightly, like there is air beneath your feet. And you hold your head high and graceful. Perhaps that is how all aristocracy walks?"

I shook my head. "No. It is the way of a ballerina. You must carry your body as though you're always lifting up, like you're floating. It has been ingrained in me after so many years." Ballet dancers could spot one another on a busy street. They walked with their feet pointed outward.

"At first, it make you seem snobbish."

"Snobbish? I hadn't realized."

"But I know better now," Mariska said and patted my arm.

How lucky was I that someone as gracious and kind as Mariska had taken me in and become my friend?

The air was cool, and it felt good to be out of the heat of the small flat. Mariska's husband, Jakab, was at home, already asleep on the sofa. I had volunteered to sleep there, but they continued to insist I have their bed. He had to rise at the crack of dawn each day to make it to the factory where he worked. Mariska always got up and made him a hearty breakfast before he left, then packed his lunch.

"I worry that he works too hard," she confessed as we walked the tree-lined street. "But we are fortunate to have food and freedom here. And America has given us even more. We will have another child soon." She rubbed her belly. "An American child."

"Oh, my," I said, embarrassed that I hadn't noticed, even though Mariska was chubby and wore peasant blouses. "What good news!"

"Yes, we are blessed. I thought myself too old to have another child. And I am craving sweets, which means it is a girl."

"I should not be intruding in your home," I apologized.

"Noblesse oblige. Those more fortunate are supposed to help the poor. Your father was known for helping many when he was alive. He opened his doors and his crops to those in need before he was captured. And the world is upside down now if the Countess Mészáros is poorer than I."

"But you have worries enough of your own."

"My worries are nothing compared to yours. At first I thought this idea was crazy, but I realize now how brave you are, Roza."

I didn't feel brave. Like everything in my life, this was another obstacle; I was just looking for a way around it.

"Yes," she said amid my protests, "you have come alone halfway across the world to make a better life. And then to have the love of your life make a fool of you like that? Anyone else would have hurried home with her tail between her legs. But not you. And now you are willing to marry a stranger in order to hold on to that opportunity. That is bravery, my dear."

"Or foolishness," I suggested. "I may indeed end up at home with my tail between my legs." It had been five days, and I hadn't heard anything from Cecil Anders since the article appeared.

Mariska squeezed my arm. "Perhaps a bit of both. But remember, if God wills, even a cock will lay an egg."

We were almost home when we saw Jakab running toward us. He had a frantic look on his face and his hair stuck up in the back. "You must return immediately," he told me, breathing heavily from the run as he pulled my arm.

"What is it?" I took in a sudden breath and held it, thinking that something had happened to Mama or János. And here I was, so far away, unable to be with them.

"There is a man come to see you. Mr. Anders."

"Mr. Anders?"

I let go of Mariska's arm and ran ahead.

I was hot and sweaty when I reached the flat, and I stopped to run a finger through my hair before opening the door. Cecil Anders was sitting on the wooden rocker that Jakab had made when Péter was born. He held a bouquet of flowers in his hands and he stood up when I entered the room.

"Roza, it's good to see you again."

"And you, Mr. Anders. Has someone replied to your column?" I asked breathlessly.

"That's why I'm here. It's the most amazing thing. I must say that our soldiers are the best in the world."

"You did receive a response," I said, putting a hand on my throat. "I am so relieved." Apprehension immediately replaced my relief. What sort of man was he? I thought of the hard life Mariska endured. Would I have to face a similar fate?

"Oh, no," he replied. "Don't be relieved just yet. We didn't get *a* response."

"No? But you said . . ."

"My dear," Cecil said, "you already have over one thousand offers of marriage."

CHAPTER NINE

O NE THOUSAND?" SURELY I HEARD HIM WRONG.
Cecil handed me the bouquet. "This is just the beginning." He bent down to retrieve a briefcase by the chair. "Not just offers of marriage," he said, as he brought out two heart-shaped boxes of candy and a thick envelope. "Telegrams, candy, and even cash has been pouring in all week," he said. "This is all for you. I have a whole bag in my car besides."

"All this. For me." I could hardly breathe. I sat down in the rocker, stunned. "This is impossible. You have done the impossible."

"All I did was relate your story. Your picture did the trick. This is the start of something wonderful, Roza. I've already received over three hundred phone calls too. But you have a big job ahead of you now. You have to read through all those letters and telegrams and figure out who you're going to marry in the remaining time."

I didn't know what to say. It hit me then, that I wouldn't have to go back. And I wouldn't have to take any man. I had choices! I could live in America.

"You stay right there. I'll be back in a jiffy," Cecil said and disappeared into the hallway.

I couldn't move. If I did it might break the spell I was in and this elated feeling would vanish. It was a thing of fairy tales, this wonderful turn of events, and I could imagine Mademoiselle Petit's surprise if she were reading my story. In her version I would go back to Hungary penniless and broken, only to be arrested and thrown in prison by the Communists. But I was writing my own tale with the help of this kind man.

Mariska and Péter arrived just then, their cheeks pink from exertion.

"What did he say?" Mariska asked.

I showed her the boxes of candy. "I have suitors," I replied, barely able to say the words, afraid they might vanish in mid-sentence.

Mariska clapped her hands together. "*Gratulálunk!* Wonderful news!"

Péter looked longingly at the candy. "Is it chocolate?"

"*Igen*, yes. Let us have some!"

Cecil returned with a large canvas bag tied at the top. He opened it and showed us the letters and telegrams. "These are all for you. Plus another bouquet of American Beauty roses."

Mariska put a hand on her mouth, unbelieving. "So many!" She started crying.

I wanted to cry too. But I was still in shock. It was more than I could ever hope for, maybe too much. "How will I possibly decide?"

"I'd organize them in piles if I were you," Cecil said. "Different regions, states, rank, occupation, et cetera. And some include pictures. That will help."

"We must begin right away," Mariska said, taking hold of the task. "We have so much to do."

Cecil put his hat on and turned to leave with the promise to return tomorrow with more letters and telegrams. "I don't doubt there will be more," he said with a huge smile and a wink.

I stood and hugged him. "Thank you. Thank you." The words were not enough.

He patted my back. "When you came to see me, you looked so full of misery that it cut me to the bone. I'm just glad I could help."

After he left I knelt down and ran my hands through the letters, my fingers caressing the coarse envelopes, feeling the weight of them all. All these men saw my picture and read my story, and were now opening their hearts and homes. I let the tears flow then. These tears tasted sweet, though, like the candy I'd just eaten.

"LOOK AT THIS!" MARISKA WAVED PAPER MONEY IN THE AIR. "This suitor send you money!"

I looked up from my spot on the floor, letters sprawled across my lap. "Why would he send money?"

"To help you. Because you are in need."

We'd been hard at work since the previous day when Cecil had delivered his bounty. Mariska sat in her rocking chair as Péter translated the writing for her. Jakab and I were smothered in letters on the floor. In the corner were two piles, one for potential suitors, and the other for rejected ones.

"*Ide, Péter,*" Mariska said, guiding him to place the envelope in the "yes" pile.

Both Mariska and Jakab reverted to Hungarian when speaking to me or their son. I hadn't realized how much I'd missed speaking my native language until I heard them speak.

"I do not like this one," Jakab said, holding up a picture of a shirtless man. "He has no decency."

"But he is good-looking," Mariska said, taking the photo from him and waving her hand in front of her as though she'd faint. I laughed.

"I will put this braggart in the 'no' pile," Jakab said, plucking it out of her hands.

"And do not get any ideas of replacing me, Mariska." He waved a finger at her.

"Do not be jealous, my husband. You are a very handsome man."

But when Jakab wasn't looking, Mariska confiscated the picture and put it in her apron pocket, then winked at me.

"I do like this one," I said, reading out loud. "'Dear Miss Mészáros, I can relate to your heartache. I was a captain in the Army and served in France. While I was away my fiancée sought company in the arms of another man. After the war, coming back home was harder than when I left. My life felt empty for a long time, but gradually I have been able to put the past behind me. My only promise to you is to always show you kindness and respect. I don't expect you're looking for love at first sight after what you've endured, but love often blooms in the most unexpected places.'"

Inside the letter was a pressed blue flower with delicate petals.

Mariska put a hand on her breast. "Very emotional. He is good writer too."

"Yes. He's now a railroad engineer in a small Minnesota town," I said. "That is a good job, no?"

"Very good job," Jakab said.

I placed that letter in the "yes" pile.

"What does divorced mean?" Péter asked while translating another letter.

"It means the letter goes in the 'no' pile," Mariska answered with crossed arms.

"This letter is in Hungarian!" Jakab held up a piece of paper. "He says 'I promised Mama I would marry a Hungarian girl in the United States. She would be thrilled with a Hungarian countess.'"

"Perfect. You should pick a Hungarian man. You share his heritage," Mariska said.

Perhaps she was right. But I was in America because I wanted something new. And even though I wouldn't admit it to Jakab or Mariska, marrying a Hungarian commoner would cause Mama even more irritation. I could do *that* back in Hungary.

I also put every letter in the "no" pile from men named Joe. I couldn't bear the thought of speaking that name every day when it held a different face than the man I had fallen in love with.

These men promised many things in the letters, including children. The thought of sharing a bed with a stranger made me uncomfortable. I was not a virgin. I remembered the tenderness of Joe, to whom I'd willingly given my virginity. How would a future spouse feel if he knew I'd made love to another man? How could I possibly have relations with a man I didn't love?

Hours later, the two piles were larger, but we still had hundreds of unopened envelopes strewn across the floor. Empty glasses of lemonade and crumbs from Mariska's *lángos* attested to the hours we'd spent on the task. A light breeze fluttered the curtain in the only window of the room. Péter was curled up in a fetal position on a pile of letters, like a homemade bed.

When Cecil showed up at the door with flowers, candy, and more letters, we all groaned.

"I told you there'd be more coming," he said in response. "You're a popular girl. You've set a world record, Roza. Perhaps an all-time record. Seventeen hundred and eighty-six proposals!"

I ruffled a hand through the pile of envelopes. "How will I ever make a decision with this many suitors? It is too overwhelming."

Cecil handed the box of candy to a hungry-looking Péter, and the flowers he gave to a wilted Mariska, who took a whiff of their scent. "This is the biggest decision of your life, Roza. I know you want to make the best choice."

"But unfortunately, it has a time restraint," Cecil added.

I sighed. "Yes, and that is what bothers me most. A letter from my future husband is somewhere in this room. I do not mean to complain. But we have little time. I want to give them all consideration in order to make a good decision."

Cecil removed his suit coat and sat down on the floor. He flashed an encouraging smile. "And you will," he said. He rolled up his sleeves and picked up an envelope. "Did I ever tell you that I was an excellent judge of character?"

CHAPTER TEN

MY HEAD ACHED FROM READING. CECIL WAS A BIG HELP, although he asked so many questions as to my likes and dislikes. He said that knowing more about me would help him evaluate the prospective suitors. We continued to read the next day while Mariska and her family were at Mass. I was grateful for the extra space.

"This letter quotes poetry," I said, smiling at the beautiful handwriting. "He must be very romantic." I put it in the "yes" pile.

"Get a load of this one," Cecil said, waving a handwritten letter in the air. "He claims he's the best fisherman in Minnesota, he's got the longest beard, and he plays the glockenspiel. He vows to keep you entertained and you'll never run out of fish to eat."

"I do not know what this glockenspiel is, but he is a definite no," I said. "I am not a fan of long beards."

I read letters from widowers who had small children and wanted a mother for them, from men who claimed they would build me a mansion with a swimming pool if I married them, and others who sent pictures of themselves in uniform. Every one of them had a story. Some were sad and tragic, others were funny. And some I didn't trust. They bragged too much.

Cecil threw an envelope in the rejection pile. "I don't want to shortchange you. But I wouldn't let my own sister marry this guy."

I stopped reading. "What is shortchange?"

"It means I don't want to deprive you of a man of good character.

But some of these . . ." He shook his head. "I guess there's always a few in the bottom of the barrel."

"So many men. I have more choices than I thought I'd have. I'm very grateful, but why would anyone want to marry a woman who is a complete stranger?"

Cecil shrugged. "Many reasons. Loneliness. Boredom. And yes, even patriotism. Some want the married life but haven't gotten around to finding a girl yet. And don't forget about your picture in the paper. I'm sure some of these guys were won over by that."

"But if a man does not work for a woman's affection, can he value the marriage as much as a man who did?" Of course, with the aristocracy, that was often the case.

"You're getting too philosophical for me, Roza. I suppose the whole courtship thing has meaning. Maybe you should narrow your list down to five and then arrange a date with each of them before you decide?"

"Is there time for that?"

"There is if we arrange it soon. Maybe we could compress it down to two dates in one day. That'll make great copy!"

Copy as in newspaper coverage? I lowered my voice. "You are going to write about it? I realize how much I owe you, Mr. Anders, but I don't think that is a good idea. My life is not interesting."

"Are you kidding me? Everything about you is newsworthy. And judging by the response we have here, everyone is interested in you. You're a remarkable young woman, and you're the only countess who's ever graced our state."

"And I am a private person by nature."

"Didn't you perform with the Vienna Ballet?"

"Yes. But dancing in front of people is different. You're part of an artistic endeavor, one in which you lose yourself in the performance. It's more about the art than the applause, although that is very gratifying. And when I was in the newspaper, it had to do with my performance, not my personal life." I paused. "My mother does not know about this."

"I see," he said, nodding. "I don't want to be the bearer of bad news, but what if she sees the article that's already out there?"

"It is unlikely that she will see it. But she may hear about it from others. She will not be happy. But to have my dating life displayed like a circus act for everyone to read about? Our family has already lost honor and social status. I do not want to cause more harm."

Cecil sighed. "I understand, but remember: You came to me first. How about we do it this way? I'll write about the dates, but I won't write any sordid details about them. Just general stuff so people will know what you did and how it went. And I won't include any names."

"Do you promise?"

He held up three fingers. "Scout's honor."

"Thank you."

We read in silence for a few minutes before I spoke again. "Do you think I am doing the right thing? Will one date make a difference?"

He wiped a hand across his wet brow. "Well, I can tell you from my experience as a married man, and having seen many other marriages, that it doesn't matter if you have one date or a hundred. There's no guarantee of happiness. After being married for twenty years, I'm still surprised by my wife. I just found out last week that her favorite actor is John Wayne! You'd think I'd know that by now, but I didn't. We just do the best we can. But there's something to be said for the physical aspect too. You may notice a spark between you and one of the men."

I nodded, thinking I couldn't expect a spark. Not like the one I had with Joe. But perhaps it would be better that way. And perhaps one of them would be easier to talk to. I thought of the Chopin score hidden in my handbag. Could I sell it if my marriage failed?

I'd hoped it would be my insurance policy if things didn't work out, but I hadn't thought it through. I had no idea how I'd go about selling it. The score was a stolen artifact of the war that I'd taken from a Nazi officer. I'd be deported if I was caught with it.

By the end of the day we had read through all the letters, and the "yes" pile had been narrowed down to thirty.

Cecil stood up and wiped off his pants. Flutters of white envelope fell to the floor. "I have to go now. If you can whittle it down to five by tomorrow, I'll make contact with them and set up the dates."

I pulled at my hair. "They are beginning to all sound alike. I keep getting them mixed up."

"I know it's hard, but the clock is ticking. After the dates, you'll only have a couple of days to decide before you get married. Look, why don't you take a cool bath and forget about it the rest of the night? Your mind will be fresher tomorrow."

"You are right. Thank you again for all your help. I don't know what I would do if . . ."

"My pleasure, countess," he said. "And my best advice is this: Trust in your own judgment."

After Cecil left, I did as he advised, soaking in the tub for a long time. The narrow white tub was stained and chipped, but it felt glorious. I dressed and went for a walk, watching the sun set beyond the tall trees.

CHAPTER ELEVEN

8✝3

RALPH JONES TOOK A HUGE BITE OUT OF HIS WATERMELON
slice, and I realized who he reminded me of: the hippo we'd just
seen. He attacked his food in the same aggressive manner, and his
round, chubby cheeks became barrel-shaped while pink juice drib-
bled down his chin and onto his white shirt.

"Watching those animals eat made me darn right hungry," he
said, his mouth still full.

I had lost my appetite. Perhaps the zoo wasn't the best choice
for our first date.

It was Péter's suggestion, and I thought it would be a good one. I
hadn't been to a zoo since Papa took me to the Budapest Zoo when
I was little. It was much bigger than this one, but the Como Zoo
offered free admission and was situated near a conservatory with
a newly built sunken garden. Mariska said that anyone could find
romance among the delicate and sweet-smelling flowers.

Mariska and Péter sat at a nearby picnic table. I flashed a with-
ered look at Mariska, who shrugged. Ralph was not at all like any of
us had imagined.

"You're different than your letter," I finally said. I'd selected
him as one of the finalists because of how articulate he'd sounded.
He wrote of how he was a war hero who'd returned to care for his
widowed mother until her death last year. And he was a successful businessman who ran the family-owned grocery store, which I
found appealing. I would never have to worry about food again!

But at our introduction, I knew something was off. Ralph presented me with a bouquet of mixed flowers and exclaimed, "Yowza! You're prettier than your picture. I done hit the jackpot!" This was the same man who'd quoted Robert Frost's poem "Carpe Diem" and claimed "Seize the day of pleasure"?

Mariska and Péter walked behind to give us privacy to talk, but I felt as though I had little to say to Ralph. Most of our conversation centered on the animals we saw; the rest on his grocery business.

He never asked about me, about my dancing or education or background. Or even what kind of flowers I liked.

While we were gazing at the lions, I commented on their magnificent muscular builds. Ralph flexed his arm in his own display of strength, then looked at me and remarked, "My mother was a sturdy woman. She used to lift twenty-pound sacks of flour every day. You got such skinny limbs, the size of a rope, like those gazelles we saw."

"A gazelle?"

"Not that I hold it against you. I bet you'd be good at sorting penny candy. And people would come just to look at you."

I felt like I was being interviewed for a job as a clerk. This man was definitely not a poet. And he expected me to work in his store? His letter had made it sound as though he were well off.

He had to stop twice on our walk through the zoo to wipe perspiration from his face with a handkerchief. "I don't like to throw my weight around," Ralph said, breathing heavily. "But I have my own store in Omaha and I plan to expand into Council Bluffs. I'm very successful, I know the value of hard work, and I aim to keep my fortune in the family. If I had a son, he'd be the one to inherit my store."

"And what if you had a daughter?" I asked, imagining a miniature version of Ralph in a dress, which made me cringe.

"I'd be hard put to allow that," he said. "Pray that don't never happen."

I quickened my step, making him run to keep up with me. By the time I'd stopped at the Monkey Island exhibit, Ralph's shirt was damp and sweat streaked his red face. His suit coat held a foul smell. How could I have selected this man from all those letters? Was my judgment that flawed?

It wasn't until we were sitting at a picnic table under a towering oak tree eating a light lunch Mariska had prepared that I finally confronted him.

"Mr. Jones, I must ask you a direct question, one I feel should be addressed after meeting you."

Ralph held up his sticky hands. "Feel free. I am an open book."

"Did you write that letter?"

"I wrote it with my own hand," he said earnestly.

"Did you have help?"

He looked away for a second, as though considering what to say. "Truth be told, my sister is an English teacher. She done told me what to write. Said it was time I settled down. But everything in it is truth, God help me." He placed a wet hand on his chest, causing me to flinch. "And I do want to get married. Having a countess for a wife would make me the envy of every man in Omaha. And seeing as how you're desperate to stay in the U.S., we'd both make out good."

I took out my handkerchief and fanned myself. "I think I've had too much excitement, Mr. Jones. It is time I return home. I apologize for having to shorten our date."

Ralph lumbered to a standing position, tucking his shirt into his tight pants. "So, when are we getting hitched?"

I stood and shook his wet hand with the tips of my fingers. "I have enjoyed meeting you, Mr. Jones. But I am sorry. I cannot marry you."

He snorted his disapproval, reminding me of the hippo once again. "Why not? I drove all the way up here from Omaha."

I was used to handling zealous ballet fans. But it was my father I thought of now, who displayed firmness and tact in all his dealings, whether it was with the stable boy or the head of a country. I missed him so much, and it was his diplomacy I summoned when I replied.

"Because," I finally said, "a gazelle and a hippo do not make a good match."

ON THE WAY HOME MARISKA SAT NEXT TO ME ON THE streetcar.

"Do not be discouraged. You still have four other men to choose from."

I watched the shady streets and stately homes blend together as they passed by. I still missed Vadvirag, the name Papa had given our mansion, although Mama refused to acknowledge Wild Flower as the name. Papa said he named it that was because we lived close to the forest and river, both wild and untamable, so that our home and its inhabitants would always hold a bit of rowdiness, no matter how Mama did her best to civilize us.

That life seemed so long ago. Even though I was no longer compelled by romantic notions of love, would it be worth living with an oaf of a man just to have the security of a nice home?

"I thought I could put aside any objections, that I would be willing to marry almost anyone. But not that man! And what if the others are like him? Or worse?" I said.

"He was awful!" Mariska agreed. "I hoped you would not pick him."

"I couldn't choose him, even if it meant deportation."

Mariska gasped. "You cannot go back. They will think you are a spy for the Americans now that your picture has been in the newspaper. You will find a husband, I know it in my heart."

I sighed. "At least it was not a wasted trip. I haven't been to a zoo in years. It was fun to see, even if Mr. Jones did remind me of the hippos."

Péter laughed at that. "I didn't like that man. He bought cotton candy and didn't even offer me any."

Mariska nodded. "Yes. He was not very kind. And kindness is a good virtue in a husband. Let us hope the next one is more kind. You will be meeting him tonight. And you have phone conversation this afternoon."

I nodded, wondering if five men were enough to choose from.

That afternoon I rejected another man after speaking with him on the telephone. He was the Hungarian suitor that Mariska and Jakab had wanted, the man they had been so excited about. He was calling to arrange our date, but after speaking to him I decided to back out.

"Why you not give him a chance?" Mariska asked.

"I could tell we weren't a match," I said. He had sounded too anxious, speaking only in Hungarian the entire time, even when I spoke in English. And our conversation had been entirely about Budapest and our relatives back in Hungary. I knew in my heart I couldn't marry a Hungarian man. He represented everything I had left behind, and I needed to start fresh.

I should not have selected him as one of my five dates. I'd only included him to make Mariska and Jakab happy.

Now I had only three left, and but a week to get married. There was a pressure inside, one that had been building up since I singled out the letters from prospective suitors. I felt my determination slipping away, and I questioned whether I was doing the right thing.

But what choice did I have?

I took in a breath and willed away my anxiety. Tonight I was meeting Jeffrey Fairbanks. With an American-sounding name like that, he would surely be a better suitor.

CHAPTER TWELVE

EVEN AS I WONDERED HOW I COULD HAVE EXHIBITED SUCH bad judgment in the choice of Ralph Jones, I had to give myself credit for choosing Jeffrey Fairbanks.

What I noticed first was his reddish-blond hair. Boyish freckles gave way to a dimple in his left cheek, a shy smile, and the deepest green eyes I'd ever seen, ones that reminded me of walks through the forests near the Buda Mountains in Hungary.

Jeffrey Fairbanks was already making a better impression than Ralph Jones.

We met in the lobby of the Lexington Supper Club in St. Paul. Jeffrey was dressed in a black wool pinstripe suit. He held out a bouquet of red roses. "I know that a countess deserves roses."

"They're lovely." I accepted the bouquet and gave him a small peck on the cheek, which caused it to redden.

"Are your hosts coming?" he asked.

"They will be joining us for coffee and dessert later." I had given Jakab some of the money I'd received to help out with expenses and to cover the costs of chaperoning my dates. But Mariska had insisted they give us time alone to talk, and I was grateful for that now.

Jeffrey explained this to the maître d', who led us to a table near the back, away from other patrons.

"I hope you don't mind. I gave him a little extra to find us a quiet table," Jeffrey said, as he held out an upholstered chair. His gentlemanly charm was welcome after my earlier date.

"No. I am happy to have some privacy."

The dark woodwork and crystal chandeliers reminded me of the elegant restaurants I was used to. When Jeffrey ordered a bottle of champagne, I felt as though I finally did have a reason to celebrate.

"Your picture doesn't do you justice," he said when the waiter left. "You're much more beautiful in person."

"Thank you." I'd purchased a new dress for my date, one I'd bought at a store off the rack, a simple black off-the-shoulder style that ended mid-calf and had a low waistline that emphasized my trim figure. It was the best I could do since I couldn't afford a designer dress.

"Your description of yourself was much too humble, Mr. Fairbanks. In your letter you said you were an unattractive version of Van Johnson. I found a picture to see what he looks like. And you are younger and much more handsome, in my opinion."

He blushed again and shook his head. "You know how to impress a guy. And my friends call me Jeff."

I watched as the waiter filled my glass with champagne. I waited until he left before I asked, "May I ask how old you are, Jeff? Your letter didn't say."

"I didn't include that? I must have forgotten." He straightened up in his chair. "I'm twenty-two."

He was two years younger than me? In the article I had requested a man between the ages of twenty-five and forty-five.

He must have read my expression. "I know you asked for someone older, but after I saw your picture and read that article, well, I've been looking for something, or rather, someone, since I got back from the war. And most of the girls I meet are, frankly, silly twits, while I feel older after my experience away. My father said that war makes a man grow up fast, and I have to agree."

"Of course," I said. "May I ask what you did in the war? You mentioned that you were stationed in Italy."

"I joined up near the end of the war and was part of the occupation forces in Europe. I didn't see direct combat, but I saw plenty of the devastating effects."

"I'm sure you did," I responded. Joe had been part of the occupation force when I met him. But he had previously fought the German army en route to Vienna.

Nevertheless, Jeff's letter had made it sound as though he'd been subjected to much more. He'd written how the experience had changed him, how he'd come to appreciate all that life had to offer after experiencing the "horrors of war." How he'd never be the same, but was now a stronger version of himself as a boy. I couldn't help but think he was still a boy compared to Joe.

It was difficult to judge what a person endured. Most would not have guessed what my life was like during the war. They assumed my title protected me, when it almost cost my life. And I'd almost been molested by a Nazi swine.

His name was Josef von Hauser, a boorish Austrian nobleman who followed his father in switching allegiances once the Nazis came to Vienna, eventually joining the SS. He sent roses to me before every performance. When he tried to visit my dressing room afterward, though, I made sure he wasn't allowed inside.

"I share my dressing room with ten other women. None of them wants you in there," I said, making sure I didn't give any impression of reciprocating his interest.

Hauser was known for helping the Nazis verify priceless artwork, although his own treasures were spared. I shared a small flat with another ballerina. One day she confided to me that she was pregnant; Hauser had recently taken an interest in her. Five nights later Greta disappeared, along with her clothes. No note. Nothing.

A few weeks later there was a knock on my door. I opened it and saw Hauser. "Greta is gone," I said, trying to shut the door quickly, but he gained entrance before I could get it closed.

"I know," he said, placing his satchel on a nearby table, as though he intended to stay.

"Where is she?" I asked.

He shrugged. "I could care less. It turns out she was a slut, sleeping with other men. I assume she left with one of them."

I knew that wasn't true. "You must leave," I said, pushing him out the door with unexpected force. He stuck his arm in the open space, but I slammed the door on his arm. He screamed. I locked the door and stood on the other side, my heart racing.

"You know what I want, countess," he said, pounding on the door. "I could have you sent to a concentration camp. Or shot."

I was sure he meant to rape me. I moved the next day to the flat of another ballerina I knew. But before I left, I searched his satchel and found the Chopin score, along with a note of authenticity. I kept it, partly for Greta, should she return, and partly in retaliation. I felt satisfaction in hearing that Hauser had been shot by the Russians just a week later, freeing me from the worry that he would find me.

The Chopin score was stolen from a Nazi thief. I felt no guilt in bringing it with me to America. Only fear that it might be taken away.

JEFF RAISED HIS GLASS OF CHAMPAGNE. "HERE'S TO NEW BE-ginnings."

Soft piano music played in the background. The aroma of fresh-baked bread and sizzling steaks wafted around us. I clinked my glass against his. "I believe you found the nicest restaurant in the city."

"It's hard to sweep a girl off her feet when you only have one date in which to do it," he replied. "My father travels for business and recommended this place. I'll remember to thank him later."

"And you work for your father?"

"Yes. He asked me to join his insurance company after I returned from Italy. I've learned a lot from him. Our firm has grown tenfold since the war, and if I'm not too humble in saying so, I had a big part in that. We've added new locations around Chicago and are planning to expand to this area too. And just so you know, my father thinks a great deal of you."

"He does not even know me."

"No, but he's the one who showed me your picture and told me to write to you. He said that someone with your background and your social grace would beat out any girl I'd come across. And now that I've met you, I can confirm that you're a woman of taste and sophistication, and great beauty. Frankly, though, I didn't think I stood a chance with you."

It was nice to know his father approved. I knew my mother would be horrified to learn I was marrying someone tantamount to a stranger.

"What about your mother?"

He took another sip of his champagne. "She passed away a few years ago. But she'd feel the same way. She supported my father in everything."

"I see. I'm sorry to hear she's gone."

"Mom followed my dad from her home state of Louisiana when they got married, and Dad always said that behind every successful man there was a great woman just like Mom."

The waiter approached to take our order.

"I'm a New York strip kind of guy. Medium cooked," Jeff said, handing his menu to the waiter. "Dad says they make the best steak in town. I assume the lady will have the same."

"What would *you* recommend?" I asked the waiter before handing back the menu.

"The walleye almondine is a customer favorite, unless you prefer steak," he said.

"The walleye sounds perfect."

"Sorry," Jeff said, after he left. "I assumed you liked steak."

"I do," I said. I left it unspoken what I wanted him to know, that I had ideas of my own, that I wasn't merely a mouthpiece for his opinions.

Jeff leaned forward. "I guess I'm just trying too hard to impress you. Ordering for you, making out like a big shot. I'm honestly just an average guy who thinks you're so out of my league that you'll see me as a putz. But I do want you to know that if you pick me, I'd do anything to make you happy. I'd take you to the nicest restaurants and clubs in Chicago. I'd buy you a beautiful home. I'd treat you like a queen."

Or a countess? "I'm sure you would, Jeff. And I want you to know that I'm just an average girl. Of course I like nice things in life, like all girls do, but I don't expect to be put on a pedestal."

He clicked his tongue, and exhaled, revealing that dimple in his left cheek. "I'd try not to, but I have to admit it'd be hard."

I smiled. He *was* trying too hard, and he was cute doing so. I tried not to make too much of it. Jeff was such a huge improvement over Ralph.

Over dinner he asked about the ballet, which one was my favorite, and what my life was like growing up in Hungary. He was attentive, almost eager for my answers, but I felt as though he'd prepared his questions ahead of time. With his father's help?

When I asked Jeff about himself, there was an awkward turn as the conversation always steered back to his father. How he'd encouraged Jeff to join the war effort, how he'd arranged for Jeff to attend business school after the war, and how he'd started Jeff in the business and encouraged him. I couldn't help but think of Jeff as a boy vying for his father's attention.

"When Mom died, Dad spoke at her funeral. He cherished her so." Jeff put his hand on top of mine. "As I would cherish you."

I wished I felt something other than the urge to pull my hand out from under his. Jeff was good and kind. So why did I feel nothing other than relief when he finally removed his hand?

When Mariska and Jakab arrived, I knew that they would fall under his spell. How could they not when he seemed so perfect?

Mariska ordered the lemon pudding cake, and Jakab had brandy, after asking if they carried the old Hungarian *pálinka*, which of course they didn't.

"I've never heard of that," Jeff said.

"It is made from fruit, often apricot or plums," I offered.

"Best brandy in all of world," Jakab said. "Remind me of old country."

Jeff also ordered brandy, and they were best friends before the night was over.

Afterward, Jeff paused outside, as though he were hesitant to leave. "I know you haven't had all your 'dates' yet." He put his fingers out in quotation marks. "But I've got to know how I did. If there's any hope . . ."

He looked desperate, reminding me of a begging dog. "Of course there is hope. How could anyone not be impressed by your charm and gentlemanly manners?"

I gave him a quick peck on the lips. It was like kissing a brother. "Thank you for a wonderful evening."

He let out a relieved breath. "I won't be able to stop thinking about you, Roza." He kissed my hand before he left. "Until our wedding day."

On the way home, Mariska couldn't stop talking about Jeff and the delicious food and music, how impressed she was with him. I was silent, staring out the window of the back seat.

"I do not see how you will find anyone better," Mariska said, turning around. "Perhaps we should call off the other dates?"

A moment later Mariska's eyes widened. "Oh, my!"

"What is it?" Jakab asked.

"I was so taken with him I completely forgot to ask if he was a Catholic."

"He will convert if he isn't," Jakab said reassuringly. "He is a good man."

Mariska nodded. "He will treat you like a countess. That is what you deserve, yes?"

I turned from the window. "Yes. But I couldn't get over the feeling that he was trying too hard to impress me. To make me think he was more mature than his age, perhaps."

"He is young," Mariska admitted. "But he does not act rash or reckless. He seems very respectful."

I sighed. He seemed to be everything I might want in a husband. He had a good job and his father's approval. And he would treat me very well. He lived in Chicago, which was a big city near a big lake, and he was an only child, and said he wanted several children, something I desired as well. But I had the impression that he was what Joe called "wet behind the ears." It made me uncomfortable to think I might be more experienced than my husband.

My biggest objection to Jeff was that I felt absolutely nothing for him, other than a fondness akin to sisterly affection. Could I raise a family with a man to whom I felt no attraction? I had told myself it wasn't important, and yet . . .

Mariska reached back to pat my leg. "You must not compare him to Joe."

"How did you know?"

"It is what I would do. What any woman would do."

Yes, of course. That was it. Jeff was a perfectly agreeable candidate for marriage. And marrying him would provide me an opportunity to live in the U.S.

I took a deep breath and relaxed back into the seat. *No matter what happens with the other two suitors, I have Jeffrey Fairbanks. He is my insurance policy, almost as good as the Chopin score.*

CHAPTER THIRTEEN

B Y THE NEXT MORNING I WAS NEARLY CERTAIN THAT JEFF would be my husband.

"Who can compare with him?" Mariska asked as she spread a thick layer of homemade peach jam onto her toast.

"I cannot imagine anyone coming close. But it would be rude to cancel after they have come all this way to meet me."

I was glad to see that Mariska was excited about Jeff, when she'd been disappointed that I had taken out the Hungarian suitor, as though it were a personal rejection. He owned a small restaurant in Minneapolis, but had started out working as a laborer, not unlike Jakab. "You were right to dismiss him," Mariska said later. "He might not be able to provide for you the way in which a countess should be accustomed." But I detected acrimony in her voice, and I wondered if Mariska wanted to keep me in the same station in life as her, as if it would make our friendship more secure.

We'd grown close in just a few weeks. Mariska felt like the sister I'd never had. She was protective and kept the nosy neighbors away from me, but she enjoyed the attention they gave her when prodding for the latest details of my dates.

What Mariska didn't understand was that I no longer cared about my aristocratic background. If ballet had taught me anything, it was that no amount of class could make up for talent and hard work. Being a countess had done nothing for me during the war, but my ballet training had saved me and kept me from starving to death.

It was Papa who'd allowed me to become a ballerina. When Instruktor Lieb approached my parents about studying in Vienna, Papa had stroked his already graying mustache, even though he'd just turned forty. He spoke in a deliberate fashion, the same way he moved, as though it were undignified to be hasty about anything.

"Since our Roza has this gift, it would be egregious not to encourage it." He turned to me, his only daughter. "Are you prepared to put in the work and effort this will require?"

"Yes, Papa. It is not work. It is my passion!"

Mama had complained. "You spoil her too much. It's bourgeois to become a professional dancer, not to mention unfashionable."

Mama looked down on anyone who obtained wealth through industry rather than genealogy.

But Papa dismissed her objections. "We do not act according to fashionable practice. She will audition, and if she is accepted, my permission will be granted."

I fought for my position in the ballet. None of my aristocratic friends could understand it. While they were off on ski holidays and relaxing in the country, I was taping my bleeding feet and performing my plié exercises. All I could think of was to be a prima ballerina, not visiting charities and attending dinners, things that normally would have been expected of me.

I remembered Mama's words, that "nobility must be wealthy. Otherwise, it won't be desirable." And Mama was now poor. What was desirable about a poor countess? At least my dancing had provided for me, until the Opera House was bombed.

"Who is first date today?" Mariska asked, wiping the crumbs from her palms.

"Finn Erickson. An engineer on the railroad. He is from a small town in Minnesota."

"I remember that letter. He was one who send you blue flower?"

"Yes. He also lost his fiancée during the war. She broke off their engagement." So we both had suffered heartache. But it was his writing that drew me in; something in the rhythm of his sentences and words. Poetic without being a poem. Wise without being cynical. Haunting without being depressing. As though it betrayed a deep soul underneath.

Hopefully he had written the letter himself.

"Where do we meet him?"

"The Minneapolis Auditorium. The Minneapolis Civic Orchestra is performing a free spring concert."

Mariska waved it off. "Ha. That is poor choice."

"Why?"

"How can you talk during concert? Is waste of time."

"He has something planned for afterward. A short lunch." We had agreed that I would spend three hours with each suitor, a stipulation that was disregarded on my first date with Ralph when I'd left early. Since the concert would last an hour, we would still have time to chat over lunch, although not as much as the other dates.

"We need to leave shortly if we're going to catch the streetcar to Minneapolis," I said, hurrying to change. I would wear the blue dress I'd worn the night I'd seen Joe. It seemed bad luck, but I didn't have a large wardrobe, and it was my best choice for a morning concert. And I had no great expectations for Finn now that I'd met Jeffrey Fairbanks.

"I will miss this adventure when it is over," Mariska said on our walk to the streetcar. The air was windy but warm as we strolled the few blocks. I wanted to relax, to enjoy the soothing breeze and sunny patches under the dormant branches of the tall trees, but I was too nervous. There was something about this particular letter that put me on edge, the rawness of it, or perhaps the fact that he shared his own heartache. Thoughts of Joe made my chest tighten.

Mariska had on a new short-sleeved jacket and skirt she'd sewn that hid her expanding figure. And she'd bought a new round hat with a pink flower on the front, one that she clung to now as a breeze swept over us. As I clutched my own wide-brimmed hat, one I'd purchased before the war from Adele List's studio on the corner of Kärntner Strasse in the center of Vienna, I thought Mariska looked more American in that outfit and less like a Hungarian immigrant.

I reflected on Mariska's choice of words. To Mariska it *was* an adventure and it had made her a celebrity in the ramshackle apartment building in which she lived. I heard her down the hall as she whispered the details of each suitor to her Hungarian neighbors, and saw how the group grew in number each day. What Mariska once saw as shameful she now delighted in, especially when she was treated to lunches and concerts.

But I also considered Mariska my best friend. She'd taken me in and given me food and a place to sleep. She'd comforted me and supported me when I'd been distraught. And she'd read through hundreds of letters, helping me discern who would be the best choice for marriage. I would forever be indebted to Mariska for her kindness and friendship, and I reserved any judgment I might normally impart on such gossipy behavior.

"It's too bad Péter couldn't join us," I said as we hurried up the stairs of a waiting yellow streetcar, inserted a dime, and found a seat. He'd joined a crew on the outskirts of the city. Each morning I heard Mariska rustling around the kitchen at five o'clock to make sure Péter started the day with a good breakfast and had a knapsack packed with food and water. He then met up with a group of neighborhood boys who hopped in the back of a truck each morning to sweep out various factories and didn't return until the sun had set.

"He want earn money to help us," Mariska said, tilting her head as she talked about her son. "He make me so proud."

They wanted to move before the baby was born into a nicer apartment with more room, one a few blocks away from their present location. Mariska's dream was to someday own a house.

My own brother wasn't much older than Péter. He would normally have been raised riding horses and reading literature and learning to be a landowner to take his father's place at the estate. But the last five years changed all that. I wondered if János was able to keep up his studies now that the estate and land were gone. What did he hope for now? Mama didn't write much about him, only that he was her great joy and he kept her going.

"America is land of opportunity," Mariska said so often that I thought I'd soon see it cross-stitched on a pillowcase. Compared to Europe, which was still struggling after the war, America was prosperous. It was one of the reasons I was eager to stay. Although I'd never be as rich as I once was, there was hope here, unlike my homeland; and someday I would convince Mama and János to come here too.

The streetcar stopped in front of the Minneapolis Auditorium, which took up an entire block on the southwest side of the city. We followed the crowd toward the enormous brick-and-limestone building, crowned with a red roof.

Mariska clutched her handbag as we waited to cross the street. "How will we ever find him? There are three doors and hundred people. So many."

"He asked us to wait outside the center door. He said I will know who he is."

"How will you know?"

"He didn't say."

"That is *nevetséges*, how you say?"

"Ludicrous."

"Yes. I already do not like this man."

It did seem an odd request. Perhaps he didn't realize how many people would be attending this free concert. A long line of people wound down the street as they waited to enter the auditorium. Would Mr. Erickson be holding something or wearing an item of clothing that would identify him? Would Mariska and I end up watching the concert alone?

I hoped Mr. Erickson had saved us a spot in the long line. I searched the crowd, remembering how I felt at the train station when I was desperately looking for Joe; how my heart had pounded with fear of being abandoned. It made me angry to have those feelings thrust upon me again due to this man's inadequate planning. Mariska was correct; this was a strike against Finn Erickson.

I turned to Mariska. "You are right. I don't care if I see him or not. Let's go."

But then I stopped and pulled her back.

CHAPTER FOURTEEN

A MAN STOOD NEAR THE FRONT OF THE LINE. IN HIS HAND he held a small bouquet of blue flowers.

Forget-me-nots.

He was tall, almost wiry in his physique, dressed in a dark gray suit. A fedora sat low on his forehead so I couldn't see his eyes, but what I did see was a face that was tan and rugged. He said he was thirty-three, but he looked older, especially when compared to freckle-faced Jeffrey Fairbanks.

When his brown eyes met mine, I knew for certain it was him. They held the same rawness in them as his letter. They were eyes that had suffered hardship and seen tragedy.

I approached him. "Mr. Erickson?"

He nodded. "I'm honored to meet you, Miss Mészáros." His lips turned up in a smile, which gave his whole face a new demeanor, a rather pleasant one.

"The perfect flowers to help me locate you," I said as I accepted them. "The same as the petals in your letter."

"They grow like weeds in Hungary," Mariska said, turning up her nose.

"They grow like weeds here too," he said. "But they're one of our most beautiful weeds."

"They're so dainty," I said. "Thank you very much. You may address me as Roza. And this is my friend Mariska."

"Pleased to meet you," he said, tipping his hat. "Please call me Finn."

Mariska gave a cold nod in return.

"Shall we, ladies?" The line was moving. He offered arms to both of us, and Mariska and I each took a side. Inside, the auditorium was huge, with an arched ceiling, and a stage at the far end surrounded by three tiers of seating that wrapped around the auditorium. In addition to that, chairs filled the floor space.

"It is so big!" Mariska said.

"It seats ten thousand people," Mr. Erickson said. "The Minneapolis Lakers play all their home games here."

"Do you follow sports, Finn?" I asked.

"Not usually. But they're the first professional sports team to come to the Twin Cities. It speaks of many good things to come for the area. And being an engineer, I know that signals more business for the railroad."

"You said in your letter that you travel a great deal."

"I do," he admitted. "Whoever marries me would be left home for stretches of time. I suppose that doesn't help my cause, but I want to be honest with you."

"I appreciate that."

He looked at the flowing crowd and quickly filling chairs on the floor. "There are a few seats to the side of the stage, if that's okay with you. We could go up into the stands, but I don't think it's very comfortable."

"We should take the chairs," I said, thinking of Mariska, who had been complaining of back pain.

He led us to three empty chairs near the side of the stage. "Perhaps we ought to have met earlier," Finn said.

I sat the bouquet on the floor below my chair. "We can still see most of the stage from here. And it is cooler on the side," I said, noting how many people in the center aisles were fanning themselves with their programs.

Finn seemed to be studying the program he'd been given.

I didn't take him for the nervous type, but the paper shook slightly.

"The Civic Orchestra is made up of seventy-one members of the Minneapolis Symphony Orchestra," he said, reading from the program. "They should give a good performance."

"Have you heard them before?"

"No," he admitted. "But I thought it was something you might enjoy. I suppose you've heard many great symphonies before, what with living in Vienna?"

"I performed to the music of the Vienna Philharmonic. They're considered the best in the world." I said this without a bit of haughtiness in my voice. It was a fact.

He looked down at the program in his hands before responding. "So you may be disappointed today."

"I'm sure this performance will be very enjoyable," I said, trying to make him feel better.

He raised his eyebrows.

"You don't believe me," I said.

"You're trying too hard," he replied. "But I thank you for it." And he flashed a small smile again, one that I thought looked out of place on his face, as though he weren't used to smiling.

I was about to say something more when the red velvet curtains parted.

The whirr of conversation ceased and was replaced by an anxiousness in the air. I remembered that feeling right before a performance, as I waited backstage for those curtains to part, jittery and excited for all that was to come. And in an instant I was back in Vienna, a young ballerina waiting for the curtains to open, filled with hope for the future, before the war. When I was young I thought the air was charged with electricity from anticipation, that a storm could form right there on the stage, and lightning would strike.

And it did strike, but not the way I'd thought.

The tuxedoed members of the orchestra sat in a semicircle around the stage, their white bow ties straining their necks, and their fingers and mouths poised on their instruments. The conductor faced the audience and bowed before turning around.

He held up the baton, pausing a moment for heightened effect. Then the band began to play.

I clutched the sides of my chair as the lighthearted music of Johann Strauss's "Roses from the South" filled the auditorium. I'd been a young student when I performed this ballet with the troupe. I remembered everything: the frilly lace of my peach dress, the lightness of the petit allegro—the small jumps, the magical moment onstage when I almost felt perfection, and the roar of the crowd afterward.

I shuddered. I hadn't expected this music. And I certainly hadn't expected this reaction. The rhythm was part of me; my toes wanted to point, my arms wanted to rise up, and my body shouted to move with the music.

This urge of movement was followed by something else. A profound sadness for all that I'd lost. What the war had taken from me. How I still missed dancing!

I looked down as a plain white man's handkerchief was placed on my lap. A tear dripped off the end of my nose. I hadn't even realized I'd been crying.

I dabbed my eyes with the handkerchief. I sniffed. How could I have let myself break down in front of this stranger? What must he think? I waited for him to say something, but when I snuck a peek at him, his eyes were on the stage.

A moment later, though, I noticed his hand at his side, his palm open, as though it was some sort of invitation.

I put my palm in his. He closed his fingers around mine, and a flood of warmth and comfort filled me.

It was a simple gesture. I shuddered again, but this time it was due to a different sensation. The first time since coming to America that I'd felt this way. No, the first time since I'd been in Joe's strong arms that reached around me like sturdy tree branches that would never break.

I felt safe.

CHAPTER FIFTEEN

Finn picked a small restaurant within walking distance of the Auditorium. He asked Mariska what she thought of the concert.

"Very good," Mariska had answered. "It was free, no? That is why so many people there. Much crowds."

"It was the first of several free concerts this year," Finn had replied. "I'm sure they will all be well-attended."

"We Hungarians know how important music is," I said. "Every occasion in Hungary must have music."

Most weekends, the Hungarian residents in Mariska's building gathered outside around a bonfire to sing, dance, and drink. I had joined them for a short time one weekend, and it made me miss my homeland that much more.

We were seated at a small table near the back of the restaurant. Mariska moved her chair closer, claiming she couldn't hear the conversation. The room was crowded, with tables almost on top of each other.

I knew that Mariska wasn't thrilled with the modest restaurant, even after Finn had opened the door, announcing, "I know it doesn't look like much, but it's one of the best places to eat in Minneapolis."

When the waiter approached our table, Finn deferred to us. "I'll let the ladies order first," he said quietly, then added, "You might suggest the wild rice soup."

"Have you eaten here often?" I asked when our orders had been taken. I'd ordered the soup, but Mariska had opted for a sandwich.

"Yes, when we don't pin for home the same day. Sorry. That's railroad talk for going home."

"Do you live far from here?" I asked.

"About an hour as the crow flies."

"Crow?" I looked around for a crow.

"It's an American saying," Finn said, smiling. "It refers to the shortest route."

"You own your home?" Mariska asked.

He nodded. "I bought it before the war. A two-story, not too fancy, but it's good-sized and sits a few blocks off Main Street. We had planned to marry and start a family when I got back. But that didn't happen, so I'm living there alone now, and frankly, it's too big for a bachelor, and the place could use a woman's touch."

"I'm sorry," I said, feeling the sting of Joe's rejection as I thought of Finn's situation.

He shrugged. "It's for the best, I guess. At least, that's how I prefer to look at it."

I wished I could feel the same way. But here I was, on a date with a stranger instead of in the arms of the man I loved.

"What has your life been like since the war ended?" he asked. "How did you survive in Vienna?"

"Like most people in Vienna I did not have much to eat. I spent my time working at an orphanage for children born during the occupation, ones who were the result of unspeakable acts. I came home to an empty apartment each night and wrote to my fiancé, telling him how much I looked forward to our life together in America."

I shook my head. "I sound bitter because I am. It is perhaps too soon, but I do not have time."

"It will pass," he said in a comforting voice.

Would it? I appreciated that Finn didn't seem as bitter as he could have been. As bitter as I still felt. He had a quiet authority about him, and I wondered about *his* experience in the war. He had written that he commanded a squadron.

"Where is your town?" Mariska asked.

"Red Wing is southeast of here, on the Mississippi River." He turned to me. "I hoped you might enjoy living near the bluffs and river."

I'd imagined Joe's homestead for so long it was hard to think of where else I might want to live. Would the river remind me too much of home, of the Danube that separated Buda and Pest, all of which was under Communist control?

"My mother and brother still live in Budapest, but they have lost everything," I told him. "It is my hope to bring them to America someday."

I held my breath, wondering how this man would feel about that statement.

"I would be honored to help you with that," he said, "although I don't know much about the process of immigration."

I nodded. Jeffrey Fairbanks might have more connections in that department. But I hadn't felt comfortable telling him when we met. Would he be receptive to helping me?

"I'm afraid the concert was my way of meeting you without letting on that I'm not much of a talker. But I am a good listener," he added.

He swept his arm toward the noisy customers. "And I know this isn't as nice a place as you're probably used to. There are some proper restaurants in Red Wing that I'd like to take you."

I caught Mariska's sideways glance, one that meant he wasn't very social *or* rich. I could hear Mariska's voice in my head wondering why he didn't take me someplace nicer if he had the money. Was he making promises he couldn't keep?

He was definitely quieter than Jeff Fairbanks, and he hadn't exactly gone out of his way to impress me. Was he miserly? Or couldn't he afford a nice restaurant?

But when our food was served, I changed my mind. After one taste of the wild rice soup I exclaimed, "This is delicious!"

Finn nodded. "It's my favorite."

"It's the best soup I've ever had, except of course for Mariska's *gulyás*," I added, not wanting to offend her.

"Here, try a bite," I offered Mariska, who accepted a teaspoon of the thick soup.

"Is okay," Mariska said in a noncommittal way, and then licked the spoon again.

I turned to Finn. "Can I ask you something personal?"

"Of course."

"I wonder why you would offer to marry me."

"Well, first off, you looked a bit sad in your picture. But it's not pity, believe me. I've been through something similar and the last thing you want or need is to be pitied. I've had this longing for some time to start over. But I needed someone I could connect with. I know this sounds simplistic, but now that I've met you, I feel that connection was more than just in my mind. I hope I'm not being too forward in saying that."

"No. I appreciate your honesty."

"Then in all honesty I can say that I'd do my best to make a good future for you."

After lunch, I paused outside the door, even as Mariska had hold of my arm.

"I enjoyed the concert and the meal, Finn," I said. "We can make our own way to the streetcar."

"Thank you for allowing me this opportunity to meet you," Finn said, taking my hand in a warm embrace. "Whoever you choose, or wherever you go, I wish you a happy life."

"Thank you. That means a great deal," I responded, and once

again I felt safe with my hand in his. It wasn't love, or passion; nothing like I'd felt with Joe. He was more of a protector, someone who would always put my well-being before his. This was what I felt as he held my hand, and the reason I let it stay there perhaps a moment too long, until he finally let go.

"I am glad you did not kiss him," Mariska said as we made our way to the streetcar.

"Why?"

"Because he is a trickster."

"What do you mean?"

"He is too nice. He shake hands with waiter when we leave, and wish everyone he meet a nice day. No one is that nice."

"But you thought Jeffrey Fairbanks was nice."

"Yes, but he is nice in different way. Jeffrey Fairbanks is friendly, but he knows not to make friends with server."

I wanted to ask Mariska if she considered me a friend. Until recently we had occupied different social positions. "How do you know that?" I asked.

"He tell him when we leave that steak was overcooked."

"Oh. I didn't know."

"He was right to say that when he pay so much money for meal."

"I guess he was."

We walked up the steps to the streetcar and found a seat near the front. "I doubt Finn would complain about a meal," I said. The waiter hadn't offered to fill his cup of coffee during our meal, and he hadn't said anything.

"Is not a bad thing," Mariska said. "Jeffrey Fairbanks knows who is waiter and who is customer. He stand up for himself. I wonder if Mr. Erickson would do same."

"That's a good question," I said. But I had no answer.

CHAPTER SIXTEEN

ARISKA BRUSHED FLOUR FROM HER HANDS ONTO HER apron. The countertop held two evenly rounded balls of dough that she was making into *kalács*, Hungarian sweet braided bread. The thick aroma of yeast and strong tea hung in the still, hot air. "I do not understand. You are a countess. You should go to fancy restaurants and attend balls. You barely speak to poor Mr. Carter. He is president of a bank! A widower who has charming little boy who needs a mother. Did you not see picture of his child? And his house? It has seven bedrooms and come with maid and butler."

I stirred sugar into my tea, thinking how commonplace it was to have sugar now in America when it was still rare in Vienna, and often sold on the black market. I knew this showdown would be coming. Mariska had been stewing all night, ever since my last date, which had taken place at Hotel Lowry's Terrace. Mr. Carter was less than attractive; he had a bulbous nose, was overweight, and had a face like a donkey, but he was gracious. And extremely rich. The food was wonderful, and afterward Mr. Carter had taken my hand and led me onto the dance floor. He'd proposed at the end of the dance. Mariska and Jakab had sat at another table, enjoying their dinner while we danced.

"He was nice. And yes, I love children. It was one of the reasons I chose him in the first place. I felt sorry for the little boy. But when I looked into his eyes, all I saw was grief. He is still in mourning over his dead wife. I do not want that complication in my marriage."

"But you can help him get over his grief."

"I lived in Vienna during the war. I have seen enough grief."

Mariska put her hand on her heart, smearing flour onto her apron. "What about that little boy?"

"Mr. Carter will have no trouble finding a wife. I am sure that little boy will have a new mother soon."

"Then you will marry Jeffrey Fairbanks?"

I paused, carefully framing my next words. "I have not made my decision yet."

"But who else would you pick? Not that man Finn Erickson?"

"It is between him and Jeff," I replied, looking away.

Mariska stood over her now, her hands on her hips. "What can he offer you? He has a small house in a small town and he travels for days. He tell you this himself. You will be all alone. Why not pick someone who can offer you nice things? He offers less than anyone else, even the one you discard at the last minute."

She was referring to the Hungarian suitor. In Mariska's view, Finn Erickson was no better. And perhaps he wasn't. But he was American, not Hungarian, and that counted for something.

"Jeffrey Fairbanks will treat you like countess," Mariska said.

"I don't want that. I'm just a woman like you."

"Every woman wants to be treated like countess," Mariska objected. "And you are an actual countess."

Mariska could never understand. I had already rejected my aristocratic role when I became a ballerina. It was unheard of for an aristocratic woman to work, much less pursue such a difficult occupation. I was supposed to attend charitable events, entertain dignitaries, and discuss the latest Paris fashions. I was supposed to arrange dinner parties for dignitaries like Mama had done.

Mama, who knew how to make proper seating arrangements and picked just the right music and food for each occasion, something I was never interested in despite her constant attempts to instruct me. I didn't want to regress into that role again, not after all

I'd done to distance myself from it. Frankly, being alone might be just what I needed now.

"You said you were not marrying for love. Jeffrey Fairbanks will buy you nice things. That is what your mother would want." Mariska was still standing over me, demanding an answer.

"I'm not in love with *any* of those men," I answered. "But it is my decision to make, and I will choose who I think is best for me."

Mariska drew back with a pained expression on her face. I regretted hurting her feelings, but this conversation wasn't one I would budge on. Mariska wasn't my mother. And when had I ever listened to my mother, anyway?

"You ask for my approval," Mariska said, her voice sounding like a whimper.

I sighed. "You are right. I did. I'm sorry. I am just anxious."

I looked around the small, hot kitchen, at the beads of sweat running down Mariska's face, a woman I might never have met if circumstances were different. My eyes fixed on the sugar bowl perched on the colorful tablecloth as I smelled the yeasty dough rising on the counter. "We are not in Hungary. We are in America now."

Even as I said that, everything here reminded me of my home country: the indigo-colored cup and saucer that her tea was in, the flowery pattern of the embroidery on the tablecloth that Mariska's aunt had sent her.

"Still, Hungarian tradition dictates."

I stood up. "I do not abide by tradition anymore," I said, my voice firm. "Things are different here. *I* am different. You did not live through the war. You do not know what it was like."

Mariska picked up a ripe apple from the counter. "Yes, war cause change. But you cannot change who you are, *really* are inside, any more than an apple can change into a peach. How will a countess make life of small-town housewife of railroad engineer? Will you learn to cook? You cannot even make the sweet bread of your ancestors. And will you wash clothes like a commoner? And clean floors and do dishes? Is this the life you choose?"

"I have already been doing many of those things for the last few years," I said. "And if I do choose that life, I will learn how to cook." I had to clear my head. I turned away. "I am going for a walk."

"And what if Mr. Anders calls?"

"Tell him . . ." I took a breath and looked back. "Tell him I will give my answer today."

As I walked, I thought of everything Mariska had said. She was right about so much, except the banker. He was nice enough, but his face made it hard for me to look at him for any length of time. His wife must have loved him very much to overlook that. He also had narrow eyes full of sadness. The kind of sadness that never went away no matter how much time passed.

Jeffrey Fairbanks was witty and social. Jeff would treat me well and Mariska and Jakab already adored him. I would live in the big city of Chicago in a beautiful home. I could attend plays and shop at upscale stores and have servants and staff to help me. Life would be easier than the farm life I had been expecting with Joe.

Joe was part of the problem. Jeff reminded me of Joe in some ways, in his outgoing manner and his promises of eternal adoration. But he was a younger version of Joe, more like a little brother. I also felt as though Jeff had selected me because I was a countess. But, of course he did!

And then there was Finn, shy and reserved. I thought of the free concert, how he'd picked a small restaurant within walking distance of the auditorium. If he didn't go out of his way to impress me now, what would he be like if I married him? How would I, a foreigner, fit into small-town life? Would I be forced to cook and clean like Mariska? What would he expect of me? I wasn't certain I was prepared for that kind of life.

I stopped in front of a pond and looked around. I'd been so lost in thought I hadn't paid much attention to where I was walking. A duck and three ducklings waddled into the weedy water.

I watched the furry yellow bodies glide across the pond in single file and listened to their peeps, glad for the distraction, even as my heart felt heavy with the decision I had to make. I was confident that staying in America was my best choice. Going back to Hungary would make for a dire life, even if I was with Mama and János. I remembered how Mama's Russian cousins had been sent to the Gulag during the Revolution.

Another memory surfaced, one from the orphanage I'd worked at. A young girl, not more than Péter's age, had arrived with an emaciated blond-haired infant swaddled in a dirty shirt.

"Is she yours?" I asked her.

The girl nodded. She had hollow eyes and a swollen belly. It was any wonder she was still alive. "I was going to drown her if she looked like the Russian pig. But I couldn't do it."

"Where are your parents?"

"Both dead." This poor child was an orphan herself.

"Did you deliver her by yourself?"

"A neighbor heard my screams and came to help. Then she kicked me out of the apartment because I have no money."

"Do you want to stay here?"

The girl looked around, as though considering. "Is there food?"

"Not enough. But you won't starve, and you'll be safe here."

The girl, who said her name was Emma, plopped down on the floor, her decision made. She wanted nothing to do with her baby, though, even after I had washed the infant and dressed her in a clean diaper and blanket. The girl watched me feed the baby from a tiny bottle.

"I thought I was going to die when I gave birth," Emma said. "I wanted to die."

"But you are alive," I reminded her. "You have survived the worst of the war."

Over the next few weeks, as the baby gained strength and started to fill out, I commented on how much she looked like Emma, and encouraged her to name the baby. When I finally left for the U.S., Emma had claimed the baby as her own and kept watch over her day and night. She'd named the infant Maria, after her mother.

I thought of Emma and Maria now, of how, despite all the brutality and suffering, there was hope for the future.

Until now, my focus had just been to survive. I had made it through the war and its aftermath.

Then I had found love with Joe, and a chance to make a new start in another country. I'd spent the past two years planning that life.

But now what? My entire future was before me. My path was not a straight line like the ducks swimming in front of me. Either path I chose would change my life. Would I look back on this moment and regret taking one path over the other?

Time was running out. Cecil Anders would be calling in few hours for a decision. An appointment was already scheduled tomorrow at the courthouse before the Justice of the Peace. But who would I be marrying?

CHAPTER SEVENTEEN

※❀※

JAKAB KISSED ME ON THE CHEEK. *"GYÖNYÖRŰ VAGY.* BEAU-tiful."

"Köszönöm. Thank you." I had opted for a white dress that hit just below the knee, one with a square neckline and short jacket. It wasn't what I'd imagined getting married in, but nothing about today was what I'd imagined. Especially the groom.

I sniffed, holding back a tear. I would miss these people. Jakab, who had been so kind to me. Péter, whose bright blue eyes and contagious laugh reminded me of my own brother; and Mariska, who'd been both a mother and friend to me. Had it really been just three weeks since my world had fallen apart?

Now I would rebuild my world.

Péter was at school today. I had left some candy for him with a note.

Mariska had tears in her eyes, which made it harder for me not to cry.

"I am glad you are standing up for me," I said. "I don't think I could do this without you."

Mariska took my hand and placed it on her growing belly. "She will remember your voice."

"I will write to you," I said. "And I will come to see the baby."

I hugged my friend, who now had a stream of wetness on her face. I continued to comfort Mariska while Jakab brought out my trunk.

"If you decide is wrong choice," he said as he placed the trunk in the car, "remember we are here."

I let a tear fall. "I am thankful for all you have done, dear Jakab." How was it that someone who had so little was willing to take me in?

We drove in silence to the courthouse. I adjusted the white hat and veil that fell over my eyes. If I were in Vienna, a horse-drawn carriage would take me to the church, where the wedding party would be waiting. If I were in Budapest, my wedding would be held in the gardens behind my parent's mansion, and at least a hundred guests would dine on pork roast and other grilled meats, chicken soup and stuffed cabbage, and make countless toasts of *pálinka*.

But neither of those was an option. Vienna was divided into four sections, still on the brink of starvation. And the mansion and gardens of my Hungarian youth were only a memory. My new husband and I would leave shortly after the ceremony to travel to our new home.

He wasn't Joe. He wasn't much more than a stranger. My heart still remembered Joe's embrace, but I wouldn't have to return home, and I had triumphed over his rejection. I should not be so glum.

"We are not going to a funeral," I said, mustering a smile as I scolded my weepy car mates. "This is a happy occasion. I do not have to go back. It is what I hoped for."

"You are right," Mariska said, wiping her eyes. "I remember how happy we were when you get all those letters."

"And I have made the best choice from them all," I said with conviction. "The past is past. Now is a new beginning."

Jakab pointed to the back. "I have bottle of pálinka in trunk. We will toast your good fortune afterward."

"And I bring something special." Mariska nodded at a bag next to her.

I let out a breath. Whatever happened, I was fortunate to have met these fine people.

The courthouse was a large stone building with pillars, but not as exquisite or detailed as the buildings in Budapest or Vienna. None of the buildings I'd seen in America could compare. As we pulled next to the curb to park, I noticed a man exit the pickup truck in front of us. He stood and patted his suit, as though straightening any wrinkles. His mouth was in a straight line, as though he weren't sure what he was getting into. If he'd been too happy, I would have doubted his motives.

I got out of the car and walked toward him. My heart was pounding, and my jacket suddenly felt too tight. Could I actually go through with this?

"Mr. Erickson," I said, and extended my hand, holding it steady despite my nerves. If ballet had taught me anything, it was that I could maintain a position in the face of fear.

A flicker of a smile crossed his face as his hand took mine. "You should get used to calling me Finn."

"Finn," I repeated. "You are ready?"

He nodded. "As ready as I'll ever be, Roza." He raised his eyebrows. "Also a bit confused. I still can't believe you chose me. I'm not exactly the catch of the year. Are you sure you don't want to change your mind?"

"You are too humble," I replied. "And when my mind is made up, I do not change it."

"You're clearly a woman to be reckoned with," he said. "And that's a compliment."

"Thank you." I felt a bit better with my hand in his. I had no idea why. I was marrying a stranger and, with him, a life I could not begin to imagine. I looked back at Mariska, who did not look too gloomy, considering that she didn't approve my choice. Once I had explained that I preferred a quiet life, Mariska had accepted my decision, even as she pursed her lips and crossed her arms. When I also mentioned that Red Wing was much closer than Chicago, which would allow me to visit Mariska more often, she uncrossed her thick arms and enveloped me in a long hug. "You do this for me?" she'd cried. "Is too much."

Of course, I hadn't picked Finn for that reason, but it didn't hurt that Mariska thought so. But how else could I explain my decision when *I* didn't even understand it?

"You have no family with you?" I asked Finn.

He shrugged. "To be honest, I didn't consider myself a contender, and then when I got the news, I decided it was best to wait until after to tell my parents. I thought of telling my brother, but he's going through a tough time right now. He lost a leg in the war."

"I understand." I hadn't written to Mama yet; I wasn't sure what I would say in a letter that would properly explain my motives.

Finn adjusted his hat and fumbled in his pocket. He brought out a small ring box. He paused before opening it. "It's not much," he warned.

It was bigger than the ring Joe had given me, although not by much. The square European-cut diamond sparkled up at me. It was small but delicate, and it had two diamond accents on the sides of the gold band. I didn't know how much a railroad engineer made, but I guessed this ring cost more than he could afford.

"It's perfect," I said. I tried it on; the ring twirled freely on my finger. I took it off and handed it back to him for the ceremony.

"I should have known it'd be too big. You can have it resized," Finn said. "That's one of thousands of details I need to learn about you. I guess we'll have lots of time for that."

I looked at him, wondering why this man would consent to marrying me when he didn't even know my ring size. But then again, I didn't know his ring size either.

"I want you to know," he said as he fingered the ring, "that I stand by everything I wrote in my letter to you. I will always show you kindness and respect."

I nodded, hoping his words were as true as his intent. I had thought the same of Joe at one time.

We ascended the steps of the courthouse, past the tall, white pillars, and Finn held open a massive door. Inside, I let out a sigh. Cecil Anders was waiting for us.

"Thank you for coming," I said, hugging him. Seeing him here made me feel less shaky.

He gripped my arm and smiled. "Of course I had to come. This is my first matchmaker wedding."

"You remember your promise?" I asked.

"No names," he assured me. "I'll just report on the happy conclusion and give them a taste of your unique experience." He turned to Finn. "And this is the lucky groom?"

"Yes," Finn said, shaking Cecil's hand. "I am indeed one lucky man."

"I'm not sure you knew that she received over seventeen hundred offers of marriage," Cecil said. "You beat very long odds on this one."

Finn flinched. "It wouldn't be the first time for me. I was one of the lucky ones to come home."

Cecil seemed to recognize the flinch. "And we're forever grateful for your dedication and service."

Finn gave a small nod.

"Shall we go in?" Cecil asked, guiding us through another door and into a small chamber.

I felt myself being pulled along. Things seemed to suddenly move so fast. I took a last glance at the lobby. Somehow, irrationally, I'd imagined that Joe would rush in at the last minute and apologize. He'd say he loved me and he'd made a mistake. He'd show me his divorce papers and we would fall into each other's arms.

I sighed. My prince wouldn't be coming to rescue me. But unlike the Princess of Krakow, I wouldn't throw myself into the river. I would make my own happiness and find a way to survive, even if it meant marrying a stranger.

I would rescue myself.

It was a bitter reminder that my childhood nanny had warned me of years ago. Mademoiselle Petit had told me I would marry someday and love would have nothing to do with it. It turned out that she was correct after all.

MINNEAPOLIS STAR NEWSPAPER

March 21, 1948

IN THIS CORNER

CECIL ANDERS

LLONA, OUR HUNGARIAN COUNTESS, the 24-year-old girl who came to America to marry her ex-GI fiancé and discovered that he had just recently married, today has probably set a world record—perhaps an all-time record. She's the only woman I've ever heard of who has had 1,786 proposals of marriage. Since the case of the countess was published here on March 7, Llona has received more than 2,000 pieces of mail, five telegrams, two bouquets of American Beauty roses, two boxes of candy, and $30 in cash from three men who wanted to assist her and lighten her burden if they could. One man who stated in his letter that he was out of work told her that he knew how hard life was and after he had read of her misery he felt she needed the dollar more than he did.

THROUGH THE WEEK Llona has been very careful about accepting dates. After all, these men were total strangers to her, she knew little of their background. She did accept five dates.

OFFERS WEREN'T ALL for marriage. One man, 42, said he recognized her plight, offered her a job, said he would loan her money, give her counsel, if she needed it. A group of 12 Minneapolis attorneys eat together every noon. They had read the story and on Monday called to offer their collective services in a legal way. A score of Hungarians living in the area wrote. They offered their help . . .

YOU MAY RECALL that Llona, when she came to my office, had lost her appetite, had been spending many a sleepless night because she was faced with the possibility of being deported to her native Hungary, now under Communist control. By the end of the week, Llona was a changed young lady. Her future seemed brighter, her appetite had returned, and when the excitement of the proposals had diminished, she began to sleep. A changed woman she was, if I ever saw one, when she came back to my office to report on the progress of her plea. Her eyes had brightened, her face looked alive, her spirit had been revived. She actually glowed. . . .

NOW LET'S EXAMINE some of the proposals. One young ex-GI used a very clever device to meet Llona. He sent her a ticket to the Horowitz concert at the University. His seat was right next to Llona's. A pleasant surrounding to woo, indeed. Unfortunately, it didn't work because the delay in forwarding the mail brought the ticket to Llona just one day too late. Several men drove in from our surrounding areas. One young man drove 200 miles. . . .

RICHES WERE WITHIN her reach too. One of the prospects wrote from California, offered to pay her airplane fare to California for the meeting. Business prevented him from making the trip but wouldn't she come out? He told her of his two homes, one in Minneapolis, a beach home in California. He has a new Buick. He told her of his bank balance, that his business was sound, his income sufficient to make them very comfortable and, he hoped, happy . . .

THERE'S A LOT of gratitude in Llona's heart today. After all, this has been an outpouring of something a little beyond romance. Evident was the American spirit to help. Llona cannot physically answer all the letters she received. She's had a busy time just reading them. She is grateful, however, and wants every one of the writers to know it. Now for the windup. She called me yesterday morning to report that this week her permanent residence in the United States will be established. Out of the 1,786 proposals, she has selected one—she hopes THE one. They plan to wed in the next few days. In order to give them every chance to succeed and lead normal lives together, we're not announcing the name of the successful candidate. After all, marriage is a personal and, in a sense, a private matter. We're going to let them enjoy the privacy they want and deserve. It looks as though her immediate problems, then, have been solved.

I WANT TO EXPRESS This Corner's thanks to those who responded. It's been quite a week for me with men sliding up to me and surreptitiously asking me for her telephone and for information about her. I'll be very happy when the routine returns to normal. We've had a couple of laughs out of it, though. This telegram came from Rochester, Minn.: "Dear Cupid—As long as you're in the business, how about a helping hand here.— Gert, Elaine and Celeste." And on that note, we write finis to the Hungarian Countess episode, and may I add that I hope a lot of happiness lies ahead for her.

CHAPTER EIGHTEEN

T HE WEDDING WAS A QUICK AFFAIR, LASTING NO MORE than ten minutes on a Monday morning. I barely remembered murmuring "yes" to my vows. But now I wore the diamond ring on my finger. Finn had managed to find some tape, which he wound around the band of the ring so it stayed in place. The kiss had been too quick to judge anything about him, and I had been too nervous to notice how it felt.

I knew that if it took too much time, I wouldn't be able to go through with it. I thought of my own mother's arranged marriage, of how she'd married a man she barely knew, and not someone she'd had the freedom to choose on her own. At least I had selected this man, although it wasn't any more intimate than an arranged marriage.

After many hugs and handshakes of congratulations, we celebrated on the sidewalk in front of the automobiles in the brisk sunshine that reminded me of spring in Vienna. Mariska reached into her paper bag and took out a loaf of her braided bread, which she put on a white linen cloth embroidered with folk art at the edges.

"Since your parents are not here, Jakab and I will do custom." Mariska tore off pieces, which she handed to each of us, saving a piece for herself.

"This is Hungarian tradition. The bread is so you never hunger or be in need. And it also represent happiness. Eat," she commanded.

We ate the bread, then Mariska gave the plate to me. "You must break the plate to scare away bad spirits. And your husband must clean it up."

I slammed the plate on the cement. Finn started to pick up the pieces, but Jakab kept kicking them with his feet. "Is custom," he explained with a smile.

Then Jakab handed everyone paper cups, opened a bottle of *pálinka*, and toasted the newly married couple.

"To marriage." Cecil offered a toast.

We all drank to that.

Jakab refilled our cups.

"Must drink in one gulp," he told us. "We have custom to steal the bride, but time prevent it."

I looked at Finn, who raised his cup to his lips. We both winced as the strong alcohol burned our throats, then we threw the paper cups behind us. Finn turned around and stomped on the cups.

"Scaring away more bad spirits," he said, and everyone laughed.

Cecil patted him on the back. "That's about as broken as a paper cup can get."

Finn turned to me. "I'm sorry we don't have more time for a proper meal. I have to report to work at three o'clock."

"I understand." I hugged Mariska one last time and told her I would write. Jakab helped transfer my luggage to the back of Finn's truck.

Cecil Anders clasped my hand in his. "Keep in touch, countess."

"Thank you for everything," I said, and felt my eyes well up.

Finn held open the door to the truck and helped me in. Then he tipped the brim of his hat to the well-wishers and hurried to the driver's side. The truck rattled to life, and we drove off, with me still waving at my friends as we left.

I turned to the front. "What is the name of your town again?"

"Red Wing," he replied.

"Red Wing," I repeated. "What is it named after?"

"It was given the name by the chief of a Sioux tribe."

I didn't hide the alarm in my voice. "There are Indians in your town?"

"Red Wing is near an Indian reservation. But don't believe the Westerns you've seen. I served with a man named Ike Eagleboy. He was a superior infantryman. He received the Bronze Star."

There was so much about this country I didn't understand.

The city landscape turned to countryside. Finn drove on gravel roads, and the dust blew so much that I had to crank up the partly open window.

"I'm sorry I'll have to leave you this first night," he said. "I've stocked the refrigerator, though, so you should be okay until I return on Thursday. Are you certain you don't mind being alone? I could ask my mother to look in on you, but I thought it'd be better if we told her we were married in person first."

"I was alone for two years after the war. I can manage," I reassured him. I wasn't ready to meet his mother yet, and definitely not without Finn.

The truck was quiet for a while, with only the sounds of the road filling the space between us. Finn was a silent type; perhaps that came from spending time on the railroad. I stole glances at his profile while he had his eyes on the road. He had a strong, almost aristocratic nose. He was good-looking without being handsome, a bit gangly, but he wore it well, and his hair had hints of gray. He looked older than thirty-three. I couldn't help but wonder if that was a product of the war.

I tried not to think too much about what lay ahead. My goal had been to stay in America and I'd achieved it. But I also remembered a wedding our family had attended before the war between Princess Marina of Greece and Prince George, the Duke of Kent. I was only ten at the time. Princess Elizabeth was at the wedding and we'd hit it off, both of us having been tutored and not exposed to many other children our own age. We both loved horseback riding and reading, and Elizabeth said she wanted to marry a farmer so she could have lots of horses. This was before Elizabeth became heir to the British throne, when she still lived on Piccadilly, and the fourteen-year-old Prince Philip, who was also at the wedding, thought we were too young to pay much attention to.

I had seen the headlines on newspapers when Elizabeth and Philip were to be married last November. I imagined how different their wedding would be from the one I just had. How far apart had our worlds become in the last few years?

I kept my hands in my lap, nervously fingering the ring. "Is this your only vehicle?" I asked. A truck, which rattled through every pothole in the road. The inside was clean and tidy, though, and I hoped this foretold what his home would be like. I couldn't tolerate a messy house.

He nodded. "But we're only a few blocks from downtown. You can walk to a store if you need anything. And you can obtain your driver's license, if you'd like."

"Yes. I'd like that." Mama didn't drive. But I vowed to learn. If I was going to live here, I would need to know things that would help me survive.

"I'll introduce you to my parents when I get back. My brother, Jack, is living with them right now," Finn continued. "Until he can manage on his own."

"You mentioned that he lost a leg?"

Finn nodded. "Yeah. Pop said he joined up two months after I did. He made it through the Battle of the Bulge unharmed, but lost his leg to a German grenade right before Germany surrendered. He spent the next year in a hospital for rehabilitation."

"He was lucky," I said quietly.

Finn turned to look at me. "Luckier than most," he agreed.

The roads turned from flat to hilly, and the river bluffs came into view. I couldn't see the Mississippi River, but I imagined it snaking its way through the city, the train tracks following the river's path down the state.

Finn was right. This reminded me of Gellert Hill overlooking the Danube River in my Hungarian homeland. Perhaps I would be able to hear the river from my new home. But perhaps it would also remind me of all I'd lost. I had put my heartbreak behind me; I hoped living here wouldn't make me feel too nostalgic.

We came to a crest in the road, and buildings glistened in the distance beneath a bright sun.

"Is that Red Wing?" I asked. It looked like a miniature toy town from up here, one that followed the Mississippi River and spread until it hit the bluffs. A steel bridge connected the city to the other side of the river, but all I could see was dense foliage on the other side.

"Yes. It's good-sized for a small town. We're about eight thousand and growing."

Then he said, "I should warn you before I forget. The furnace makes a rumbling noise when it turns on, so don't get scared when you hear it. And Minnesota weather can turn on a dime, even in the summer months."

I nodded. Was this his way of preparing me for a house that he knew I would not like? I didn't expect it to be a mansion, but I hoped it would be a home I could be proud of, one where I would find a happy respite from the world.

Finn drove onto a paved road, a busy street that wove past businesses and factories. He pointed at a large building made of reddish-brown brick. "That's Red Wing Potteries, where they make crockery and dinnerware."

In America I had noticed that there was no aesthetic quality to their buildings. The factory was built for function, and other than a sign out front with the name of the company, it looked rather plain.

Even street signs were ugly, not like the ones in Vienna. The businesses we passed were all like that; storefronts with large signs that did little to lure a person inside. And the wide streets had no character either. They were all paved the same way, with no personality.

Then he turned down a residential street. I studied each house we passed, trying to guess which one was Finn's. They were small homes shaped like little boxes, some with peeling paint and unkempt yards. A few had screened porches. I held my breath as we passed each one, hoping the truck would continue past.

Then Finn turned down another street, one that was lined with tall oaks and maples. The homes were large and stately. He drove another two blocks until he pulled up in front of a yellow two-story home. It was framed by a white wraparound porch with decorative railings. Beneath the railings were neatly trimmed shrubs. A dormer and large windows lent a Victorian charm to the house. Two black wrought-iron chairs occupied the large porch, adjacent to the front door.

"It's beautiful," I said, feeling pleasantly surprised. It was by no means a mansion, but it was bigger than I had anticipated. "How many bedrooms does it have?"

"Four. I got a good deal on it with the GI Bill. I know it's a lot to keep up with. I have a woman who comes every Thursday to help clean. She's real nice, and if you want, we can keep her on. I thought I'd ask you first."

He got out and hurried over to open my door. A stone path led to the front porch. I could see myself sitting on the porch, a cup of tea in my hands, and an open book on my lap. I sighed with relief.

Finn carried my trunk up to the porch. He left it there while he opened the door. He paused. "We had a quick wedding, but some things are tradition in our part of the country."

He reached down and scooped me up in his arms. I let out a small gasp. "What is this?"

"I told you. It's an American tradition." Finn carried me over the threshold. The front entry had a rug and a closet and met with another door. Finn grasped for the other door, swinging it open, then set me gently down inside.

I stepped into a room filled with warmth, from the wooden floors that opened to a large sitting room on the left, to a staircase on the right that led upstairs. Directly in front of us was another door, which was partly opened and revealed a mahogany dining room table and buffet. Flowery red-and-green wallpaper lined the walls, which I thought made the rooms darker than necessary. Thick beige curtains hugged the tall windows.

The sitting room held a piano and two chairs that didn't match.

"Do you play?" I asked, pointing at the piano.

"I used to, a long time ago."

"Mama made me study piano, but my heart wasn't in it. I only liked subjects I excelled at, and piano wasn't one of those. I do speak four languages, though. Who helped you decorate?"

"No one. I haven't done much with it since I bought it," Finn said. "The previous owners left most of the furniture that's here, including the piano. I haven't had much inclination to replace it. Until now. Like I said, it needs a woman's touch."

I can do that, I thought. It would give me something to keep busy.

The living room held two high-back chairs that had seen better days, and a beige sofa flanked by a table with a square radio on a lace doily. Opposite the sofa was a stone fireplace that took up much of the wall. Finn led me through another pocket door to the expansive kitchen, where a breakfast nook was tucked into a bay window. There were many cupboards and a black iron range. I had no idea of how to work such a thing.

"There's another stairway to the bedrooms," Finn said, motioning toward a smaller stairwell to the side of the kitchen. "But I'll take you up the front staircase."

I followed him up the staircase, which turned abruptly after a few steps at the front of the house and ended at a small landing, and headed to the second level, clutching the wooden banister and noting the tall radiators.

A long hallway had doors on each side. Finn opened each door as we passed. Two rooms were empty of furniture. The last three held a bathroom, a guest room with a twin bed and simple dresser, and the master bedroom, which had a larger bed topped with a heavy Scandinavian printed bedspread, rounded dressers carved with a leaf design, and a rounded mirror atop another dresser carved the same way. A smaller version of the downstairs fireplace occupied the far wall. A door to the side opened up into a master bathroom.

Finn patted the bed. I froze, overcome with a sudden nervousness.

"It's not the most comfortable mattress. I've been thinking of getting something new." He cleared his throat. "I guess now is as good a time as any to talk about our wedding night."

I held my breath, wondering if he wanted to consummate our marriage right now.

He looked away a moment, as though he were embarrassed. "Since we're pretty much strangers, I thought it might be best if I slept in the other room until we're more comfortable with each other. I don't want to rush you into anything."

I tried to hide the relief I felt. I choked up, unable to do anything but nod.

"That's not to say I'll settle for a platonic relationship," he added. "I married you in good faith, and expect you did the same." He turned toward the door. "I'll go get your trunk."

After he left I sat down on the bed and forced out a breath. "What have I gotten myself into?" I murmured.

CHAPTER NINETEEN

❧

I BARELY HAD TIME TO ASK HOW ANYTHING WORKED. FINN handed me a piece of paper with some numbers written on it before he left. "You can call the depot if there's an emergency, and they'll get hold of me. I also wrote my parents' number on here, and the number of an elderly couple next door, Mr. and Mrs. Mennen." He paused. "I'm sorry we don't have more time."

I followed him to the door. There was an awkward moment before he reached down and kissed me on the lips. It wasn't as quick as the earlier kiss. His lips lingered for a long moment. "I'll see you in a few days, Mrs. Erickson."

"Goodbye. Don't worry. I will be fine."

I closed the door behind him and smiled. It didn't feel at all like kissing a brother. For that I was grateful.

The first thing I did was to unpack my clothes. Finn had left the two top drawers empty. I hung up my dresses and noted that Finn's clothing was neatly pushed to one side, but that, even with his modest wardrobe, he still had more clothing than me. That would have to be remedied.

I changed into a casual, button-up shirtdress that belted at the waist and spent the rest of the afternoon searching for a place to hide the Chopin score. I imagined a big house like this would have plenty of hiding spots. But first I took the manuscript and laid it flat, then I wrapped the score in a plastic bag to make sure it didn't get damaged. I took out an old Hungarian Bible I'd brought with me from Europe and placed the plastic-covered score inside so it would stay flat. Then I wrapped the Bible in plastic as an added protection.

I dismissed the basement for fear of mold or dampness. I also had to be careful of the radiators, which I feared would set the manuscript on fire. A folding stairwell led to the attic, where the dormer windows looked out the front of the house. I could see the Mississippi from here, wider than I'd imagined, its rushing waters carrying boats downstream. I stood for a while enjoying the view, then left. I would have to find another spot to hide the Chopin score. There were boxes in the attic, which meant that Finn sometimes came up here.

It wasn't until I'd looked in all the bedrooms that I finally found a loose board in one of the closets of an empty bedroom. I tucked the plastic bag containing the book and manuscript beneath the board, then put it carefully back, stepping down on it to secure it in place.

I was famished. I went down to the kitchen. Finn had left a $10 bill on the table with a note that read:

> In case you need anything—you can also go to Koplin's Corner Grocery and have them put it on my account.

I studied his handwriting. Small letters, neatly written, concise with no flair, as though he purposely didn't want to draw attention to his handwriting.

I opened the refrigerator and found an assortment of lunch meats, and some cold chicken under plastic wrap. I ate a piece of chicken and poured myself a glass of milk. I took the glass with me to the backyard, which I had yet to explore. I was surprised again to find that the porch wrapped completely around the house and had steps leading down to a grassy area with mature trees. Beyond that were distant trees that hinted of more homes.

A row of tall lilac bushes separated Finn's house from the neighbors, and on the far side of the house was a low garage that made the other neighbors more distant. That was fine with me; I wasn't the type to talk over backyard fences or have coffee klatches. I preferred to keep busy in other ways. I would plant a small garden like Mariska had done. I would decorate my new home. I would get a dog, and maybe start riding horses again like I used to do when I was young. I would learn to cook.

And perhaps one day I would even have children, although their faces in my dreams wouldn't be the same. Because when I dreamed of children they still looked like Joe.

CHAPTER TWENTY

B EFORE ANYTHING ELSE, I WOULD EXPLORE THE TOWN. I
put on my coat, wrote down my new address on the sheet of
paper Finn had left on the table, just in case I got lost, and placed
it in my pocket. Then I picked up the $10 bill and tucked it in my
handbag.

Finn had said we lived a few blocks from downtown. I looked up
at the dormer window, which pointed east. That was the direction
I needed to go, toward the river. The streets here were straight, not
like the winding ones in Vienna, where some were more cobblestone
alleyways than paved roads. If I could find my way around Vienna, I
was certain I'd have no problem in Red Wing, Minnesota. I walked
down the street lined with elegant homes, most of them larger than
the one Finn owned. Finn had said the homes in this neighborhood were older, but what did Americans know of old? To them
anything more than one hundred years old qualified as historic.

It made my heart hurt to know that no one would recognize
Vienna now. The center of the world reduced to rubble, where I had
once reveled in all the churches, monuments, and museums, where
every house was old and had a touch of elegance, perhaps a window
seat or brocade curtains, or a crystal chandelier. Where culture was
everything. How would they rebuild, and what would it look like
after they did? Hopefully, not like what I'd seen so far in America.

It was late afternoon and still chilly, but the sun hugged my back
as I walked, and I was perspiring by the time I reached Main Street.
I passed by restaurants, shops, insurance companies, a bowling alley,

law offices, and a nice hotel. So much space between buildings, not like the ones in Vienna and Budapest that were propped against one another, with mazes of alleys where artisans hawked their wares.

People walked past and nodded and smiled. I took it all in. The chubby-cheeked babies. Everyone so clean with such healthy, white teeth. They all looked happy, their arms filled with packages. A door opened and I was overcome by the strong aroma of cooked meat and fresh vegetables. And fresh fruit! I almost burst into tears at the sight of an orange.

All this prosperity. All this food. An unbidden memory surfaced from last year in Vienna. I had spent hours in line waiting for a loaf of bread. I was the last to get one before they ran out. I tried not to look at the desperate faces behind me, and when I did they haunted me; mothers with small, fussy children, men with protruding stomachs and listless eyes. I remembered the shame of walking away with the loaf, unwilling to give it up.

But looking around now it was as though the war had never come to Red Wing, Minnesota. I wondered if the people living here during the war were aware of it all, if it never happened except in newspaper headlines.

But I knew that Finn served, and that his brother did too. Finn's brother had lost his leg.

I could see the river in the distance, another two blocks away. But my legs felt suddenly wobbly, and I was thirsty. It had been a long, stressful day.

I went inside a corner café called Nellie's, where only one other customer was sitting in a small booth. It was dark compared to the bright sunlight outside and I could barely see. There were a few booths, and opposite those, a laminated counter that stretched the length of the café. I sat on a stool at the counter.

Across from me a chocolate cake sat under a dome. An older woman, who was as wide as she was tall, came out from the kitchen carrying a plate. She sat it before the other customer, a man who had been reading a newspaper.

"Better eat this before it gets cold," she scolded him. "I don't fancy anyone not appreciating my cooking."

"Yes, ma'am," he replied, and dutifully put the paper down. His dinner looked to be some sort of beef and noodle dish, which smelled delicious.

The woman took her place behind the counter, swiping at a stray gray hair that had come out of her bun.

"What can I get you?" she asked.

I pointed at the cake. "Is that made with real sugar?"

"Of course it is. You think I'd use corn syrup for my cakes?"

"Then I will have a piece of cake. And a glass of lemonade."

The woman put her hands on her hips. "I didn't hear a single 'please' with that order."

I was taken aback. "I am sorry. Please may I have a piece of cake and a glass of lemonade?"

"That's better. Where you from?"

"Originally Hungary. I have been living in Vienna for the past few years."

"That explains why you asked about the sugar. I heard rations are very restricted over there. Doesn't explain the rudeness, though."

"Daily rations are very little." I didn't try to explain that I still sometimes forgot the manners I'd been taught as a child.

"I'm Nellie, by the way. I've owned and run this place ever since my husband died eleven years ago."

"I am Roza."

"Good to meet you." She took out the largest slice of cake and put it on a plate.

"A skinny thing like you can eat this," she said, placing the plate and a fork in front of me. "I'll get you the lemonade."

"Thank you," I said, not forgetting my manners this time.

The cake was rich and moist, and the frosting creamy. I ate every morsel, leaving no crumbs on the plate. *This is my wedding cake,* I thought. *And I'm eating it alone.*

Several other customers entered. I watched them as I finished my lemonade. Nellie knew them all by name. She even knew what they wanted before they ordered.

Nellie gave a ticket to a man in the kitchen, then wiped her hands on her apron. She handed me the check. "You must have liked the cake."

"It was delicious. Please give my regards to the chef."

Nellie chuckled. "Gus does most of the cooking, and I have a couple of young men who help with the heavy work. But I make every cake and pie that's eaten."

"You are very gifted," I said.

"And you're kind. Sorry I snapped at you earlier. Some days wear at you more than others. Today was one of those. It's my wedding anniversary. You'd think I wouldn't get sentimental after all these years. It's just another day on the calendar, after all."

"I understand." I looked around to make sure no one was listening. "It is my wedding day today."

Nellie's eyes widened. "So what are you doing sitting in here eating cake by yourself?"

"My husband had to work."

"He couldn't take a day off to get married?"

I paused, then shrugged. "It was sudden, our marriage."

I stood up and took out the $10 bill.

"Hold on," Nellie said. She cut another slice of cake and put it on a plate, then wrapped a napkin over the top. "You think I'm taking your money today? We share the same wedding day. I wish you as much happiness as Ned and I had. And take this home for your husband."

"Thank you," I said, accepting the gift. "I will return the plate."

"No hurry," Nellie said, then left to attend to her customers.

I walked home, thinking how my first impression of Nellie had been wrong. Her gruff exterior hid a tender heart. I wondered about the men I'd met this week, if I'd been too rash to discount the banker with the children, or Jeffrey, who seemed too young. I'd only had time for one impression.

And what of my new husband, Finn? He was very quiet, a man who confessed to not knowing anything about ballet or symphonies or theater. I thought I wanted quiet. But was he too unrefined? Would our life together be dull and repetitive?

I almost walked past my new home. I caught myself at the neighbor's hedge and turned around. This was the right house. But something was wrong.

There was a car parked at the curb, and the front door of the house was slightly ajar. I'd closed it tightly before I left.

I entered cautiously, the plate shaking as I walked through each room. A movement in the kitchen stopped me. I took another step and peeked around the corner. A man sat at the kitchen table drinking a bottle of beer. He slid his other hand through messy brown hair. Dark stubble lined his face. He wore a short-sleeved plaid shirt and dark trousers. A crutch was propped next to his chair.

He almost dropped the bottle when he saw me.

"Who the hell are you?"

I stood up straight and walked into the kitchen. "I'm Roza. You must be Jack."

He tipped his head. "Have we met? Because I think I'd remember a dish like you."

"Not formally." I put the plate with the cake down on the table. "Finn is at work."

"I'm aware of that. I only come here when he's gone to check on the place and steal a few beers. But why are you here?"

I took a breath. This wasn't how I wanted to be introduced to Finn's brother. But I had no choice. "I am his wife."

"Wife?"

Then Jack fell off his seat.

CHAPTER TWENTY-ONE

※※※

IMADE A MOVE TO HELP HIM UP, BUT HE WAVED ME AWAY. HE shakily righted himself back in his chair, keeping his leg stiff, then took a long drink of his beer.

He was a shorter, stouter version of Finn, like a family version of Laurel and Hardy. He had Finn's narrow nose, but his eyes, cheeks, and chin were different, and he was not nearly as attractive as his brother.

Jack shook his head and let out a deep belly laugh.

"Good one. You had me going for a minute."

"But it's true."

"Listen, lady. I know Finn. My brother wouldn't go and get married and not tell anyone."

"We were married earlier today," I said. I held out my hand with the ring on it.

Jack stopped laughing. He took hold of my hand and stared at the glistening ring. "You're not joking me?"

"It is no joke. But I'm sure he didn't mean for you to find out this way."

"Well, I'll be. Old Finn got himself hitched. And he did well for himself, I might add. Did you meet in Europe?"

All these questions. Finn should be here to answer them. I removed my hand from his. "No. I am from Hungary originally. I have been living in Vienna the last few years and moved to St. Paul a few weeks ago."

"So you've only known each other a few weeks?" he said. "I don't get it. What was the big rush?"

I wasn't prepared to answer this. I didn't want to tell Jack about my visa expiring. But what if he read the newspaper article and saw my picture? Eventually he might find out, and then what?

I made a casual gesture with my hand. "Why wait? We both survived the war. We didn't want to waste more time."

He took another swig of his beer and wiped his mouth with the back of his hand. "That doesn't sound like Finn. Not after what happened with Pearl."

"She was the woman he was engaged to," I guessed.

"So he told you about her?"

"Yes."

"He told you she threw him over and ran away with another railroad man, and when that didn't work out she moved back six months ago, but Finn wouldn't have anything to do with her?"

I didn't answer.

"Didn't think so. He'd never admit it, but he's been pining over her ever since he came back. We figured eventually he'd get over the hurt, and his pride, and marry her. I mean, he wouldn't sell the house, even though he's all alone in it."

"He is no longer alone."

"So, you don't mind being a rebound wife?"

"I am not, what you call it, a rebound wife." I wasn't sure what that was, but I was not one.

"If you say so. What's in this marriage for you?"

I took a breath. "My fiancé married another woman. Finn and I have that in common."

He shook his head. "Really? What a fool. Your fiancé, I mean." He paused, studying me. "I think there's something more to this," he finally said.

"I am sorry to disappoint you, but . . ."

"What do you really know about my brother?"

"I know enough," I said and turned away to put the cake on the counter. I could feel his gaze on my back.

"Did he tell you he came back shell-shocked after the war?"

I abruptly turned back around. "What is that?"

Jack had a smirk on his face. "Seems you don't know as much as you think about the man you just married."

I felt my hand curl into a fist. Jack was taunting me, and he was enjoying it. But I took the bait. "What are you talking about?"

"He lost his entire squad in France. Only Finn survived. He had to write letters to the families of all those men. He's never gotten over the guilt. He used to be a carefree, happy guy. The Finn who came back was a different man than the one who left."

I reflexively put a hand on my abdomen. "That is horrible."

"Yeah. Well, that's war." He stood up and patted his left leg. "At least he came back in one piece. I got this baby. Might as well put me out to pasture. Not too many women are gonna be attracted to a one-legged man."

He grabbed the crutch and put it under his left arm. As he made to leave, I put a hand up. "Please don't tell your parents. Finn wants to do that himself."

He took a step toward me, close enough that I could smell his breath, the metallic stench of stale beer. "Your secret is safe with me."

He paused at the door. "Welcome to the family, Mrs. Erickson."

After he left, I sat down on the chair he'd occupied just a moment before. I didn't like Jack. He was bitter and mean, as though he enjoyed telling me about Finn being, what did he call it? Shell-shocked?

I put my head in my hands. Had I made a mistake marrying this man? Was that why Finn was so quiet? He was fighting demons from his past?

He should have told me. It was dishonest not to reveal such an important piece of his background.

But how much had I kept hidden? I had not told Finn that I wasn't a virgin. Would it have made a difference? Would he have changed his mind about marrying me?

Perhaps.

What would I have discovered about the other men I'd chosen: Jeffrey Fairbanks, or the banker, or hippo-faced Ralph Jones, who hadn't even written his own letter? Everyone had secrets. Everyone had a past.

Finn hadn't asked much about my past. He'd revealed that he'd been hurt by a woman, and that he'd served in the war. He knew that I'd been hurt by another man, that I wanted to stay in America. He had offered me a home.

I wanted to forget the war and take refuge in this small town, far away from the starvation and destruction of Vienna, and Communist-occupied Hungary. I wanted to heal, to put the past behind me, and never think of Joe or war or foolish love again.

And for now I *would* put the past behind. I would not mention to Finn what Jack had told me. I would concentrate on the future.

I looked into the living room. I knew just how to start.

CHAPTER TWENTY-TWO

❧❧❧

LOVELINESS FOR LIVING ROOMS AT A PRICE YOU CAN AFFORD. That was the sign that greeted me on the second floor of Ferrin's Furniture Store, located on Main Street. I had walked past the store the day before, but I was too preoccupied at the time in finding my way around town to stop in.

I meandered through the selection, noting the different styles, the lighter shades of fabric, and the new contemporary designs that reflected a Scandinavian influence. I wasn't a fan of the modern furniture, although I did appreciate the practicality. I was accustomed to the darker wood used in Europe, but I liked the thought of something lighter. Not blond wood, exactly . . .

"May I help you?" An older man appeared at my side. He had a name tag on his suit coat that identified him as Clarence.

"I am looking for a living-room suite," I said.

"Well, you've come to the right place. We have some beautiful overstuffed sofas on display. Others that can be custom-made in a variety of coverings: damask, mohair, jacquard velours, or leather. It's the hidden qualities you can't see that are important. The high-carbon wire springs, the seat cushions filled with the best cotton and moss. And the mohair and wool fabrics are given moth-proofing treatment."

He gave the cushions a pat to show me what he meant.

I enjoyed hearing him talk about things I would never have noticed or considered. Mama was the one who selected all the furniture in our home, except for Papa's study, which he insisted needed a man's influence. I didn't remember Mama ever concerning herself with these things, either, although with thirty-three rooms to decorate, she did have outside help. Mama was more worried about whether the pieces she bought were authentic heirlooms, not whether the seat cushions had good springs.

I wouldn't have that problem. This furniture was in a different class entirely. And as much time as Mama had spent in acquiring such extravagant possessions, I knew that none of them were now in her possession. Even as Mama refused to believe her husband was dead, she wailed at the loss of her furniture and house as though she couldn't bear the heartache.

I had no idea how much to spend on this sort of thing. I'd never been furniture shopping before. Mama never thought of the price.

"Is your husband with you?" Clarence asked.

I huffed at his comment and stretched out my neck. "No. He is busy working. But he trusts me to make proper decisions on furniture purchases."

"I'm sorry . . . I didn't mean to insult you. I usually see the husbands in tow behind their wives."

Really? Was this an American custom I was unfamiliar with? In any case, it was not my custom.

"I am not looking for anything too ornate," I said, although I didn't see anything that qualified as such. But all of it was better than what currently occupied the living room.

"I want something that can be delivered tomorrow," I stated in a voice that suggested this could not be compromised. "Something that is well made. But affordable."

"And where do you live?" he asked.

I showed him the piece of paper with our address.

"Depending on what you choose, I think we can accommodate that request. But we may have to sell you a floor sample in order to do so."

I nodded. "If it is in good condition, and if you also offer a discount for it being a floor sample."

Clarence's eyes widened, but he flashed a small smile as he bowed his head. "I'm sure we can work something out."

"Good. I also have another small sitting room with a piano." I paused, thinking. "And where can I buy window coverings?"

TWO DAYS LATER, I PACED BETWEEN THE SITTING ROOM AND living area, wringing my hands as I waited for Finn to walk through the door. I hoped he'd like what I'd chosen for the decor. I wanted to show him I was ready to be a wife, to make his home more desirable.

The new curtains made the room so much lighter and accentuated the white sofa and green-and-white upright chairs I'd chosen. I couldn't help but feel proud at having accomplished so much in just a few days. I hastily straightened the vase of flowers on the new round glass coffee table and adjusted the position of the silver bucket, which held a bottle of champagne in thawing ice.

Then I turned on the radio to calm my nerves. Music filled the room, a song of love, dreams, loneliness, and sentimental reasons. I turned it off, because any music that spoke of love still reminded me of Joe.

I'd purchased pictures of dainty flowers in vases to hang on the bare walls. Except for a small family photo on Finn's bedroom dresser, the only picture that occupied any of the walls was one that hung on the landing of the steps going upstairs. It was a photo of Finn's platoon posing in front of a jeep. I shuddered every time I passed it, thinking of how they were all dead except for Finn. And I couldn't help but wonder if he was punishing himself with a daily reminder.

Finn was still very much a mystery to me. Whereas I knew why the other three men had written to me, and what they expected of me in return, I had no idea why Finn had answered that article in the newspaper.

I jumped at the grumbling sounds of a truck engine. I was tempted to run and peek out the window, but I refrained. Instead, I went to the door and waited.

The outer door finally clicked open. Feet stomped on the rug before Finn opened the inner door.

"Hi," he said, removing his boots. "I'm sorry I'm late. I had to go over next week's schedule." His face looked drawn, with dark shadows under his eyes, as though he hadn't slept in days.

"I understand," I said.

"How have you been?"

"Fine." I gave him a small smile. "I have been busy."

"That's good. What have you . . ." He noticed the sitting room, where the piano now had two matching floral chairs to the side of it, and a low table between them. The window covering had been replaced by willowy sheers. "What's all this?"

"I did what you asked me to do."

"Where did it come from?"

"A store. Ferrin's. They were very helpful."

He walked in farther, where he noticed the living room. He wasn't smiling. He didn't even look particularly happy.

"Do you not like it?" I asked, confused by his reaction. "I only have time for these two rooms. But it is a start."

His eyes scanned the room. "Where's the old couch?"

"They took it when they delivered the new furniture."

He finally looked at me. "We can't afford this."

"I did not purchase expensive items."

"You have to return it."

I took a step back. "I don't understand. You have a big home. It needs furniture. The cost was very economical."

He closed his eyes for a second, then reopened them and spoke as though he were explaining something to a child. "Usually, at least here in America, or Minnesota anyway, a woman asks her husband before she makes a large purchase."

"I did not think this was a large purchase." Mama didn't usually consult my father about furniture purchases. "Decorating is women's work," I said.

"I left you money to buy groceries. I thought that would keep you busy."

"Busy? I am to be kept busy?" What did that mean?

"I didn't mean it like that. Listen," he said, putting his fingers over the bridge of his nose, "I know you're probably used to being able to buy whatever you want without thinking of the cost. But I'm not rich."

I folded my arms. "I *did* think of the cost. As I stated, it was economical. You asked me to do this, did you not?"

He sighed. "I suppose I did. Look, I'm going to take a shower. We can discuss this later."

I fought back tears as I watched him go upstairs. This hadn't gone at all as I had expected. I thought he would be happy.

I picked up a pillow off the couch and threw it across the room. I was not some spoiled aristocrat like he made me out to be! The audacity! How dare he! He knew nothing about me or my situation. He knew nothing of all I'd been through.

I would go pack my things and make Finn take me back to Mariska's apartment. If he thought he could treat me like that after all I'd done, after how hard I'd worked . . .

"I'm sorry."

I wiped my eyes with a finger before I turned around. "I thought you were in the shower."

"I need to apologize first."

Finn took a tentative step into the room. He was still in his work uniform, the striped bib overalls and red bandana that smelled of oil and steam.

He waved his hand around. "It's really nice. Better than nice. It's grand, really. You have a real knack for knowing how to make the place look beautiful."

"It is wasted time," I said, looking away. "If you are returning everything."

"I misspoke. We don't have to take it back. I'll figure out a way . . . I can work something out."

I looked at him. Thoughts of leaving vanished. "I am sorry. I did not realize that we were poor. This house is very big and I assumed—"

"We're not poor," he interrupted. "We're not rich either. We're sort of in between."

"In between," I repeated with furrowed brows.

He shrugged. "Let's just say that I make a decent wage, and I have some savings set aside. That's about the most anyone can strive for."

He didn't elaborate. I still didn't understand. I'd gone from having so much to having nothing in such a short time that I had no idea how any of this worked.

"I'm not a miser, but I am conservative when it comes to money. I do want to be consulted about purchases. I mean big purchases like furniture."

"I have much to learn about living here," I said in an apologetic voice. "I should have asked you first." I remembered how the salesman had asked about my husband. I should have heeded that warning, but I wanted to assert my own authority.

He shrugged. "We both have a lot to learn. Married life? I'm the first to admit I have no idea what I'm doing."

An awkward silence followed. It reminded me of how easily Joe and I used to talk, of how we couldn't wait to see each other, how we burst into each other's arms, eager to talk and kiss, to share our day, and how there weren't such uncomfortable silences.

Finn noticed the champagne. He picked up the dripping bottle. "Is this to celebrate? Why don't we have a toast?" he said.

I nodded, but all enthusiasm had left. There was no longer anything to celebrate. I wasn't supposed to be here, apologizing for doing what I'd been asked to do. I was supposed to be a prima ballerina for at least another five years, if I didn't get injured. And after that, for I knew that few dancing careers lasted beyond one's early thirties, I would settle down with a man of good standing who I loved, and who wouldn't be making me ask for permission to buy furniture.

But the war had taken all that from me. In its place it had left death and uncertainty, and worse, dependence on other people. And now I had made a decision to marry this man, the one I deemed to be the best of all the men who'd proposed. I was determined to be a normal American housewife, but I was already failing.

Perhaps because I had no idea what a normal American housewife actually was.

The champagne left a bitter aftertaste, and Finn soon excused himself, saying he was tired and needed a shower.

I was relieved when he left.

CHAPTER TWENTY-THREE

❧❀❧

SAT UPRIGHT IN BED. LOUD SOUNDS HAD AWOKEN ME. Screaming and wailing at such a high pitch it sent a cold chill through me. I jumped out of bed and put on a housecoat, my heart pounding. I stopped at my bedroom door. I remembered the Gestapo marching through my apartment building, yanking people out into the hallways. I remembered their screams, the sound of gunshots that echoed off the walls. Now, in my panic, I grabbed a chair to put in front of my door to secure it.

But then I remembered I was in Red Wing, Minnesota, not Vienna. The sounds continued. What if there was an intruder? What if someone was murdering my husband? I turned the knob slowly, careful not to make any noise.

The screaming was coming from Finn's room. It turned to incoherent yelling, and I realized he wasn't being attacked, at least not here, but in his dreams. He was having a nightmare.

I knocked on his door. "Finn. Are you all right?"

Now he was moaning and crying. I knocked again. "Finn?"

The sound of creaking bedsprings was followed by a muddled voice. "Who is it?"

"It's me. Roza. May I come in?"

I waited a long moment, until I thought he might have fallen asleep again. "Just a minute," he said.

I pulled a hand through my messy hair, suddenly aware of my appearance.

The door opened, and Finn stood on the other side in a plaid housecoat, his hair disheveled. He wiped at his eyes, which had a dazed look, and didn't immediately let me pass through. I took a step forward. Finally, he allowed me in. There was a chair near his bed, and a pack of cigarettes on his nightstand. I sat down on the chair.

"May I?" I picked up the pack of cigarettes.

"Help yourself. I've been trying to quit."

I put a cigarette in my mouth and lit the end, then inhaled, closing my eyes. It would be so easy to become hooked on these again. I let out a slow puff. "I quit when they became too costly. What little money I had went for food and rent."

He didn't say anything.

"I wanted to make sure you were all right," I said.

He shoved his hands in his pockets, but not before I noticed them trembling. "I'm sorry. I must have had a bad dream."

I tilted my head. "I still dream of the bombs. I wake up thinking I need to run to the air-raid shelter. I remember when the Opera House was destroyed. The beautiful auditorium and stage. More than one hundred thousand costumes! Gone in an instant.

"But worse than that, I still see the gray, lifeless bodies on the boulevard, their mouths open as though they are about to say something, but full of muck, their words lost in the whine of the warning sirens. In my dream I am trapped under the rubble with them, my mouth full of dust, unable to breathe."

He nodded. "I guess even if we leave the war behind, it follows us home."

"Were you afraid when you were fighting?"

"Every man is. Fear is contagious, though. You have to keep it in check when you're leading a platoon. Otherwise it warps judgment, breeds mistakes . . ." His voice trailed off.

"Do you have these dreams often?"

He looked away, as though he were somewhere else, someplace

he didn't want to be. I remembered what Jack had told me, how he was "shell-shocked."

When Finn looked back at me, his eyes held the same steadiness as when I'd first met him. He had regained his composure. "More often than I'd like, I'm afraid."

"Have you ever talked to someone?"

"I saw a British doctor during the war. He gave me some sleeping pills. He said I should keep busy, try to forget. . . ." His voice trailed off again.

I knew that wasn't so easy. It had been two years, and hadn't I awoken from such a nightmare on the train just a few weeks ago? But what else could a person do?

I knew I should ask Finn about his war experience. But I suspected he didn't want to share his horror stories any more than I wanted to share mine. And I had moved here to escape the war, not to be reminded of it again.

I nodded at the photo perched on the top of his dresser. The black-and-white portrait was taken outside in front of a large bush, and showed a boy around seven years of age standing between his parents. A younger boy stood on the other side of the mother, his chubby hand grasping the fabric of her dress. No one was smiling, although the older boy, who I guessed was Finn, had a pleasant expression on his face. The younger boy, Jack, was scowling. Both parents had somber faces.

"I didn't have a chance to tell you earlier. Your brother, Jack, stopped by on Monday."

"He did? What did you tell him?"

"I had to tell him we were married."

Finn smirked. "I'll bet he was more than surprised by that news."

"He was. I asked him not to say anything to your parents until we'd had a chance to tell them ourselves."

"Right. We'll do that tomorrow. Or today, I guess. I should let you get some rest."

I snuffed out my cigarette. "Yes. Of course."

I stood, feeling suddenly vulnerable in front of him. My bare leg showed through the front of my housecoat, but I didn't move to cover it. We were married, after all. I looked at his tangled bed-sheets, and wondered if I should ask him if he wanted me to lie next to him, to comfort him. What would it feel like to climb into his bed, to be pressed up against his warm body?

I fought a sudden desire that shivered through my own body. I turned to go. "Good night, Finn."

"Good night." His voice was soft, and I was tempted to look back at him. But I didn't trust myself to do so. Finn didn't make a move either. He didn't ask me to stay.

I left. As the door closed behind me, I thought of all that we couldn't say to each another. We were still very much strangers. But I had also never confided in Joe, who was my fiancé, about the atrocities I'd seen and experienced. They felt too raw, too painful. I just wanted to forget.

And it seemed that whatever demons Finn was fighting, he preferred to fight them alone.

CHAPTER TWENTY-FOUR

THIS IS THE HOUSE JACK AND I GREW UP IN," FINN EXPLAINED as he parked in front of a small, white, one-story home on a dirt road. The street was on the other side of the highway that divided Red Wing. Three blocks away the houses butted up against the bluffs, leaving little room for expansion. Two cracked steps led to a covered porch that poked out the front. A tall ash tree hovered over one side, and the bare branches of lilac bushes, which I recognized from the photo on Finn's dresser, lined the other side.

"Dad works for Marigold Dairy. We always had fresh milk growing up. When it was hot out, my brother and I would sleep on that porch because it was cooler there."

"It sounds delightful," I said politely, wondering how there was room enough in that tiny box for four people.

Finn cleared his throat. "I'm sure it's nothing compared to where you must have lived."

I remembered the porch that occupied the rear of our country estate, of how I played between the arched columns and peered out across the gardens toward the stables, where my filly Sabina waited, a Wielkopolska breed that Papa had selected for me. That porch was larger than this entire place. What could I say that wouldn't insult Finn's childhood home?

"Hungary is an ancient country," I said. "Everything is big and old. The home I grew up in was built in the early 1800s."

"Was your home destroyed in the war?"

"No. The last I heard it is now used for Communist headquarters."

"It must have been huge."

"It was," I admitted. "Our family estate sat on ten thousand acres of land."

Finn let out a low whistle. "That's a lot of land."

"Was. It is no longer ours," I reminded him.

He got out and opened the door for me. He held out his hand and I took it to exit the truck. He didn't let go afterward, and I kept my hand in his, finding reassurance and comfort as I had before, wondering if he felt the same way. We needed each other's strength right now.

It was cool outside, although I hadn't figured out the American Fahrenheit system, so I didn't really know how warm sixty degrees was. With the Minnesota humidity, it felt like twenty degrees Celsius.

Finn was wearing a jacket over his short-sleeved button-down shirt, and casual slacks. I had on a sweater over my sleeveless top and a loose-fitting skirt that hit at mid-calf, which made me feel like a Hungarian peasant. But my skirt was a plain blue color, not like the bright patterns worn by Mariska.

As we approached, Jack came to the screen door, his face expectant. I thought I saw a smirk.

He opened the door and gave his brother a smack on the arm. "I hear congratulations are in order."

"Not now," Finn said, shushing him.

"Right. Got it." He nodded at me. "Good morning, Mrs. Erickson. Nice to see you."

Finn shushed him again. "Where's Mom and Pop?"

"In the kitchen."

"Has Pop left for work yet?"

"No, he's still here."

"Has he had his coffee yet?" Finn asked.

"He's drinking it now. You know him. He's got to have his morning habit before he can make small talk. Or," he added with a smirk, "big talk."

Finn nodded. He seemed hesitant to go any further than the porch.

"Don't lose your cool now," Jack said, prompting Finn to move. "Even though you know how much Mom loves Pearl."

I noticed Finn flinch at the name. I glared at Jack. It was bad enough to bring up his brother's former fiancée. But to do so in front of me was thoughtless and rude.

Finn opened another door, which led to a small sitting room where a worn sofa sagged beneath a crocheted blanket next to a rocking chair and table, on which stood a radio and lamp. Behind it was the kitchen. A hallway led to two other rooms, which I guessed were the bedrooms. A bathroom sat off the kitchen.

Jack followed us in. He half whispered, "I don't know what he's nervous about. Finn is the golden boy of this family."

That made me more nervous. How would they feel about Finn marrying me without telling them first?

An older man sat at the table in an undershirt and pants, but no shoes or socks, his toes pink and wide set. He had Finn's lanky build and a full head of white hair, which I noticed was parted the same as Finn's. He wore thick glasses and held a copy of the *Red Wing Republican Eagle*, the town's newspaper that appeared on Finn's front porch each morning.

The room smelled of sausage and eggs, which Finn's mother was making at an old black stove. She was in her housecoat. She was smaller than her husband, and her movements were quick and graceful as she flipped eggs and moved the sausage links around, each of them occupying their own space in the pan. Her grayish-brown hair was tied in a bun at the back of her head.

Even though she was turned away from us, it was as if Finn were a magnet, drawing her attention. She noticed him before her husband did.

"What a pleasant surprise, Finn. You want some breakfast?"

Then she saw me, and patted her hair. "Oh, my. You should have called first and let me know you were bringing someone. Earl, we have guests."

Her husband looked up from his paper and clicked his tongue. "Finn isn't a guest."

"No. Not Finn," she said, touching his arm and motioning toward me, a rounded spatula in her other hand.

"Oh, I didn't see her." Mr. Erickson stood and clasped my hand. "Good morning," he said, with more exuberance than I felt this early in the morning.

"Hello, Mr. Erickson."

"Call me Earl. I take it you're not from Minnesota, judging by your accent."

"I am Hungarian."

"Mom. Pop. This is Roza," Finn said, tipping the back of a kitchen chair as he gave it a hard squeeze.

"Hello," his mother said, giving me a limp nod, while squinting at her son, as though she was confused. Finn's brother took after his mother, with the same solid build and deep-set eyes, ones that narrowed in on me now. "How do you know Finn?"

"We met," I said haltingly, "at a concert."

"Roza is a ballerina," Finn said.

"Ballerina? Well, that explains why you're so skinny. Are you performing somewhere?"

"No. I have not performed since the war."

Mrs. Erickson gave a sad smile. "So many lives affected by this horrible war. Thank God we defeated those Nazis. But our poor Jack lost his leg, and his livelihood."

"Jack can work if he wants to," Finn said.

"What would you know about it?" Jack spat out. "You think a ballerina would marry a cripple like me?"

"She would if you'd stop feeling sorry for yourself all the time," Finn replied.

"Marry?" The smile on his mother's face instantly vanished.

Finn froze. He nodded. "This isn't how I wanted to tell you. Roza is my wife."

No one said anything for ten seconds, which seemed an eternity. I had imagined what it would be like meeting Joe's family. It was never as bad as this. Finally, Jack broke the silence. "Roza and Finn got married earlier this week."

"You knew about this?" his mother asked, her voice rising.

Jack's cheeks reddened. "I sorta found out when I stopped over."

That brought a scowl from his mother. "My God, Finn. Married? To a woman you just met? When did this happen?"

Finn shot Jack a dirty look. "Monday. We would have told you sooner, but there wasn't time."

"Well," Earl said at last, "that's the last thing I expected to hear on a Friday morning. Finn has always been impulsive that way, don't you think so, Bernice? Remember when he joined the Army the day after Pearl Harbor?"

Finn's mother didn't answer. I thought she might cry.

Earl didn't look very happy either. "I guess congratulations are in order," he said reluctantly. He shook Finn's hand, and gave me a peck on the cheek.

"What about Pearl? We thought you were seeing her again," his mother said, looking at her son as if to make sure this wasn't a joke.

She was frozen in place, the spatula in her hand held up, egg dripping off the end.

Finn shook his head. "It was just that one time. It was nothing serious," he said, looking at me.

"Pearl thought it was," his mother said, "and so did we. I mean, you've known Pearl for years, and you marry someone you just met? No offense, Rose." She sniffed, then suddenly remembering the sizzling food behind her, she turned her attention to the sausages, which were now burnt on one side. She moved all the food onto a plate, then cleared her throat. "Do you want to stay for breakfast?" Her voice was less than inviting.

Finn looked at me. I gave an imperceptible shake of my head.

"No. We're eating at the St. James Hotel."

His mother frowned. "Dressed like that? Isn't that a fancy restaurant? Not that I'd know. We've never eaten there."

"Uh, no. I'm going to change. But we wanted to tell you the news first."

Finn hadn't mentioned eating there. I wondered if he'd just now decided, or if he was saying that because he couldn't think of any other excuse.

"Why don't we go in the living room," his father suggested. "And you can fill us in on this . . . unexpected event."

Finn nodded and led me to the sofa. Finn's father sat in the rocking chair. Jack's fake leg made a stomping noise, and he jerked to one side as he pulled a kitchen chair in to sit on. Finn's mother was busy putting ginger snaps on a plate, which she passed around the room, the eggs and sausages now forgotten. She sat on the other side of the sofa, next to Finn.

Her mouth stayed in a straight line as she reached across and patted my hand. "You'll have to excuse us. This is such a shock. We expected that Finn would be marrying Pearl. He would have if the poor girl hadn't gotten so scared about losing Finn during the war.

She was a nervous wreck worrying about him, and then when her brother's friend died, she said she couldn't take it any longer. She upped and married Dale Carter, even though she didn't love him the way she did Finn."

"Mom." Finn's voice was a warning.

"It's true. Her mother told me. And that's why it didn't work out. Thank God they didn't have any children. And she moved back to Red Wing, but Finn, well, he went through a lot in the war, and he's always been proud, and now he's so quiet that we never know what to expect . . ."

"Mom. That's enough." Finn reached over and took my hand. "I'd hoped you'd be happy for us."

"Well, it's just such a shock, like I said. Not what we expected." She adjusted her housecoat. "Of course we're happy for you, Finn." But the words sounded hollow, and I wished we could leave right then and there.

"So, how did you meet again?" Jack asked, and I wanted to hit him for bringing the subject up again.

We had decided earlier to tell his parents the truth. Finn said he couldn't lie to them about something this important. Besides, what if someone recognized me from the newspaper article and showed it to them later?

I had my doubts now. I wasn't sure about Earl, but telling Finn's mother that I only married Finn to be able to stay in America would not endear me further. Although a marriage of convenience was common among aristocracy, I had learned that it wasn't what most American parents wanted for their children. The last thing I wanted was to start off my marriage with a mother-in-law who despised me, but it seemed destined.

"As Roza mentioned, she was a ballerina before the war. She performed in Vienna."

"Didn't Austria side with the Nazis?" Finn's mother asked, but it sounded more like an accusation.

"They didn't have a choice," I said, trying to explain. "My family was from Hungary. My father was killed during the occupation."

"I'm sorry," Finn said. "You didn't tell me that before."

I shrugged. I wasn't used to having to defend myself against accusations lobbed at me across a sofa.

"What did your father do before the war?" Mr. Erickson asked.

"He was a landowner, and the Hungarian minister to Austria. Before the war."

"A landowner? You mean a farmer?"

"Not exactly," I said.

"Roza is a countess," Finn said.

"A countess?" Finn's mother looked around the room, as if suddenly seeing it through the eyes of royalty. Normally when people heard I was a countess, they automatically assumed I was rich.

"My family lost everything in the war," I explained. "All we have left is our title, which means little to nothing now."

"But you're still sort of like a princess, right? You're royalty?" Jack said, sitting taller.

I nodded. "Technically."

"Anyway," Finn continued, "she met an American soldier in Vienna and came to Minnesota to marry him, but he threw her off and married someone else. Her visa expired in two weeks, and then she'd be sent back to Hungary, her birthplace, which is under Communist rule now."

Finn's father nodded and clasped his hands together, as though all this finally made sense. "So you married her so she wouldn't have to go back?"

"Actually, I saw her picture in the newspaper. And I wrote to her. We met last week for a date. Afterward, Roza agreed to marry me."

It was then that I noticed Finn's mother had a handkerchief pressed against her nose, and heard her sniffing. "I don't understand," his mother said. "Why did you write that letter, Finn? Was it because you were still mad at Pearl?"

This couldn't have gone worse. I wanted to bolt, to run away. Or shrink into the chasm of this ratty sofa with its expanding cushions. I had survived bombs and starvation only to face these rude people who didn't like me before they even knew me? Why had Finn brought me here? To be interrogated and insulted? To be compared to another woman?

Finn might be good at hiding his own anger, but I wasn't. I stood up, ready to tell off these rude people and walk out the door. I looked down at Finn. He should be defending me. His family had spurned me even as his mother accused me of helping the Nazis.

"Pearl had nothing to do with it, Mom," Finn said quietly. "I fell in love with Roza the moment I saw her picture."

I felt my breath hitch as I sat back down. I hadn't expected this.

Finn gave me an intense look, as if he wanted me to understand. "And then, when I met you, I fell head over heels in love."

CHAPTER TWENTY-FIVE

❧

I WAS SPEECHLESS, BUT FINN'S MOTHER JUST KEPT SHAKING her head.

"It doesn't make sense," she said. "You don't marry someone whose picture you see in a newspaper. I just don't understand, Finn."

Finn finally stood up. "You never will, then," he said, and grabbed my hand and stalked out, slamming the door behind him.

I was happy we'd left, until he opened my car door for me. It occurred to me, then, that this wasn't what I wanted for Finn, to turn away from his family for me.

"We shouldn't leave like this," I said, refusing to get in.

"My mother is hopeless," he said, running a hand through his thick hair. "She sets her mind on something and won't change it for the world. Going back inside won't change anything."

I didn't want to go back inside either. I just didn't want to come between Finn and his family. "At least call her later and apologize. This is not the way to start our married life."

He sighed. "You're right. I'll call her later."

We went home and changed into more appropriate attire, but when we finally arrived at the St. James Hotel, we were turned away because we didn't have a reservation.

"I know a good place," I said, and led him down the street to Nellie's. It was busy there as well, although it was a more casually dressed crowd. The smell of sizzling meat, eggs, and the fresh aroma of coffee filled the small space. A booth opened up just as we walked in.

"So, this is your husband?" Nellie said after seating us in the booth. "I was beginning to think he was a figment of your imagination. He's handsome too. You make a nice-looking couple."

Finn blushed and stammered his name. "Finn Erickson," he said, holding out his hand.

Nellie put both hands on her hips. "Are you the Finn Erickson who used to deliver groceries for Koplins when you were a boy?"

Finn nodded. "I remember delivering your groceries every Tuesday, Mrs. O'Donnell."

"I haven't seen you in years." She turned to me. "Finn had the gift of gab as a boy. I swore he was an Irishman. He talked nonstop about trains. He memorized the train schedule and could tell you just by the whistle what train was coming into the depot. That and baseball. Who was that fellow you admired so much?"

"Lefty Gomez. He pitched for the St. Paul Saints before moving to the Yankees."

"That's right. Well, I'll be. What are you drinking? Coffee?"

"Please."

"I'll be back in a jiffy."

"How do you know her?" he asked when she left.

"She was the first person I met," I explained. I'd eaten several meals here, and every dish I'd tasted was delicious.

"She hasn't changed a bit," Finn said. "She had gray hair back when I was delivering groceries as a kid."

Nellie returned with coffee and a cup of tea for me. "What'll you two have?"

"What do you recommend?" Finn asked, looking at the menu posted on a nearby chalkboard.

"He's a smart one too," Nellie said, directing her comment at me. "You're never disappointed when you ask what's good. Of course, that depends on whether you like fluffy pancakes, or fried eggs and bacon. Or both. They're the special today."

"That sounds very good to me," I said and nodded at Finn.

"I'll order the same," he said.

"Good choice," Nellie said, and added, "Just nod at me and I'll bring more coffee. Don't be shy about it either."

She left to attend to other customers. The sound of clinking silverware and nearby conversation made the silence between us awkward. I could not reconcile the boy Nellie described, who liked to talk, to the quiet man sitting across from me. Jack said he'd changed during the war. Was his quiet demeanor hiding something darker? Is that why he had such horrible nightmares? How was it that Finn had survived when everyone else in his platoon had died?

"You're not disappointed that we're eating here instead of the St. James?" Finn finally asked.

"Not at all," I replied, feeling in a better mood when I saw Nellie wink at me. She had that effect on me. I didn't know if it was her forthright attitude or her no-nonsense rules. Or the fact that everything she made was delicious.

"We'll have dinner there soon. I promise."

"I am not a picky eater," I reassured him.

"I noticed that about you right away."

"You can only be picky when food is plentiful. I have learned to appreciate any dish. Of course, I am afraid I will turn into a pumpkin with all this delicious food."

"That's okay. You could stand to gain some weight," Finn said.

I added a sugar cube to my tea and stirred it until it dissolved. "I am sorry that our marriage has caused problems for your family." I kept coming back to what Finn had told his parents; that he fell in love with me at first sight. How was that even possible? Or was it just a line he'd prepared ahead of time?

"No. I should be apologizing to you. I didn't know what to expect, but I'd hoped it would have turned out better than that.

They're really not that bad, but I guess we caught them off guard. Maybe if I'd told them ahead of time, but then . . ."

"They would have talked you out of it?"

"They would have tried. My dad said I was impulsive because I enlisted the day after Pearl Harbor. I wasn't impulsive; I knew exactly what I wanted to do, had been planning to join up if we went to war. I just didn't want to have to explain it to them. My mom gets emotional and makes a scene, like she did today. I figured she'd be better after the fact. Unfortunately, that wasn't the case today."

"And what of your father?"

"Dad always wants to move in slow motion. Said he took three years to ask my mom to marry him. It's funny, though; they didn't object to Jack enlisting. Maybe because he didn't have a good job at the time. He was pumping gas at the Phillips 66. He's never had a lot of motivation to pull himself up in the world, though. And now, after losing his leg, he's less inclined to try."

This was the most Finn had said since I'd met him. He seemed to recognize this, and he looked embarrassed that he'd spoken ill of his family, because he quickly added, "Don't get me wrong. They're not a bad lot. My parents gave us a good upbringing and made sure we went to church regularly. Both Jack and I took piano lessons, although Jack gave it up after one year. He was like a puppy who followed me around when he was little. Always trying to keep up. He even took up baseball just because I played in high school. He wasn't much good at it, but he made an effort. I know he enlisted only because I did."

"Does that make it your fault he lost his leg?"

Finn looked down before he answered. "He makes me feel like it was. He can really get under my skin sometimes. Mom said he's always been jealous of me. I'm not sure why."

"I think there is always competition for a parent's love. But family is important," I said, even as their treatment of me still caused anger.

"How do you think *your* family will feel about our marriage?"

"My mother will disapprove, of course. But she lives in a fantasy world built upon ages of elaborate tradition when her titles meant something. She thought that when the war ended Hungary would end up the way it was before. The realization that her former way of life has disappeared forever will cause her many regrets. My marriage is minor compared to that. Actually, I worry for her sanity if she ever does accept the truth of her situation."

"Life is full of regrets, though. Isn't it?" Finn said, looking down at his coffee.

"I suppose it is." Did I regret coming to America? Did I regret the war that took everything away, including my precious papa? Did Finn regret joining the Army? Did he regret his brother enlisting?

And as Nellie placed our food upon the table, it seemed as though another question was laid down with it. Would our marriage be one of regret?

CHAPTER TWENTY-SIX

WHILE FINN WAS GONE FOR DAYS AT A TIME, I SPENT much of it exploring my new home. I remembered how our mansion in Hungary had concealed tunnels that connected with the stables, and hid Papa's wine collection as well. I loved playing in the tunnels and exploring every room of the mansion, including the servant's quarters, and finding numerous out-of-the-way stairways, cupboards, and tiny closets tucked behind armoires and bedposts, as if their whole purpose was to be hidden, which made them especially interesting to a child who considered herself a sleuth.

Now it felt as though I were eavesdropping on my new husband, and I didn't feel the same thrill of exploration, but just the same, I wanted to make sure the Chopin manuscript was in the safest hiding spot, as I hadn't spent much time that first day securing its safety.

That was how I found the letter, tucked in the back of Finn's closet in a box containing his war medals. There were other letters in the box, all of them from his mother, and I read those too. But this one was from his fiancée, Pearl. The paper was crinkled, as though Finn had crumpled it into a ball to throw away, then changed his mind later. Finn had told me very little about her. I hadn't shared much about Joe either. It felt safer to distance myself from memories of Joe, and I suspect Finn felt the same. But I had burned Joe's letters the night before I married Finn in the bonfire behind Mariska's apartment building.

I read the letter several times, trying to decide what kind of person this Pearl was.

Dear Finn,

I was shocked to hear that you were injured. But I heard through your mother that you're going to recover. Just don't be going back to the front now that you've done your part, okay?

I don't think your mom wrote you about this, but Finn, you know how hard it is for me to wait for things. And how frantic I get when I'm worried. And I worried so much about you all the time that I couldn't even put on fingernail polish without streaking it all over my hands. And then my brother's friend Hale Smith died and I could barely breathe. It got to be too much for me, Finn. I was getting worry lines fretting over you all day and night.

I would have written sooner to tell you, but I didn't want to do it when you were fighting. While you were gone I got a job at the snack bar at the Sheldon Movie Theater and started spending time with Dale Carter, who worked the ticket booth. You remember him from school? He was a couple years older than you and would have been in the war, too, but he's got bad eyes and wears thick glasses that look like Coke bottles.

The movies were my only release and I spent almost every night there, and well, to be straight up with you, Dale and I got married last month.

I know this will come as a shock. I know we were supposed to get married when you got back, but to be

honest, I've spent more time with Dale than I did with
you before you left for the war, and I think maybe we were
just caught up in all that war nonsense and if you hadn't
left things might have been different.

I'm so sorry to have to write you and not tell you in
person, but you deserve to know. Please forgive me for
not waiting, but I couldn't take it. I'm not that strong of
a person. I will continue to pray for you and hope for you
return in good health.

Best wishes,
Pearl

Fingernail polish? Worry lines? War nonsense? After reading the letter again, I decided that Pearl was a selfish, uncaring girl who took advantage of Finn. He was lucky to be rid of her. But why did he save this letter? Was he still in love with her?

I jumped at the sound of a knock on the downstairs door. I hurriedly put the box away and ran out of the room, wondering who it could be. I'd lived here three weeks already, but barely knew anyone. My only friend was the owner of a café. Most days I wandered down to Nellie's to have a lemonade and chat, trying to time my visits to when the café wasn't too busy. Sometimes I walked the extra few blocks to sit and watch the swirling waters of the Mississippi River, which made me feel homesick.

Another knock. I almost tumbled down the steps. This was the first time anyone had knocked on my door.

A postman stood on the doorstep. He held a letter in his hands. "Are you Roza Mészáros?"

"I used to be. I am Roza Erickson now," I answered breathily from my jaunt down the stairs.

"I heard something about Finn getting married. I'm Sid Preston. I've been delivering mail on this street for the past fifteen years. Congratulations are in order."

"Thank you."

"I have a letter for you. It's all the way from Hungary. It was forwarded from an address in St. Paul."

Mariska must have sent it. I reached out to take it.

"I need you to sign something first," he said and held out a clipboard with a form. "Just some paperwork."

I signed the form without reading it. Then he handed me the letter. I recognized my mother's tight handwriting.

"Are you from Hungary?" he asked.

"Yes. I grew up there."

"I thought I heard an accent, although you speak very good English. I used to know someone who was Hungarian who lived in Miesville. Could barely understand the poor fellow. I don't suppose you know where that is."

"No, I don't."

He pointed with his finger. "Well, it's about fifteen miles west of here on highway sixty-one. Of course, I don't know anything about Hungary. I might be able to pick it out on a map, but that's about it, so you shouldn't feel bad not knowing where Miesville is."

"Oh, I don't feel bad about it."

He laughed. "You have a good sense of humor, Mrs. Erickson."

"Would you like to come in for some lemonade, Mr. Preston?"

"Well, I'm on a schedule, but it is a warm one out today. I'll gladly take a quick glass, if you're offering."

"I am offering." I led him through the dining room into the kitchen. I'd started buying frozen lemonade and making up pitchers to have on hand so that Finn could have a cold drink when he came home from work. I'd yet to master cooking, though. Most nights we ate sandwiches, or I would bring something home from Nellie's that I could heat up. Finn's schedule was such that he was gone for days in a row, only to come home for one day, or even less, sometimes just twelve hours, and then he'd leave again. I didn't feel the need to cook for myself.

"This is a very nice house you have," he said, setting down his knapsack of mail. He was older, perhaps in his forties, and he had an easy manner about him, as though he truly enjoyed his job.

"Thank you." I'd accepted Finn's offer of a housekeeper once a week to keep up with the cleaning. Our relationship was still fragile, as though we were flatmates trying not to get in each other's way. I didn't mention the frequent shrieking nightmares that woke me during the middle of the night. Finn didn't mention my lack of cooking abilities.

He also didn't make overt physical gestures, as though he were waiting for me to initiate them. He kissed me when he left for work. They were nice kisses, I had to admit; I didn't, however, admit how much I looked forward to them.

"Have you met your neighbors yet?" Sid asked.

"No. I introduced myself to Mr. and Mrs. Mennen next door, but other than them I have not met anyone else. I have only been here three weeks, though."

"You don't say! Well, that is not the town I live in. People should have brought over cookies and almond cake by now. I happen to know that Belinda Johnson hosts a Women's Club at her house once a month. I'll mention you to her to make sure you get invited."

"That is very kind of you."

"Well, delivering mail is more than a job. I tell my wife that it's a way of keeping our community together."

"Do you have children, Mr. Preston?"

"Call me Sid. I have a daughter, Alice. She's nine years old, a spitfire, always climbing trees. So much energy my wife can't keep her dresses and pants mended."

"She sounds like me when I was young. She needs a way to focus all that energy."

"I'm not sure how she would do that. How did you focus your energy as a young girl?"

"I learned ballet. I eventually became a ballerina and danced with the Vienna State Opera Ballet."

"You don't say! That's a great idea. But I don't think we have any place to take ballet classes in Red Wing. We have the Skyline Ballroom south of here, but that's about all for dancing."

He finished his lemonade and set the glass on the table. "Thank you for the refreshing drink, Mrs. Erickson. I hope you receive good news."

"Call me Roza," I replied. "It is a letter from my mother back in Hungary. I miss her and my brother a great deal."

"Well, if you ever open a ballet school, I'll be the first to sign up my child."

I showed him to the door. As I closed it behind him, I thought, *Ballet school? What a novel idea.*

CHAPTER TWENTY-SEVEN

❦❦❦

THE ROOM SWIRLED WITH GOSSIP: WHO WAS GETTING married, who was having babies, whose daughter was pregnant and *had* to get married, who was sick and on the verge of death, who had been seen in the company of another man, and whose husband had been seen with another woman. I didn't know any of the people they were talking about. After explaining that I was from Hungary (*your accent is so cute!*) and was a former ballet dancer (*that explains your figure*), and that yes, ballet took a great deal of practice, I resorted to small talk.

"Do you like the weather here?"

"Yes, it is very pleasant, but colder than Budapest weather."

"Do you like to garden?"

"Yes, that is something I plan to do."

Didn't any of these women attend the opera or ballet? Hadn't any of them traveled abroad? Did they know anything of fine art? Their topics of conversation revealed that none of them had a proper education. They even talked about their ailments, which no one in polite society would do.

"We can't invite Mrs. Johnson to our meetings. She attended the Ladies Lutheran Seminary, and I know she wouldn't approve of our cocktails."

"That place burned down before I was born."

"Yes, she's that old. But she's still a prude, and so are her daughters."

And so it went.

"Did you make this yourself, Belinda? I have to get the recipe." A woman with tight black curls framing a round face picked up another chicken salad sandwich. Her red dress pinched her bulging thighs, and she complained that her sciatic nerve was acting up. Was she Grace or Ann? I couldn't remember any of the names of the women I'd been introduced to, except for Belinda, who had issued the invitation, thanks to Sid. He'd delivered it personally, giving me a wink as he handed me the beige envelope, with a scallop-edged beige note inside stating that I was cordially invited to a neighborhood tea. This would be my first real social event, and after the disaster with Finn's parents, I wanted to be sure nothing went wrong. With Finn's permission (even though he told me I didn't have to ask to buy clothes), I bought a new outfit, a slimming skirt and jacket that hugged my waist.

I thought of Mama as I dressed, purposely leaving the white gloves at home, which Mama would have insisted I wear. I imagined America, and especially this small town, to be less formal than any social gathering I was used to attending in Europe. In her letter, Mama had acted bewildered by my marriage to Finn, wondering how I could have changed my mind at the last minute. (I neglected to tell Mama that Joe had married someone else.) Instead, I'd told her I'd fallen in love with Finn, and that even though we'd only known each other a short while, we had decided to marry.

Mama hinted that things were getting worse in Budapest instead of better. While she had many gracious friends who continued to send her food and money, for the most part she now had to wait in food lines twice a week for basic items like bread and meat, which she saw as a terrible indignity. Members of the Communist Party received rations before everyone else, leaving them picked over. And after being forced to study German during the occupation, János now had to learn Russian in school!

Perhaps this was why Mama wasn't as harsh in her judgment of my marriage. There was not the denouncement or anger that I had anticipated. But she did want to know of Finn's heritage, of his parent's ancestry and bloodline, and their standing in the community. None of which I could possibly write about. I hadn't had contact with his parents since that awful first meeting, although I heard Finn speaking to his mother on the phone a couple of times.

Perhaps I would write about this social occasion, where I met Grace and Alice, and Elsa and Yvonne, and many others, who were all a blur of incessant talking, including descriptions of which houses they lived in, which I couldn't keep track of. In my letter I would have to make it sound better than it actually was.

I excused myself to use the lavatory. I did admire Belinda's decorating style, especially the black and white tiles in her kitchen. Belinda also had good taste in clothing, sporting a modern knit belted sweater over a plaid skirt with a chic kerchief around her neck. Her blond hair boasted a perfect flip.

After I returned, the hostess held up her drink, a Gin Rickey topped with a slice of lime. "Ladies, it's just come to our attention that we may have royalty in this room."

I wanted to slink back into the hallway, but Belinda caught my eye and held it.

She came over and took my arm, guiding me to the center of the room. "Roza, dear, why didn't you tell us you were a countess? We've never had royalty at our Women's Club before."

How did Belinda find out? Had Jack told people? Or Finn's parents? Should I recount how our family could trace its lineage to the warrior leaders of the Árpád dynasty? How my ancestors had owned twenty villages and estates? Should I tell them how I'd gone from magnificent splendor to poverty and despair, and now to this small town that didn't even boast a single art museum?

I could have told her that it was considered improper to brag about one's lineage to commoners, but I held back. Mama had taught me that the only thing worse than raising your voice in a social gathering was to insult the hostess.

"That was in the past. I am just a housewife like you now," I said.

"You mean you're a commoner like us now?" the woman in the red dress said. It sounded spiteful, as though I had said something snobbish.

"I will always have my title. That is something that cannot change," I said, trying to explain.

The woman pinched her red lips together in a smirk. "Of course. And perhaps you can ask Princess Elizabeth to join us for tea at our next meeting."

A few women laughed.

"Alice is joking," Belinda said, putting an arm around me. "We're just not used to having nobility in our little town. But you must have some wonderful stories to tell," Belinda encouraged, as though she needed something, or someone, to raise this party above the mundane event that it was.

"I'm sure you would not be interested," I said.

"But we are! Please tell us," Belinda said, and everyone waited for me to speak.

"Very well. I first met Princess Elizabeth when I was a child. We played together at the wedding of Princess Marina of Greece and Prince George, the Duke of Kent," I said. There was instant regret when I saw their faces. A few raised their eyebrows in disbelief; the rest looked at me as if I'd just sprouted an extra nose, as though I was doing precisely what I'd determined to avoid: bragging about my social status.

"My, but that must have been memorable," Belinda said, with a forced-looking smile. "Do you have any good scoops to dish out?"

"I do not understand," I said. "Scoops?"

"You know. Any royal gossip about the newly wed Elizabeth?"

I shook my head. If I did, I certainly would not share it with these narrow-minded, simplistic women.

"You actually met Princess Elizabeth?" Alice asked with a laugh. "Why ever would you marry Finn Erickson then? His family heritage consists of potato farmers back in Norway."

"I know why," said another woman wearing a black-and-white polka-dot dress. She looked like a cow stuffed into a dress.

I held my breath.

"Do tell," Alice encouraged her.

"I saw her picture in *The Minneapolis Star* weeks ago. She was looking for a husband to stay in this country because she got thrown over by her fiancé and her visa was expiring."

There was an audible gasp at this announcement.

Alice smirked. "I guess Finn was the only one to answer the ad."

I wanted to tear Alice to shreds. My fists clenched at my side. "Actually, I received one thousand seven hundred and eighty-six offers of marriage," I said, tilting my chin up. This was followed by another round of gasps.

"I chose Finn Erickson because he is a good man. I do not care about his background."

Belinda was wringing her hands. "Oh, dear," she murmured.

When someone announced that they'd run out of gin, Belinda smiled gratefully and the attention turned to cocktails.

I left then, telling Belinda I had another engagement. She followed me to the door and thanked me for coming.

She patted my arm in a condescending manner. "I'll be in touch about the next meeting."

Be in touch?

I did not care if I never heard from her again. Those women were cruel. They couldn't understand my aristocratic upbringing or my situation. They acted like royalty in this small town, looking down on others, when all they had ever accomplished was getting married and having children.

But isn't that why I'd come to America in the first place? To be just like them?

No. I'd come because of love, which no longer existed in my world.

Instead of going home I walked downtown to Nellie's Café. I knew that if I went home, I would shed a fountain of tears onto my pillowcase. I wouldn't give that woman the satisfaction.

I viewed the river in the distance and heard the sound of a distant train whistle. Finn would be home late tonight, but he would have to leave again tomorrow. When he said he would be gone a great deal, it was the truth, one I had welcomed at first. But now I felt lonely, especially after reading Mama's letter, which mentioned the annual Easter festival, a tradition in Hungary for hundreds of years. It sparked memories of egg painting and dancing in my innocent and happy youth before the war.

"You look down in the dumps today," Nellie remarked as she plunked a tall glass of lemonade on the laminate countertop.

Something else I didn't understand. "What is down in the dumps?"

"It means you're upset about something."

"It is nothing."

"Nothing is nothing. This is something."

I sighed. "My life is not what I thought it would be."

Nellie let out a deep chuckle. "You and a million other people. Me included."

"I do not fit into this town."

Nellie clucked her tongue. "I'm an Irish woman in a town that's filled with Scandinavians. You have to make your own way. That's what I learned."

Nellie had made a life here. She knew everyone in town. She was not afraid to tell a grown man to mind his manners and eat her stew without slurping, and she even boxed raucous boys behind the ears when they got too loud. But I was not like Nellie.

"I thought I wanted this life. Now I am not so sure."

"Some women are made for more than running a house," Nellie said. "God gave us all different gifts and blessings. When I married Ned I *had* to help out at the restaurant. I didn't have a choice. We couldn't afford to keep the place going without my help. And then when we weren't blessed with any children, this place and the people who stopped in became my kin. And when Ned passed away, I was thankful I had it.

"A woman like you, who's used to being a performer and a ballerina, you must be bored to death with a husband who's gone days on end. You have more energy than you can handle, and no place to put it. I think you need to use the gifts God gave you. It's a sin not to. And even though I'm Irish, that's more truth than blarney."

I remembered what the postman had said. "Sid Preston suggested I open a ballet school."

"That's not the worst idea I've heard. There's an empty building behind the barber shop. Used to be a candy store. Might be just the place for a dance studio. Our town could use a little culture."

I didn't know how Finn would feel about me opening a ballet studio. And was I prepared to teach others? Would anyone in this small town besides the postman enroll their child in lessons?

I shook my head. "No. I cannot think about it."

Nellie picked up a wet rag to wipe off an empty booth. "Sure you can't. But you're the one who brought it up. We have a saying in Ireland. 'Where the tongue slips, it speaks the truth.'"

She winked at me and left.

CHAPTER TWENTY-EIGHT

I T IS EXPENSIVE," I SAID, BUT I HOPED FINN WOULDN'T change his mind.

Nellie had said that dinner at the St. James Hotel was something most people couldn't afford, but if you had a special occasion, it was the classiest place in town.

"We never had a proper wedding dinner," he replied.

We walked hand in hand the few blocks as it was a perfect evening, with a slight wind that cooled the top of my bare shoulders. I let my shawl rest in the crook of my arms.

I noticed that Finn had a habit of swinging his left arm while he walked, a mannerism that made him seem more carefree than he usually came across, and a bit more boyish.

I was still conflicted about my life here. But when I held Finn's hand, my heart settled. I felt reassurance that he was by my side.

We walked past other couples taking strolls, the pace less hurried tonight, a few pushing carriages with sleeping babies inside. Would that be me someday? Right now I could not imagine it, and that alone was cause for concern. I couldn't forge a life with a man I barely knew. He lived in a home that was almost empty of anything that reflected who he was, as though he were a temporary guest instead of the owner.

Music floated out an open doorway of a local tavern, a jazzy tune, and I felt my step lighten.

"Do you miss dancing?" Finn asked, as if he'd noticed the change in my gait.

"Very much. It was everything to me for so many years. It was my identity. Like the train is for you," I said.

Finn flashed one of his rare grins. I wished I could make him smile more often. It made him look younger when he did, and more attractive. I resolved to try harder.

"Why didn't you return to ballet after the war ended?" he asked.

"The Americans bombed the Opera House. It was still in disrepair."

"What about Hungary? Could you have joined a ballet company there?"

I stopped walking. "Are you speaking of my home country that Stalin turned into a Communist puppet state? Do you think I would dance for those Communist pigs?"

"I'm sorry, I don't know much about ballet, and I didn't mean . . ."

"No." I closed my eyes. Why did my anger flare so quickly? This was not the way I wanted the evening to go. "It is not your fault. I am the one who should apologize. You did nothing but serve your country with great honor. If not for your sacrifice, we would still have those horrible Nazis in control. Please, let us talk of something else. What did you do before the war?"

Finn frowned, as if talking about himself was something he didn't enjoy. "I went to college, then took a job with the railroad. I started as an engine watchman and worked my way up."

"What is engine watchman?"

"My job was to keep water in the boiler and keep the fire going in the firebox."

"I did not know you were an educated man," I said, surprised by this new knowledge. He had not mentioned it before, but I was learning that Finn never bragged about himself. Who was this man, and why had he offered to marry a woman he didn't know? Was he trying to rescue me, or was he lonely? He didn't reveal much, and was so humble that I had half expected to live in a shack instead of the nice home he owned.

I wasn't used to this type of man. Joe had sometimes acted humble, but I knew it was an act because of the way he carried himself. Joe knew he was attractive, was aware that women's eyes followed him, and even though he pretended he didn't know, I could tell he enjoyed it. He often winked at women when he thought I wasn't looking. I'd never once seen Finn wink.

Finn shrugged. "I went to the University of Minnesota and earned a degree in mechanical engineering. That's why I was made a captain in the army."

"And then you have to start at the bottom job on the train?"

Finn took my hand and led me across the street. "That's how it works with the railroad. You have to work your way up the ladder."

"That is somewhat the way of ballet as well. But not the way aristocracy works. You simply take your place on the ladder. There is nothing to climb. I know it seems contrary to the American dream I hear talk of, but my father believed that his position carried responsibility to care for all people, to respect every person, and to use his wealth for the good of his country."

"Your father sounds like a good man. I wish more people were like that. My father taught me that if you want to get anywhere in life, you have to work hard, because no one is going to give you anything. I've found that to be true here in America."

In Hungary, noblemen took care of others. In America, you took care of yourself. Papa believed you must learn from the past, that the downfall of the Russian aristocracy was due to injustice, and he vowed not to make the same mistake. But in America, a land of dreams come true, was hard work the only requirement? What of those whose predicaments were less fortunate? Who took care of them?

"So you worked very hard and were gone frequently. Why did you want to marry?"

"I wanted what every man wants: a wife and home and children. And freedom. It's what we fought for."

I knew that marriage was something I wanted, but only after my ballet career had fizzled out. Papa had allowed me to study ballet and dance with the Vienna Opera with the understanding that someday I'd marry someone of my own standing. The war had not only hastened my departure from dancing, but removed most of the eligible bachelors of my class.

"Aren't you the one who says the past is past?" Finn asked, and I knew he didn't want to talk about his history any longer.

"Yes," I admitted. It was a beautiful evening, and I would soon enjoy a delicious meal. Tonight would be a new beginning.

We approached the three-story brick building through a side entrance tucked off Main Street. There were women in furs, ones who got out of fancy cars on the arms of well-dressed men, and I looked down at my simple black dress, the one I'd bought off the rack for my date with Jeffrey Fairbanks, feeling a rush of inadequacy. It was nice enough, but not as dressy as those.

Finn wore a plain gray suit, one that looked a bit worn, but he seemed oblivious to the presence of the fine-tailored men who stood outside the entrance. He smiled and led me up the steps and into the lobby. A dangling chandelier lit the entrance, and an elegant library with stained-glass windows and a cozy fireplace sat off to the side.

"It's nice, isn't it?" Finn squeezed my hand, and I smiled up at him.

Then Finn's face froze. I followed his line of sight to where Finn's brother stood. Jack's suit was even more worn than Finn's, but he had cleaned up well; his hair was neatly combed and he'd shaved. He held on to the cane at his side. A woman stood next to him. She had platinum hair and bright red lipstick on her pale face, and a white dress that was low cut, revealing a birthmark above the ample cleavage of her left breast.

"Jack. What are you doing here?" Finn asked in a terse voice. His eyes briefly darted to the woman next to Jack and flicked back to his brother.

"Wanted to check out how the other half lives. Mom said you were planning to go here tonight. Thought we'd join you, if that's okay."

Finn's face shifted, became stonelike. "We?"

"We've been seeing each other a couple of weeks. I hope that's okay."

All eyes were on Finn. I didn't understand. Why did he need Finn's approval?

Finn finally answered. "It makes no difference to me."

"So can we join you?"

Finn flinched. "We hoped to dine alone."

I remembered how poorly our last meeting had gone. But Jack had a date tonight. That was encouraging. Surely we could be accommodating, even though it was inconvenient.

"It is fine," I told Finn, then looked at Jack. "We would enjoy the company."

Jack smiled. "It's settled then." He approached the maître d', who nodded.

"Your table will be ready in just a moment," he told Finn, whose face remained taut, his mood now changed.

I extended a hand toward the woman. "I'm Roza."

The woman glanced at Finn, as though requesting permission to shake my hand.

Finn looked away.

The maître d' held out his arm. "We are ready to seat you now."

The woman in white gave a quick shake of my hand. "I'm Pearl."

Pearl?

Of course. She was Finn's former fiancée.

I would not have asked them to join us if I knew.

I followed my husband to our seats. Finn held my chair, then sat next to me. Pearl was seated on my other side, with Jack opposite.

I glared at Jack. He seemed determined to undermine our marriage. Is that why he'd brought this woman to dinner? He was just a spiteful, jealous man trying to ruin everyone else's lives.

"Your bracelet is very sparkly. Is it real?" Pearl asked, nodding at the diamond heirloom on my wrist.

"It was a gift from my grandmother, the Countess Maria Katarzyna Mészáros," I replied, more haughtily than I'd intended. "What do you think?"

Pearl rolled her eyes. "I'd heard you were some sort of royalty. But Jack said you didn't flaunt it."

I already didn't like this woman. In fact, I hated her just from reading her letter.

"She doesn't flaunt it," Finn said, defending me. "She just wasn't prepared to meet you tonight."

"Well, if you want me to leave . . ." Pearl made a move to stand, but Jack grabbed her arm.

"No," Jack said. "I know it's awkward. But we're all adults, right?"

He looked at his brother. "You'll have to get used to it. I plan to bring Pearl around with me."

Finn nodded. "Like I said, it makes no difference to me."

His voice was flat, and I couldn't help but wonder if he meant what he said. How would I feel if I saw Joe with someone else? And how much worse that it was Finn's brother?

I was glad the room was noisy with laughter and chatter, the clank of silverware on dishes, and the sound of piano music in the background. Perhaps no one would notice the drama at our table.

Jack relaxed back into his chair and opened the menu in front of him. "I'm starved." His eyes jerked to the right and he let out a small breath. "They should give you a whole cow for these prices."

"I'd like a drink," Pearl said.

"Order whatever you want. We're celebrating." Jack took out a cigarette and lit it.

He looked at me. "Don't you want to know what we're celebrating?"

Not particularly. But I took the bait. "What is the occasion?"

"I'm getting a place of my own."

"Congratulations," I said.

Finn set down his menu. "You don't have a job."

"I got a loan through the GI Bill. I get some disability pay, and who knows, maybe someday someone will have sympathy and hire a cripple."

"You don't need more sympathy," Finn said. "You pile plenty on yourself."

"Sorry I didn't come back in one piece like you," Jack spit out.

How he could say that when he knew of Finn's nightmares?

"Please, boys." Pearl gave Jack a pleading look. Then she turned to Finn. I saw her bat her eyes right there in front of everyone. *How dare she!*

"The war caused all this," Pearl said. "We've all been hurt. But we have to forget all that's happened and pick up the pieces and move on."

Forget, as in forget that Finn was now married to me?

The waiter approached, and Pearl said in a hushed voice, "Let's play nice now."

"I'll have a highball," she told the waiter.

"Whiskey sour," Jack said, then added, "make it a double."

Finn ordered a beer.

I wanted to go home. "Ginger ale," I said.

"You're not a teetotaler, are you?" Jack asked between puffs of his cigarette. "Because you won't fit into this family if you are."

"No." I picked up the menu and pretended to study it. "I just don't want a drink right now."

Jack turned to his brother. "You ever see Mom drunk?"

Finn frowned at his menu. "Can't say that I have. I didn't think she was much of a drinker."

"Well, when she does, it's a hoot. Dad had to put her to bed because she could barely stand, and she only had two beers. She can't keep a secret either. That's how I found out that you were coming here tonight. She said you didn't come right out and say it, but you didn't want your new wife to think you were cheap."

Finn's cheeks reddened.

"Of course, Finn was always the one who saved his money. Dad used to complain that anytime I got a penny I'd hustle down to the drugstore to buy candy. Not Finn, though. He saved like he was gonna *buy* the train, not just work on it."

"I don't know what you consider cheap, but Finn was always generous with me," Pearl said, and held out her arm, on which a blue bracelet dangled. "He bought this for me, and I've kept it ever since. Couldn't bear to get rid of it when I married Dale, and I'm glad I didn't, as that was a terrible mistake. Of course, it's not diamonds, like yours. But I still treasure it."

"I do not think my husband is cheap," I said, even as I remembered Mariska's cautioning me about that, and worried that he might be after the incident with the furniture.

I wanted to grab Pearl's arm and cut it off. So that's why she'd asked about my bracelet. And now she shoved Finn's gift in my face. It was insanely obvious that this woman was clearly using Jack to get to Finn. Only Jack seemed oblivious to it.

I felt a sudden twinge of sympathy for Jack. He was collateral damage from the war, just as Finn and I were, in different ways. And now he was a pawn being used by Finn's ex-fiancée. Even though I disliked his self-pitying attitude, he didn't deserve this.

Finn's neck muscles twitched and he clenched his menu the same way I used to hold on to the sides of the Prater Ferris wheel in Vienna.

The drinks arrived, and Jack took a long sip of his. "Don't go too far," he told the waiter.

"Did you always want to work on the train?" I asked Finn, picking up a thread Jack had mentioned.

His grip loosened. "Ever since I was a tot. The railroad tracks are just a few blocks away from where we grew up. I'd hear the whistle, see the curl of steam, and I'd go tearing outside to watch them pass by. I didn't just want to work on one. I wanted to drive it."

"I hear diesel units are replacing the steam engines," Jack said.

Finn nodded. "The old steam locomotives are being retired and replaced by diesel. We've been getting trained for them."

"Maybe they need new people for that?" Jack asked, and I could hear the hope in his voice.

"Maybe. But we're losing people too. Diesel doesn't require as much support personnel. They're probably going to furlough some mechanics."

"You got older guys ready to retire, though," Jack said. "You must need help somewhere."

Finn stared at his brother. "Is that what this is all about? A setup to ask for a job?"

Jack drained the rest of his drink. "Why wouldn't you help your own brother? You're the one who's always telling me I can do things, that I can't let this wooden stump stop me from working."

Finn hesitated. "It would require a lot of climbing up and down . . ."

"So you're saying I can't handle it? After all your bullshit about getting a job?"

"You *can* get a job. I just don't know if the railroad is the right job."

"Sure you don't. You're just as highfalutin as your wife. You don't want me on the railroad because then you'd have to acknowledge a gimp for a brother. I got a bum rap in the war and I'm getting a bum rap now."

Jack reached into his pocket and threw two dollars on the table. Then he stood and grabbed his crutches. "Let's go, Pearl."

Pearl stood up but didn't move right away. "I'm sorry, Finn." The way she said it, I wasn't sure if she was referring to tonight, or to something else. She was looking at Finn with an expression that I recognized. It was one I used to see reflected on my own face when I looked in the mirror and thought of Joe. Pearl was still in love with Finn.

CHAPTER TWENTY-NINE

❧✦❧

I WOKE WITH A JOLT. FINN WAS SCREAMING AGAIN.

I threw on the silky blue housecoat that matched my nightgown, hurried down the hallway, and stood in front of Finn's bedroom door. The screaming had stopped, but I could hear him panting; loud, uneven breaths of panic and desperation.

I knocked and waited.

"Roza?" came his voice, and the sound of creaking bed springs.

"Is everything okay?" I asked through the door.

"Yes. Just a bad dream. I'm fine now. You can go back to bed."

"Very well." But he didn't sound right.

I knocked again. "Please open the door, Finn."

"I'm all right, Roza."

"I am not leaving until I see you."

The bed creaked again, and I heard the soft thump of his feet on the floor. Then footsteps. The door finally opened. Finn's hair was disheveled and his eyes and cheeks were red. He was drenched in sweat.

"Thank you for your concern," he said gruffly. "I'm okay now."

"You were . . . louder than usual. I was worried."

The room was dark behind him, and the light from the hallway cast a harsh glare on his face, making him look more drained than usual.

"No, it was just . . ." He closed his eyes a moment. His whole body shook. "Nebly was so young, so brave, so . . ."

He suddenly moved past me. "Nebly? I'm coming. Stay down!"

I grabbed his arm and pulled him back. "No, Finn. He's not there."

He looked at me, confusion still in his eyes. He turned toward the empty hallway and let out a breath.

"Oh, God, I thought . . ." It was as if all his strength suddenly left him. His body shook and he was sobbing. He fell to his knees. He looked so vulnerable, his face so distraught that I knelt and wrapped my arms around him and brought his head down to my shoulder. I held him tight.

"It's okay, Finn."

"He was just a kid. Too young. It should have been me. Not him!"

"Shh." His sobs echoed in the hallway. "It is done. The war is over, Finn."

But he couldn't stop. It was as though a dam had burst open. "It's not right. It's not just. It's all wrong."

His sobs melted into a soft whimper. "I'm sorry," he said over and over again.

Was he apologizing to me or to the boy who'd died? "You need not apologize," I admonished him while stroking his hair. "I know what it was like. I remember the first time I saw the burned-out buildings from the Kristallnacht, the graffiti on buildings, and the people they took away. Give yourself time, Finn. It is not easy to leave the memories behind."

I knew it was harder to leave guilt behind, to forgive yourself for living when others had died. I thought of my roommate, Greta, of how I'd let her down. I thought she was old enough to make her own choices, but did she really understand what a monster Hauser was? I should have insisted she stay away from him.

And Finn. How much harder was it for him to forgive himself when his whole platoon had died?

Here he was, three years later, a blubbering mess on the floor.

Finn finally pulled away, looking embarrassed by his sudden outburst. He swiped a hand across his nose. He stood and helped me up. "Thank you, Roza. I swear that's never happened before. I've never done that. I mean, broken down in front of anyone. I . . . appreciate your understanding."

"Who was Nebly?" I asked. "Was he in your unit?"

His eyebrows knotted together. "Floyd Nebly. He was the youngest in my squad. They gave him the nickname 'Newby' because he was the newest recruit and he'd never kissed a girl besides his mother. He carried a Bible with him and used to read it all the time. He took down a German during the attack but got hit in the gut at the same time. I held his hand as he . . ." His voice faded.

"That must have been so hard."

He nodded, but didn't speak.

"I am here if you want to talk, Finn."

Finn shook his head. "No. I'm okay now."

"Are you sure?"

"Yes. I promise. Thank you."

There was nothing I could do for this man other than offer my comfort. He felt he had to carry the burden of his guilt privately, without confiding in others. How many times would he revisit this battle in his dreams, hoping to change the outcome?

I put a hand on his cheek. "I wish you a dreamless sleep. Good night, Finn." I turned to leave.

"Roza?" I stopped and turned back. "Uh, I just wondered what kind of perfume you're wearing."

"Perfume? It is Chanel." I noticed then that my housecoat had come open while I was hugging Finn, that my low-cut nightgown revealed more than I'd realized. I gathered the robe at my neck.

"It smells really nice," he said, and the grief in his eyes had been replaced by something else: a longing I recognized. Finn's grief had left him vulnerable, but not in the pitying way the banker had been.

It made him seem more appealing, and his opening up to me a bit had brought about a dizzying attraction to him, especially when our bodies were pressed together. But the encounter with Pearl and the letter he'd saved reinforced what I suspected: that Finn wasn't over her yet.

And I wasn't ready either. Even as I was attracted to Finn, I still couldn't think of making love to anyone other than Joe.

Finn leaned against the doorway. "I never told Pearl this, but I hated her perfume. It was like sticking your nose in a lilac bush. And she was wearing that same perfume tonight. It brought everything back."

I couldn't hide the anger in my voice. "I cannot imagine that your own brother would date her, knowing your history with her."

"I don't blame Jack. He's feeling low, thinking no woman will ever want him. But Pearl should have known better. I got her Dear John letter when I was recovering in the hospital. It smelled of that same perfume. She said she got a job at the snack bar at the Sheldon Movie Theater while I was gone and started spending time with Dale Carter, who worked the ticket booth. He was a couple years older than me in school. She wrote that they got married, that it was better this way because she was getting worry lines fretting over me."

He gave a scoffing laugh. "Worry lines. That was her biggest complaint."

I already knew this from reading the letter, but I shook my head and swore softly in Hungarian. "*Kurva*."

Finn let out a long sigh. "I memorized every word of that letter before I threw it away."

Threw it away?

"How long did you know Pearl beforehand?" I asked.

"I knew her in school, but we didn't start dating until I was in college. When I came home we'd go out. Then after I graduated and got a job with the Northern Pacific, we spent that summer together. We were engaged at Thanksgiving, and I left in December after Pearl Harbor."

"And you were gone for several years."

"I wrote her every week. Her letters became more infrequent, until that last one . . ."

"Do you still care for her?" I avoided the word "love," because I didn't want to know.

"When she moved back six months ago, she said she wanted to see me. I met her to make peace, not to get back together. She's too fickle for me. I can't say it doesn't bother me seeing her with Jack, even after all this time. But I don't love her anymore. That much I can say as fact."

He reached down to kiss me, but I pulled away, patting his chest as I gave him a sad smile. Finn had lied to me about the letter, and that made it worse than admitting he'd kept it. Finn would take me to his bed for comfort right now, as a substitute for Pearl, and he would be a substitute for Joe. I required more than that, and I did not want to think of Joe as I made love to my new husband.

I remembered the way Pearl had looked at Finn. I put my hands into the pockets of my housecoat and turned toward my room. "I know you believe that," I said, "but does Pearl?"

I left before Finn could answer.

CHAPTER THIRTY

ℬ❧ℬ

IT WAS THE FIRST TIME I'D SEEN FINN LOOKING TRULY RE-
laxed. I'd come down to find him sitting on an aluminum chair on
the back porch, a beer in his hand, chatting with his friend, who'd
dropped by unexpectedly.

The lilacs were in full bloom and bees hummed around the pe-
tunias I had finally gotten around to planting. It was warm out, and
our postman Sid said that a warm June promised a hot July.

"This is Chet Maguire," Finn said, introducing his friend. "He's
the conductor, the chief of the train, the one who makes everything
happen. I just blow the horn occasionally."

Finn is lankier than Chet by several feet. Chet was shorter than
me, and had a pleasant chubby face, a round pink nose, and neatly
trimmed white hair.

Chet laughed. "Don't let him fool you. Finn is in charge of running the train; I just do everything else."

Finn let out a belly laugh. Who knew he could make such a
sound? Was this what the old Finn was like? The lines around his
eyes softened, and I smiled, even though I didn't understand the
joke. I'd never heard Finn laugh like that before. I'd never met one
of his friends before.

"How long have your worked as a conductor?" I asked Chet.

"I didn't start out as a conductor. No, I spent years working
my way up, first shoveling coal into the firebox, then working as a
brakeman, and then eighteen years ago I made conductor. Finn, on

the other hand, is one of the youngest engineers we've had. He's a real prodigy."

"It was the war," Finn said. "Some of the more senior engineers didn't come back, and they needed younger ones to fill in."

"True, but I've never met anyone who has as much railroading in his blood as you do," Chet said.

Finn took a swig from his bottle of Grain Belt to hide his reddening cheeks.

"That is a great compliment to my husband," I said. "He would never admit to it, though."

"You don't have to tell me that," Chet said. "He's always been a humble guy. More so after coming back from the war."

I wondered if Finn confided in Chet. It didn't sound as though he did. I had my roommate, Greta, and then Mariska, and now Nellie. It would be so lonely never to have someone to talk to.

Chet motioned toward Finn. "But old Scout, she was love at first sight. Right, Finn?"

Finn nodded and took another drink.

"She? Who is this Scout?" I asked, raising my eyebrows.

Chet waved his hand in the air. "Sorry, didn't mean to lead you on. All steam locomotives are 'she.' Always been that way. And personality? Every locomotive has one, which is why you have to name her. The screeching, hissing, clanging? It's her talking to us all the time. Sometimes complaining, sometimes giving us a scare or two, but believe me, she's alive."

"I have never thought of a train that way," I admitted. "Are you married, Chet?"

"Forty-two years next month," he replied, looking a bit wistful. "She's a saint, my Shirley. I suppose every railroad wife is, though. You're discovering what it's like. What with our stretches of being gone for days; missing holidays and birthdays, and having to raise the kids mostly on your own, it can be a tough life for both of you."

"But it is a rewarding job, yes?"

"Absolutely! The best in the world." Chet raised his beer into the air, as did Finn, and they clinked their bottles together. "Not bad pay either. There's an old blues song that goes, 'When you marry, marry a railroad man, every day Sunday, a dollar in your hand.'"

Chet reached into his pocket and drew out a round watch on a long, gold chain. He squinted as he looked at it. "Speaking of marriage, I'm due home for dinner soon."

He stood up and took my hand. "I'm happy to meet the woman who captured Finn's heart."

Then he handed me a flat, rectangular box wrapped in white paper. "A small gift from me and Shirley to celebrate the occasion."

I accepted it with a smile. "May I?" I asked, holding the box up in the air.

"Of course."

I carefully removed the paper to reveal a sterling silver picture frame. "Thank you. This is very thoughtful."

"You're welcome. I hope to see a picture in that frame next time I visit."

Finn showed Chet to the door, and I followed behind.

"We must have you and your wife to dinner," I said before he left. I noticed Finn wince at that suggestion. Two days ago I'd attempted to make a roast in that cavernous oven. I hadn't understood the temperature setting, though, and when Finn came home, I was helplessly waving at the smoke that was pouring out of the kitchen. He'd turned off the oven, which he said had been set to five hundred degrees, and opened all the windows and the back door. Then he took out the remains of the roast, which now looked like a piece of hardened coal, the blackened chips next to it barely recognizable as potatoes.

I'd started crying then, embarrassed by my ineptitude. But Finn took my hand.

"I should have explained the settings to you, Roza. Look, it's not that bad."

And he picked up one of the burnt potatoes and took a big bite.

"How can you eat that?" I exclaimed.

"I had worse during the war," he said, and picked up another one. I grabbed his hand before he put it in his mouth.

"Stop. Please."

"I will if you stop beating yourself up about it," he said with a grin. "It's just a little well done."

"Well done?" I tried to put a fork in the dried-up meat, but couldn't puncture the hard crust. I burst out laughing then, and Finn joined in.

After Chet left, I put the empty frame on the side table, next to the lamp. We had no pictures from our wedding to put in it. I hadn't even thought to take one at the time. Perhaps I could instead place a picture of Mama and János, if they would send me one. The only picture I had was dated. Papa was in it and János a young child of six. I would ask Mama for a new picture, although I dreaded to see what Mama looked like now that she was impoverished. Mama had written that poverty did not suit her at all.

A while later I joined Finn on the back porch. He held another cold beer in his hands; this was the third I'd seen him drink today. He didn't drink when he was scheduled to work, but when he had two days off, I would find six empty beer bottles in the trash, or an empty whiskey bottle. He was leaning back; his eyes were fixed on a tree in the distance, one with drooping branches and long spear-shaped leaves.

"What is English name for that tree?" I asked.

"A weeping willow."

"Did you plant it?"

"No. It was here when I bought the place. I figure it's probably a good twenty years old."

I sat next to him. "May I have a sip?"

Finn's eyes widened and he tipped his head. "I didn't think this would be the choice of drink for a . . ." He stopped, and handed it to me. "Sure, if you want."

I took a long swig, not caring for the bitter taste, but appreciating the coldness that rushed down my throat. I wiped a hand across my mouth and handed the bottle back to Finn. "You think I act too high class?"

Finn raised his eyebrows. "Is this your attempt to prove you're not?"

"No," I said, but felt a blush on my cheeks.

"You're cultured, certainly. It comes through the way you talk and carry yourself. But I don't think I've ever seen a less fussy eater. You're not . . . what I expected."

I wasn't sure if that was a compliment. But it deserved an explanation. "The last few years I have had so little to eat. I am just glad to have food now. And a cold drink in this hot and humid weather."

"You continue to surprise me, Roza."

"Good," I replied, and Finn held a soft smile at the corner of his mouth.

"I enjoyed meeting your friend. He was very nice. You should invite him over more often."

"I would, but our schedules don't always match. Someday I will, though. Just so you can meet his wife, Shirley."

We settled into an easy silence as a slight breeze rustled across the yard, and I felt the wind lift my hair.

I nodded at the weeping willow. "I used to see them in Budapest when I would peek over the wall into the garden of the Carmelite monastery. Those trees always made me sad."

"I guess that's why they're called weeping willows. They are kind of lonely looking, aren't they?"

We both sat there for a long moment staring at the tree. *It reflects the loneliness of the home's occupants*, I thought. Had the previous owners experienced sadness? Is that why they planted one lone tree, so different from the pine and oak trees surrounding it?

"I hope Chet's talk of hard marriages didn't bother you too much," Finn finally said. "I know it's not always easy being married to a railroader, but it isn't as bad as he made it out."

"It did not bother me. I knew what your job was when I married you." But I still felt entrenched in the loneliness of the moment, thinking of the endless stretches of days when Finn was gone.

As if he felt it too, Finn reached over and took my hand. There it was, the sensation that always came with his touch. Reassurance. Safety. How was he able to make me feel that way when he suffered such terrible nightmares?

I touched my other hand to my eyes, feeling moistness. I did not want Finn to think a tree would make me cry. But it was the remembering of a simpler time that had done it—my youth in Budapest before the war, the carefree days of my childhood. When my ballet dancing held such promise. When Papa was strong and I thought he would live forever. All I'd lost came rushing back.

I sneaked a look at Finn, who was still staring at the tree. But I felt his hand tighten around mine, squeezing it ever so slightly.

And this time I felt more than just comfort. I looked away, afraid to show my face to Finn. My skin tingled with desire.

CHAPTER THIRTY-ONE

Y OU KNOW, YOU CAN ASK FOR HELP. MY MOTHER WOULD help you."

Finn stood at the entrance to the kitchen, his hands in his pockets, not daring to enter the floury haze that blanketed the room.

I sneezed and dabbed my nose on a powdery sleeve. Until this moment, it was the only spot left on my body that wasn't splotched with white dust. I could barely see the blue of my apron under the floury mess.

I stopped kneading the dough and looked at him. "I cannot ask her," I answered. "I will figure it out myself."

As if I would give Finn's mother the satisfaction? It would add fuel to the fire and give her further cause for thinking Finn had married the wrong girl, someone who could not even cook. The fact that I couldn't cook made no difference.

"Why not?"

I didn't look up. "I do not want her to think of me any worse than she already does."

"She doesn't . . ." Finn started, but his voice trailed off. It was no use denying what was obvious.

"Look, it's just a church social picnic."

Now I pounded the flour on the table.

"Do you understand the oven settings now?"

"Yes," I reassured him, but he looked skeptical.

"I could always go to Nellie's and buy a pie."

I stopped and put my hands on my hips. My eyes flared.

Finn stepped back. "Sorry. It was just a suggestion. I think I'll go clean out the garage."

I heard the floorboards creak and the front door slam. Good. He would not bother me anymore. I looked at the pathetic mess of dough on the table. It was hopeless. If only Mariska was here to help. Perhaps I should have tried to make something from my own country instead of an American apple pie. The Hungarian version that I remembered, *almás pite*, was more of a cake or cobbler, and I was certain it didn't involve rolling the dough into a perfectly thin, flat circle. Mine looked like a triangle, and bits of butter and egg stuck out. Perhaps baking ability was inherently transferred to those pastries that were customary for your particular country of origin? Or perhaps I just had no ability at all.

In fact, I hardly ever entered the kitchen of my childhood mansion; I barely knew where it was. Food just appeared, as if by magic. I knew the names of the servants who served the food, and Emese, the head cook. That was all I needed to know, as far as Mama was concerned, who would rather starve than prepare her own food. Who was cooking Mama's food now? Perhaps János had taken over those duties in order to have something edible to eat.

During the war, I had managed to make soup when I was poor, but little else. I had certainly never baked pastries. Emese made delicious *dobos torta*, six layers of sponge cake filled with chocolate butter cream, and *kalács* that made my stomach growl just at the thought. They were even better than Mariska's, although I would never tell her that.

During my ballet years, we were forbidden to eat pastries, and during the war, since sugar was rationed, there weren't many desserts. I had never much concerned myself with cooking. Only with eating.

But now cooking seemed an important ability in a housewife. Especially at a church picnic.

My first church social. It was important I not fail this time.

I pushed a stray hair back into the hairpins that held it off my forehead, the dough sticking to the strands. Not only did my pie look awful, but so did my hair. I would have little time to clean up.

Somehow I managed to produce something that resembled the picture in the cookbook I'd borrowed from Nellie. It was too lumpy, not like it was supposed to be, and the edges were too brown, a rusty coffee color with cracks. Perhaps overly crisp? And the apples I'd bought at the store and put in the pie were smaller than I was accustomed to. But I held it proudly as we drove to the Lutheran Church that Finn's family had attended dating back to his father's birth. I'd made this one thing, at least, a symbol of my ability to be like any other American housewife.

I had on a freshly washed cotton dress, one that had a white rounded neckline, not too low. My pillbox hat and Oxford shoes lent a conservative touch.

"Are you sure you're okay with going to a Lutheran social?" Finn asked, knowing I was Catholic. "St. Joseph's Church is not far from our house."

"Yes, I want to go to this event," I reassured him. His mother had called to invite us, and to reject their church community would mark me as even more of an outsider.

Finn had explained that St. Paul's was the first English-speaking Lutheran church in Red Wing. The Germans, Swedes, and Norwegians had founded churches that preserved their own traditions and language. But when this church was established, they wanted to embrace all settlers in the language of their new home. I hoped that meant it would be more welcoming.

"Will your brother be there?" I asked.

"Most likely."

I didn't ask the follow-up question, whether Pearl would be there too, but it was implied. I thought back to our last encounter.

We hadn't stayed for dinner at the St. James that night; Finn had paid for the drinks and we had eaten cold bologna sandwiches at home. What had started as a promising night of dinner and dancing ended with strained silence between us.

Anger flashed inside at the thought of Pearl, who had made a choice to marry someone else; the fact that she'd made a poor choice was her own mistake. Why should she try to ruin Finn's marriage now?

I would have difficulty maintaining a civil tongue when I saw her. But I would make an effort not to cause a scene only because of Finn, who I sensed desperately wanted his family to accept me. If it were up to me, I did not care one bit what his family thought of me. Not after the cold welcome they'd given me. But I knew that family was important.

All the time I'd spent worrying about Joe's family? Wasted time. What good had it done after all? I had never even met them.

I was confused when we parked in front of the church. In Hungary, events like this were usually held outdoors on the grounds of the church. But no one was milling about; instead people were walking into the church. "Where is this picnic?"

Finn opened my door. "It's in the church basement."

"On a beautiful day like today?"

He shrugged. "Minnesota weather is finicky. You can't always trust it to be nice outside."

I rolled my eyes. To me, "picnic" meant a meal outdoors. I took Finn's arm and he led me up the stairs to the brick church framed with ornamental stone trim and through the heavy oak door.

An adjacent door opened to narrow stairs that led to the basement.

I felt a renewed embarrassment at my contribution when I saw the creations heaped on the tables: lemon and chocolate pies covered with cloud-white meringue, cakes topped with straight lines of pineapples with little cherries in the middle of each yellow circle, plates of mincemeat pie and molasses cookies, beautiful chiffon cakes, and worst of all, perfect apple pies, each of them flaky masterpieces with pleated rims of golden crust that could have come straight from Nellie's café.

I turned around, holding the pie close to my body. "I have changed my mind. I will leave this in the truck."

A woman with short, tight curls intercepted us. "The pies go over on this table," she said, plucking it from my hands. I put a hand on my mouth in horror as my bumpy, dark monstrosity was placed in the middle of those gorgeous desserts.

"Mine is *szörnyű*, awful," I said in a small voice.

"It's fine," Finn said reassuringly. "And there are so many desserts here no one will notice yours."

That was little comfort. As I stared at the other pies, I remembered that I had forgotten something in mine. I'd meant to ask Finn to buy some because I couldn't remember how to say it in English when I was at the store, and the grocer didn't understand my Hungarian pronunciation of cinnamon. Would it make a huge difference if I'd left it out?

"Finn Erickson, you have to introduce your new wife to the Ladies Aid Society," another woman said, taking my arm and pulling me away from the table. She guided us toward a group of women gathered around pots of coffee and pitchers of lemonade. Most were elderly, older than Finn's mother.

"I'd like to introduce my wife, Roza," Finn said. "She came to the United States from Vienna, where she was a professional ballet dancer. But her country of origin is Hungary."

"How do you do?" I made a sweeping motion with my hand that came from muscle memory. I had learned long ago that a dancer's hands are the most eloquent part of her body, the language of ballet. In my nervousness, I resorted to the ballet hand position:

fingers separated and rounded in a straight line, index finger slightly elongated, thumb tucked inside, wrists lifted to continue the line of energy. The result was a delicate movement, but one that drew several raised eyebrows and comments such as "Oh my, aren't we fancy?" No one made a move to shake my hand.

I withdrew my arm, wishing I could have a do-over. I hadn't meant to come across as haughty.

"Well, it's nice to see you ladies again," Finn said, tipping his head as he led me away, and I could see the pink on his cheeks, which made me feel worse.

I felt myself being pulled across the hall until we were in front of a nervous-looking man about Finn's age. He had on a long-sleeved flannel shirt over wrinkled slacks, and had pressed himself into a corner, as though trying to avoid any conversation. I wished I could join him.

"Roza, this is Lou," Finn said. "How are you doing, buddy?"

Lou looked up at Finn, as if startled to hear his name.

He grabbed Finn's shoulder. "You're home. When did you get back?" His words were slurred.

"I've been back for a year and a half. Remember? We both came home about the same time."

He let go of Finn and slouched back into the corner. "Oh, yeah. Time flies, doesn't it?"

"Are you working?" Finn asked. "That job sweeping out the hardware store? You still doing it?"

Lou shook his head. "Nah. Old man Hager let me go. It's been tough. You know what it's like."

"Well, I'm glad to see you here at church," Finn said.

"The pastor dragged me here," Lou said, then shrugged. "It's a free meal."

Finn nodded. "I'd like to introduce you to my wife, Roza."

"I'm happy to meet you, Lou," I said.

Upon hearing my voice, Lou's face shriveled up like a rotten tomato. "You sound just like them. Those poor sons a bitches that didn't stand a chance."

I drew back. "I do not understand."

"So many of them. I never expected it to be so bad."

Finn patted his shoulder. "It's over now, Lou. Been over for three years. You gotta get some help."

Lou wiped his bloodshot eyes and nodded. "Yeah. I know."

"Call me if you need anything," Finn said.

Finn led me away. "I'm sorry about that."

"What is wrong with him?" I asked, when we'd gotten out of earshot.

"His troop liberated a train of Polish prisoners. They'd been locked in and left by the Germans. Most of them were dead. Stacked like pancakes on top of each other. He must have confused your accent with them."

I put a hand on my mouth. Tears stung the corners of my eyes. "How awful."

Finn nodded. "Your accent probably brought it all back. We deal with the memories in our own ways. Lou tries to drink them away."

I sniffed. "And you suffer nightmares and little sleep."

He looked at me. "As do you."

I didn't think Finn heard me at night. My war dreams weren't as frequent as Finn's and had lessened since our marriage. But the bombs still fell in my sleep.

His face was near mine. I felt a shiver at his closeness, one I didn't expect. Other than the kisses he gave me as he departed for work, our relationship was still on shaky ground. His biggest detriment was that he wasn't Joe.

Finn located his parents, and standing next to them, his brother and Pearl.

"It's nice to see you again, Rose," Finn's mother said, but she wasn't smiling.

"It's *Roza*, Mom," Finn said.

"Shouldn't she start using the English version? And wouldn't that be *Rose*?" She turned to everyone as if confirming this, and looked at me with questioning eyes. "Am I right?"

Right? About *my* name? I pursed my lips together to keep from making a spiteful comment. I used all the grace I could summon at the moment. "You may call me Rose if that suits you, Mrs. Erickson."

Finn's hand gave mine a grateful squeeze.

Jack had his arm around Pearl's waist, and he pulled her close. "Did the St. James have a waiting list today?" he asked.

Pearl nudged him with her elbow. "Be nice. You're brothers, after all."

Finn's mother scowled. "I saw you talking to Lou. He's a disgrace. Anyone can tell he's been drinking. He's been nothing but a drunk since he came back."

"That's what happens sometimes," Jack said. "A man goes batty and never recovers. They find him dead in the gutter years later. It's usually the quiet ones. Right, Finn?"

Finn ignored the jab that his brother lobbed at him. "Let's hope Lou doesn't end up there," he said. "This is a step in the right direction."

I remembered that last week I'd awoken one morning to find a half-empty bottle of Jack Daniel's on the counter and a dirty shot glass in the sink. Finn's nightmares were becoming more frequent.

Bernice made a tsking sound. "Jack didn't turn out like that, and heaven knows he coulda after losing his leg."

"Everyone handles it differently Mom," Finn responded.

"What Lou needs is a girlfriend," Pearl said. I noticed she'd moved away from Jack, closer to Finn.

"Or a wife," I said, taking my husband's arm.

"Earl, didn't Lou used to date a girl at the Dairy before he went overseas? You know, the cross-eyed one?" Bernice asked.

"Shh. The reverend is talking." Finn's father shushed her. I noticed he'd refrained from bashing Lou, as though he had no opinion. Or did he let his wife speak for him?

After a twenty-minute benediction that had some women worrying over their now-lukewarm casseroles and platters of fried chicken, we finally filled our plates. We sat with Finn's family. Finn had made a point of taking a piece of my pie, the first to cut into it. He nudged his brother, and Jack followed suit. I noticed no one else took a piece.

Bernice sat next to Pearl and spoke to her the entire time, ignoring me completely. I tried to listen to their conversation from across the table, but it was too noisy. The men were talking about two sports teams, the Minneapolis Millers and the St. Paul Saints, which I couldn't follow, having no knowledge of baseball.

Finn did little to help. He didn't pay much attention to me, and when Pearl asked him to pass the salt, I saw their hands touch. Pearl's eyes met mine after that, and I saw Pearl's lips curl up. How could my husband act this way? Why did he not object to Pearl sitting at the same table?

It wasn't until Jack's lips puckered up that I noticed he'd taken a bite of my apple pie. "What's the matter, Jack?" Pearl asked, her attention suddenly turning to her date.

"This is crabapple," he said, scrunching up his nose. "It tastes bitter."

Pearl hooted. "Who would make a crabapple pie?"

Oh, no! I shrunk back.

A moment later Finn started choking. His cheeks flushed red, and he coughed loudly, until his father hit him square in the center of his back. Finn spit up the contents of his mouth onto the table. One of my hairpins rested in a piece of soft apple.

"What in God's name is that? Who made that atrocity?" Finn's mother yelled, calling the attention of nearby tables.

Finn just shook his head, still coughing.

I didn't wait to hear anything more. I bolted from my chair, then found the stairs and ran up, hurrying out the church door, where I sat down on the steps and sobbed, unable to hold it in any longer.

I was a fool to think I could slip into a new life in America. And this simpleminded family and uncultured town was horrible. How could I possibly be expected to fit in when they were all against me? I was not used to being treated like this.

If only Joe had married me like we'd planned. At least he didn't have nightmares, and he'd written that his family was looking forward to meeting me.

It made no difference now. Life with Joe was not a possibility. I was stuck in a loveless marriage to a man who might end up like Lou. What would happen to me then?

Finn appeared at my side, his hands in his pockets. "Roza, please don't cry. It's not as bad as you think."

How could he say that? Of course it was! "Please let me be. I do not want to talk about it."

"Won't you just come inside?"

I shook my head, unable to answer.

"Roza . . ."

A woman's voice interrupted Finn's pleas. "Perhaps I can help. Why don't you go downstairs, Finn?"

Finn's footsteps retreated. A dainty handkerchief, one with embroidered pink flowers, was placed in my lap. I looked up to see a woman I hadn't met before. She was older than me, perhaps in her late thirties, with a wide face, kind blue eyes, and soft blond curls that hit her chin.

She sat down on the steps next to me, gathering her skirt around her knees. "I'm Henrietta Preston, but everyone calls me Etta. My husband, Sid, is your mailman."

I wiped my eyes with the handkerchief. "Sid is a nice man. Thank you for this."

"You're welcome. Are you ready to come back inside?"

I shook my head. "I am humiliated. I cannot return."

Etta patted my arm. "Embarrassed, yes. Humiliated, no. When I was first married, I accidentally put a casserole in a wicker basket in the oven, and didn't realize my mistake until smoke came pouring out of the kitchen. The neighbors called the fire department. I almost started the house on fire. Now *that's* humiliation."

I'd also had a similar incident, although no fire department had been called, thanks to Finn. I felt a smile tug at my mouth, but I pushed it back. "You did not have an entire church congregation witness your mistake."

"Oh, my dear. You're exaggerating. Most of them were so busy gabbing they didn't see the commotion. Only a couple of tables noticed, and they'll forget soon enough. If you've ever tasted Mrs. Patterson's tuna noodle casserole, you'll know what I mean. People take it to be kind and then throw it in the trash. She brings it every year and it keeps getting worse. She added onion and cheese to it this time."

I sighed. "I would like a few more minutes please. I cannot face them yet."

"Then I'll sit with you. I happen to make a very good apple pie, by the way, only because I grew up on a farm and my parents had an apple orchard. I've been making apple pies and apple crisp and apple strudel since I was ten years old. I'd be happy to share my pie-making tips with you if you want to come visit. That way next year you won't be compared to Mrs. Patterson."

I sniffed. "That's very kind of you."

"Not at all. By the way, when they called the fire department on my burning wicker basket, it was in the newspaper. Sid even saved a copy. He said someday I'd look back on it and laugh. You know what? He was right."

I could not imagine ever doing that after what happened to me.

"You're thinking you'll never consider this funny, aren't you?"

I nodded.

"Well, Sid follows football and he always says the best defense is offense."

"I do not understand."

"It means that when you're ready you should dry your face and we'll go in laughing like I just told you the funniest story. Okay?"

"Yes," I said, "okay." This time a smile found its way out.

CHAPTER THIRTY-TWO

"THE SECRET IS TO USE VERY COLD WATER, AND FOLD THE lard into the flour until it's pea-sized. And don't overmix the dough. Then you refrigerate it for a few hours."

Etta's proficient hands formed the dough into two perfect balls, which she placed on a countertop dabbed with flour. I watched as she sprinkled the top of a ball with flour and rolled it out, turning it as she rolled so it formed a perfect circle.

"Your turn," she said after she'd transferred the circle to a pie dish. Etta wiped her hands on her apron.

I tried to duplicate what I'd seen, but my circle didn't flatten like Etta's.

"It's okay, but you can do better." Etta crumbled the dough back into the shape of a small plate. "Start in the center and roll toward the edges. Think of it as a clock."

I tried again. And again. Etta took more dough out of the refrigerator and had me roll out more crusts. By the time I'd finished, I had made many attempts and we had four pie plates filled with smooth crust. We added apples, sugar, and cinnamon, something called nutmeg, a pinch of salt, and a larger dab of butter. Then we topped the bloated fillings with crusts pinched at the edges. It looked remarkably like the pictures in the cookbooks.

"During the war, I had to use honey and corn syrup in place of the rationed sugar," Etta said. "But those pies got eaten just the same."

"Rationing was more restricted in Vienna," I said. "There were no pies." The ration cards gave more food to physical laborers, and men in general. Greta and I lived off bread and dried peas. I often spent my mornings pulling worms out of every single pea.

"These pies look beautiful," I said, admiring our work. "You are a great cook and teacher."

Etta placed the pies on the lower racks of the heated oven. "You're a quick study. You'll be making delicious meals in no time. The saying that the key to a man's heart is his stomach is really true, you know."

Her kitchen was painted lemon yellow, and bright curtains dotted with sunflowers framed the windows. It was the kind of place that made you feel warm and happy, that spoke of the attributes of those who inhabited it.

Although I had confessed a bit of my aristocratic background to Etta, I hadn't divulged many details of my marriage to Finn, only that we'd married quickly before we knew each other, and I did not feel welcome in his family now.

I sighed. "I never took the time to learn how to cook. We had servants who cooked, cleaned, and did our laundry. If war had not broken out, my family would still have servants. And I would still be a ballerina, perhaps performing all over the world."

Etta crossed her arms. She wasn't what I would consider a pretty woman; her nose was too wide, and her face was plain, but she exuded a great deal of self-confidence. "Self-pity is a poor bedfellow. It doesn't make you feel better, and it keeps you from doing things. After Alice was born, when we found out we couldn't have more children, I was depressed for a long time. Then one day I made six pies; one for every additional child I'd planned to have. I gave each pie to a woman friend in the hope that they would have the children that my body couldn't have.

"Then I moved on with my life. That was nine years ago, and since then I've had a very happy life. I love my husband and my rambunctious daughter, and I love having time to play bridge and do gardening, and serve on the women's auxiliary. Yes, I might be happier with more children, but my life is so much richer than I'd imagined it could be."

Alice came in just then, a bouncy girl with blond pigtails and the same easy composure as her mother. Her checkered romper ended above grass-stained knees and bobby socks that were also soiled.

Etta made a tsking sound. "Just look at you, Alice Marie. Were you climbing trees with Jimmy Foster again?"

Alice's cheeks reddened. "Jimmy wanted to."

"That's what I thought. Go wash up and change into decent clothes. And say hello to Mrs. Erickson on your way."

"Hello, Mrs. Erickson," Alice said.

"Please call me Roza. I am happy to meet you. Your father is my postman."

"Everyone calls him Sid the mailman," Alice said. "But I call him Daddy."

Etta nodded. "We're very casual here, and Sid likes to be called by his first name. He says it makes it easier for people to get to know him."

I remembered how easily I'd connected with him. How he'd helped me get invited to Belinda's party.

"Off to get cleaned up, young lady," Etta said with a jerk of her finger, and Alice left.

"She's really not that much of a tomboy," Etta explained, "but there are only boys to play with in this neighborhood. Not a single girl her age."

She poured us each a cup of tea. "It's too bad Alice doesn't have something to channel all that energy into. Like dancing. Or ballet."

I gave her a sideways glance. "Sid told you to say that?"

"No. But he did mention that you would make a wonderful ballet instructor, and we don't have a ballet school in Red Wing. I know of several girls Alice's age who would love to attend. You have such a wonderful gift. Just think about it."

"I will think about it," I said, remembering how Nellie had mentioned an empty building just around the corner from her café. How much I missed ballet in my life.

Etta smiled. "Good. Let's check those pies again."

AN HOUR LATER I WAS HOME WITH AN APPLE PIE COOLING ON my kitchen counter while I was searching the back of the bureau, beneath my nylons and underwear. I brought out the pale pink pointe shoes, ones I'd worn only enough to soften, but not wear them out. This was my last pair, the shoes I had worn that last day when the Opera House had closed due to the war. No one was surprised by the closure. The air-raid warning sirens had gone off so often that we seldom made it through an entire performance anyway.

I bent the shoes back and forth in my hands, then banged them on the floor the way I used to, seven times for the right softness. Then I put them on, groaning at the pain in my toes and feet. I had lost strength in my toes; they were mushy now, not used to the strain or tightness. But I knew that with time I could harden them again. I tied the strings and took a few tentative steps.

I had been ten years old when I had graduated from ballet slippers to pointe shoes, and I still remembered how proudly I'd carried them around, knowing my years of hard work had prepared my feet and legs to finally stand en pointe.

It was dancing that had defined me. It was my life for so many years. And it was my identity. I had let the war take that away from me. Perhaps by teaching I could reclaim some part of myself?

I tied my hair back into a bun. It felt good to get the hair off the back of my neck, to do these simple tasks that I had taken for granted for so many years.

After taking a broom to sweep the floor of the garage, I mounted the broom between two sawhorses and stretched before I started my "routine." Every pain and tightness felt good, somehow, as though reinforcing that my muscles needed this, that they still responded to my movements.

But it was too dark in the garage with the single overhead bulb. I opened the creaking overhead door, and natural light flooded the space, which now looked grimier than the light bulb and small windowpane first allowed. A high shelf above held old paint cans, a kerosene lantern and oil, and tools that I couldn't name. A rusty bike was propped in a damp corner that had lime growing up the side of the wall.

I continued to practice, but was interrupted by the sound of giggling. I turned to see two little girls staring at the broom and sawhorses, and at me, dressed in a sleeveless shirt, pajama pants, and pointe shoes, my leg suspended in arabesque position.

"What are you doing?" one of the girls asked. They were young, about five or so, and holding hands. They both wore short, collared dresses with puffed sleeves and ruffles. One dress was red plaid, the other a smocked anchor-blue dress with a blue knot in the front.

"It is called ballet."

The girl's eyes widened. "Are you a ballerina?"

"I used to be." I looked out toward the sidewalk, seeing no adults behind them. "Who do you two belong to?"

"I'm Judy. I live that way," she said, pointing left.

"And how about you?" I asked the other girl, a little thing with dark braids who had yet to speak.

She moved back, too shy to speak.

"She's Tammy, and she's my next-door neighbor. Can you show us how to do that?"

"Perhaps," I said. "Are you willing to listen and to work hard?"

Judy looked at Tammy and they both nodded.

"I will show you the first position," I said, arranging the girls several feet apart from each other. "But you each need your own space. Put your arms out to make sure you have room to move."

They did as I instructed, although the giggling continued.

"Now you must stand straight and tall with your heels together and your toes apart. Like this," I said, showing them the stance. Judy mastered it, but Tammy had trouble placing her toes apart, and I had to help move her feet, even as the little girl looked on the verge of collapsing.

"Very good," I said. "Keep your arms out to help with balance. Now you can perform a plié, which means to bend your knees like this."

That's when Tammy fell down. But she instantly jumped back up and tried again. I had to admire her tenacity, and the fact that she didn't cry when she hit the hard garage floor.

I was so occupied that I didn't hear the truck approach or the door slam as Finn got out.

"What's going on?" he asked.

I put my hands behind my back, overcome by a sudden nervousness. "We are stretching," I said.

"Stretching," he repeated, a blank look on his face.

"Yes. Go along, girls," I said, bustling them out of the garage. "Thank you for visiting me today."

"Can we come back tomorrow and learn some more?" Judy asked.

"Perhaps. We shall see."

Finn watched them go. "Are you teaching them ballet?"

"I was doing basic exercises when they came by."

"In your pajamas?"

"I didn't pack any leotards."

He took his hat off and scratched his head. "And what is the broom for?"

I reached over and touched the wooden stick. "This is a make-shift barre."

"I see."

But it was clear he didn't see. Finn didn't know what a barre was. He knew nothing of ballet. He'd told me so many times.

"There is no ballet school in this town," I noted.

"Red Wing isn't a sophisticated place, Roza."

"Ballet is not just about dancing or sophistication. It gives you good physical training, and poise and confidence. You learn patience and hard work, and balance. It is healthy. Every town should have a ballet school."

"And you plan on opening one in our garage?"

"No, of course not. The girls were passing by and were curious. That is all."

"Because they saw you out here in your pajamas?"

My explanation had not helped. Finn still didn't get it.

"I made an apple pie," I said, changing the subject, and saw him grimace. "Go try a piece. I think you will be surprised."

"Okay," he said. "Will you be long doing," he paused, "whatever it is you're doing?"

"No. I am quitting. You may park the truck in here now, if you wish."

"Good. I mean, I don't know." He turned, then stopped. "Roza. Is there anything you want to tell me?"

He was not ready to hear what I wanted to say. So I said what he *was* ready to hear.

"Yes. I am learning how to cook."

CHAPTER THIRTY-THREE

I RISH GINGER COOKIES WERE NELLIE'S SPECIALTY, AND IT was her insistence that Etta and I learn how to properly make them that bound the three of us as good friends.

"I'm old, and who am I going to pass this down to?" Nellie said as we crowded into the kitchen of her small apartment above the restaurant, too warm with three people and but a slight breeze ruffling the white curtains.

In Hungary we ate *mézeskalács*, gingerbread cookies painted with delicate patterns and designs, but they were rolled out flat, unlike Nellie's round mounds of chewy moistness. I had become addicted to them at her restaurant, and when Etta met me there for lunch, she'd asked Nellie for the recipe.

"I don't have a recipe. It's all in here," she said, pointing to her head. "But if you two want to come over and watch me make them, you're welcome to do so."

Now we were listening to Doris Day on the radio while Etta wrote furiously on a notepad as Nellie threw ingredients haphazardly into a bowl.

"You're so fast," I commented, watching her roll a round ball of dough in sugar before setting it on the baking pan.

"I can't afford not to be," Nellie replied. "I get up at dawn and make two batches every day, and still run out before the dinner rush. All except Sundays, when we're closed."

"Why don't you make them in the restaurant kitchen? "Etta asked.

"This oven is the best for cookies," Nellie explained. "It's got the right touch. The one downstairs gets too hot too fast."

I had no idea. There was so much to learn about baking.

Once Nellie had two pans of cookies in the oven, she made us cups of tea and we sat at her small table.

"How do you keep doing this every day?" I asked. I wasn't sure of Nellie's age, but Finn had thought her old when he was a boy.

"My birthplace was a seaside village in Ireland," Nellie answered. "I was born with the tides, and I go on like the tides. If I ever stop, then it will be time to worry."

"This town is lucky to have you," Etta said, taking a sip of her black tea, in which she'd added a good dose of milk and sugar. It was the only option, I thought, as the tea was the strongest I'd ever tasted. But I noted that Nellie did the same.

Nellie nodded. "And your husband as well. Good people make the town."

"It must be very rewarding to own a restaurant," I said.

Nellie shook her head. "I don't think of it like that. It was my husband's, and I only kept it going because of him. But I have to admit, it makes me proud to say we've done better business now than when he was alive, and that's including the war, when so many men were gone."

"You have a good mind for business," I said, because it was true. Nellie ran a tight ship with both her employees and customers.

"Anyone can learn," Nellie said, her sharp eyes holding mine. "Especially someone with an education like yourself."

"I do have a desire to open a ballet studio," I admitted, twirling the spoon in my cup. "I know I could learn the business duties. And I could be a good teacher. But I do not, how do you say, make good connections with people, especially other women. You two are my only friends in this town."

Etta made a tsking sound. "If you're referring to the church social, you needn't worry about those women. Their opinions turn faster than their hot dishes go cold."

I felt my cheeks heat up. "It is not just them. The neighborhood women think I am scandalous. And perhaps they are right. I did not tell either of you how I came to marry Finn."

"If it's to do with that newspaper article, we already know," Nellie said. "The cookies are done."

She jumped up, displaying her uncanny ability to know the exact moment when the cookies were at their peak, before the tops cracked.

"You knew?" I drew back, unable to contain my horror. I'd been so worried about them finding out.

"Course we did," Nellie said, her back to me.

I looked at Etta. "You, too?"

She shrugged. "Your brother-in-law told everyone about you being a Hungarian countess, and, well, we put two and two together."

I was beginning to hate Jack.

Nellie turned from the oven to face me. "If that gobshite who proposed to you hadn't turned you over like that, you'd just be another war bride. Heartbreak like that cuts sharp as a razor blade. Fair play to ya for not letting him get the best of you."

"She's right," Etta said, placing her hand on top of mine. "You found a nice fellow in Finn. And mark my words; once all the little girls in town are prancing around in their leotards, those uppity women will be clamoring to get their children signed up."

"Just make it reasonable for plain folk to afford too," Nellie emphasized. "Not too highbrow."

I sighed. "You are both very persuasive. And kind. I could not ask for better friends."

Nellie set a plate of cookies in front of us. "I was an immigrant to this town too. I had no one but my Ned, so I understand how you feel. This is as good a place as any in Minnesota. God never closed a door without opening another. If you're ever lonely you can knock on my door anytime."

"And mine as well," Etta said.

I looked down. My eyes were moist. I didn't know what to say. But Nellie brought me out of my sadness.

"You two going to eat those cookies or just stare at them?" she barked. Then she let out a laugh. "Don't be telling anyone I'm going soft, now."

CHAPTER THIRTY-FOUR

ELLIE AND SID INSPECTED THE ABANDONED CONCRETE building that had once been a candy store, and before that a shoe store, and before that a hardware store. The walls smelled of wood and fertilizer and leather infused with peppermint, as though each use had imparted its own character and fragrance upon the space. The empty store now sat between a floral shop and a dentist's office.

"The wooden floor has a few cracks, but that can be repaired," Sid said, dragging his shoe across the planks. "I think it's oak."

Nellie pointed to the large plateglass window that looked out on the street. "Little girls will be pressing their faces up to the glass to see all those pretty pink ruffle outfits they could be wearing. You'll be the talk of every schoolyard."

I could picture it: a long mirror on one side, a barre running in front of it and another on the opposite wall. Some good lighting, and pictures of famous ballerinas on the walls. Perhaps even a picture of me? It would not cost too much, if the rent was as cheap as Nellie thought.

"You should bring Finn down here to see it," Sid said. I looked down. I hadn't even mentioned the idea to Finn yet.

"He does not understand ballet," I said.

Nellie held her handbag in the center of her robust body. "He doesn't have to understand it. But he has good business sense. That's what you need to impress on him."

I didn't reply. As far as I knew, Finn didn't have any great ambition or knowledge of business either. He loved his job; he loved trains. He was a simple man.

I left with information about the building and a number to call if I was interested in renting it. Sid offered to help paint the walls. Nellie would show me how to do bookkeeping. I was grateful for their help, but I would make no commitment until I had discussed it with my husband. Finn wouldn't be back for two more days.

Finn might not have the money to finance a ballet school. I would have to detail the cost and expenses involved to determine how much I could charge so that I could make money for the time and effort I would put into it. And the cost needed to be reasonable, as Nellie had reminded me.

I arrived home to an empty house. Sid had delivered the mail earlier in the day, but I hadn't had time to look through it. I did so now, hoping to see a letter from Mariska announcing the birth of her baby. I was excited to see a letter addressed to me, but there was no return address. I quickly tore it open.

I gasped as I started reading. I should have recognized his handwriting after two years of correspondence. But I hadn't been expecting this.

Dear Roza,

Don't blame Mariska for giving me your address. I begged her for it several times before she finally relented. I was surprised to learn that you hadn't returned to Vienna, or to your mother's home in Hungary. Even more surprised that you'd married.

I know this is asking a great deal, but we last parted on bad footing. I owe you more of an explanation and, frankly, would like the opportunity to apologize properly.

You do not owe me this, of course, and you may put me out of your mind forever as you said you never wanted to see me again.

> *But I beg you to reconsider. I don't believe this is the ending each of us needs. Rather than make you have to write back, I have arranged to be in Red Wing at the top of Mount La Grange on Thursday at ten o'clock a.m. I will wait one hour. If you cannot make the time or date, I will understand that my bold request is being denied.*

> *In any case, please accept my regards for your well-being, and know that I truly still care about you.*

Sincerely,
Joe

I held the letter to my chest. Just the thought of seeing Joe again made my body pulse with desire. Could I face him again, after all that had happened? Did I even *want* to see him? And what would it accomplish?

We were both married now. It would only make things harder to see him again.

Finn would not be home until Thursday evening.

It would be wrong to meet Joe. Every thought in my head struggled against the idea.

But my heart longed to see him again.

Just this one time, I told myself. *What could it hurt?*

CHAPTER THIRTY-FIVE

❧❦❧

So MANY STEPS! I STOPPED TO REST BENEATH A COVERED landing before tackling the stairs that now mounted to the left. I looked up at another landing in the distance, where more stairs could be seen.

I removed the sweater I'd worn over my sleeveless dress and headed up, feeling glad that I'd only seen one other couple going up the stairs ahead of me. There could be other people on top, of course, but at least Joe hadn't asked to meet at Nellie's (God forbid!) or some other heavily populated location. There was less chance I'd be recognized by anyone I knew up here.

I swatted at a fly and held tight to the railing. I'd never been up here, but had heard of this bluff, how it looked down upon the entire downtown area, as well as the Mississippi River, and Lake Pepin to the south.

My breath came out in short spurts. How long had it been since I'd pushed myself physically? I did a great deal of walking. But I found myself gulping air by the time I'd reached the top of the bluff.

The couple I'd seen ahead of me was standing near a plaque with information about the bluff. But no sign of Joe. I kept to the path. The view up here was remarkable. I could see the Mississippi bridge that crossed from Minnesota to Wisconsin. And I could see down Main Street, the wood mill and flour mill, the railroad depot, the Ben Franklin store, and the St. James Hotel, all of them looking like little toy blocks from up here. The entire town spread out before me.

"It's a beautiful view, isn't it?"

His voice was like smooth Hungarian brandy, the kind that poured pure down your throat and didn't burn.

When I turned around, I thought I was prepared to see him again. But there he was, the easy smile, the same chiseled chin, a wisp of his dark hair caught in the breeze. I stopped myself from reaching out to pat it down.

"Yes. It is. How are you?" Despite steeling myself ahead of time, I still heard the choked emotion in my voice. My own body betrayed me.

"Okay. And you?"

"I am well," I replied.

The silence was awkward. I remembered how easily we had talked to each other, how I'd felt I could tell him anything. Did time make us strangers? Or was it our current situation?

"You look beautiful," he said, scuffing his foot on the dirt path. "I'd forgotten how beautiful you are."

The other couple had wandered close by. Joe put his arm out. "Shall we explore this bluff a bit more?"

I took his arm, just like I'd done so many times before. I thought of the first time he'd walked me home from a dance, when we'd stopped on the banks of the canal, where the black water of the Danube swirled between the American and Russian sections. That was also the first time he'd kissed me. It seemed a lifetime ago now.

We walked along the overgrown path, occasionally batting off a tall weed or bush. We came to a clearing, where a ledge looked down at the Mississippi River. Black smoke roiled above a steamboat making its way down the river.

"I'm glad you came," he finally said. "I didn't really expect to see you here."

Why had I come? I couldn't say. His betrayal still made my stomach roil. Had he come to seek forgiveness?

"I'm not here to ask your forgiveness," he said, as if he'd read my mind. "I don't deserve it."

"No. You don't," I said, but the satisfaction of seeing the hurt in his eyes turned to sadness. "It does not matter now."

"I don't suppose it does. You're a married woman now. What's he like?"

"Finn is a nice man. Very quiet." It was hard to talk about him in front of Joe. To explain why I'd done this. Was it for revenge, to show Joe that I could find a husband despite his rejection? Or was it really for my own survival, as I had rationalized at the time?

"And how about you?" I asked, not sure I wanted to hear about the woman who stole my fiancé.

"Lily is, well, she's Lily. Don't get me wrong. She's a great gal, perfectly fine." He looked at me and his eyes were moist. "But she's not you."

I needed to tape my feet down to keep from rushing to Joe's arms. I reminded myself that I was a married woman now, despite the fact that we had not yet had sexual relations. I was attempting to make a life here. And Joe had betrayed me.

"It's funny how life doesn't turn out the way we think it will," he said. "I decided I didn't want to be a farmer after all. I'm a salesman now."

This surprised me. "You always spoke so fondly about your farm."

"I know. I guess I was just homesick. But after all I'd seen, I couldn't settle down and be a farmer. That wasn't for me. But I'm glad you're happy."

I looked down at the water below. "After all that has happened, I would not characterize myself as being happy."

"That's all I wanted for you," he replied. "It kills me to think you're not."

I looked up at him, wondering how he could say that. This was all his fault. "Do not worry about me. I am a survivor," I said, standing taller.

"That's what I most admired about you, Roza."

Hearing my name on his lips took me back to that moment when he proposed. Yes, I was happy then, even when there was destruction all around us.

"I mean, even when you lost so much, you looked for the best in life. No one here understands what it was like over there. Certainly not my wife."

"It is not easy for me either," I admitted. "I do not fit in here."

"And you shouldn't. You're a countess, and a famous ballerina. Why would you want to change? You have more class in your little finger than this whole town has. They're the ones who should be welcoming you with open arms."

"I am thinking of opening a ballet school for children," I said. Etta had spoken to other parents and six girls had already promised to enroll.

"That would suit you perfectly."

"Yes. I think it would. But it costs money to open such a school, to buy equipment, and such. I do not think a bank will loan me money."

"How much would it cost?"

"Perhaps five hundred dollars."

Joe took my hand in his. I felt a jolt of recognition, of the passion that passed between two people in love. It was still there, as if waiting for his touch. "I recently came into a small inheritance from my grandfather's estate. It's not huge, but I could lend you the money."

He kept talking even as I shook my head. "I want to do this, Roza. It would be a way of helping you with your life in America, and I owe you that much."

"No. I cannot accept your money."

"Yes, you can. I want to do this."

"We should not even be here, Joe. Does your wife know you are meeting me?"

"No," he admitted.

"And how would she feel if she knew?"

"She'd feel lousy, I guess. But I feel lousy every day. Do you want to know why?"

I wasn't sure I did, but I let him talk.

"I feel lousy because I caved in to pressure to marry someone who everyone said was good for me, and who I thought I could love even though she'd written me off during the war, someone who was familiar. And you know what? I made a mistake."

He kicked at a weed dangling in the tall grass surrounding the path. "There. I said it. I went with safe instead of what was a little bit scary. I let people talk me out of what I knew was true."

He looked at me, his face pleading. "I made a terrible mistake, Roza. I love you. And I'm not asking you to forgive me, or feel sorry for me, or upend your life because of it. But I had to tell you how I felt."

I closed my eyes. The childhood fantasy of the prince riding up on a white horse to save me had finally come to pass. Here he was, not quite on his knees, but certainly he was here admitting his mistake, admitting he still loved me. But where was he on my wedding day? Now it was too late.

"Please, Joe," I said, feeling wetness dampen my eyes. "Do not say these things. It is too hard."

He let out a long breath. "I'm sorry. But please let me at least lend you the money."

"My husband would never allow it," I said, pushing out the thoughts.

"He doesn't have to know. You could say you had it stored away or got some money from a relative."

"No. It is a kind offer, but . . ."

"You can pay me back just as soon as your school takes off, which I'm sure it will. Like I said, no one has to know where you got the money."

Was Joe doing this out of guilt? Either way, he didn't have to offer. And if my school did succeed, I would have no trouble paying him back.

Finn wouldn't like it. But did he have to know? Finn would be more likely to approve my request to open a school if he didn't have to invest money. Money I wasn't sure Finn even had. And I couldn't get a loan. I wasn't even an American citizen yet. This was a way, perhaps the only way, to make my dream come true.

"It is a gamble," I said. "What if my school fails?"

Joe let out a sigh. "I've made enough mistakes in life already. This is a bet I'm willing to take. If it fails, then I'm out the money. But you're someone I'd bet on any day."

"Are you certain?"

"I'm positively sure about this, Roza," he said.

I nodded. "Okay," I finally said.

CHAPTER THIRTY-SIX

FINN FOLDED HIS ARMS. "I THOUGHT YOU WERE JUST PRAC-
ticing for the fun of it," he said. "Are you thinking of performing
again?"

"No. I want to teach dance to young girls. I would like to open
a ballet school."

Finn grimaced. "It's an admirable undertaking, but I'm not sure
something as highfalutin as ballet will be of much use in our small
town."

"How do you know if no one has ever tried it before? I already
have six girls enrolled. I expect more will join."

His eyebrows shot up. "Oh. Well, it seems you have this all
planned out. You didn't think this was something you could talk
to me about beforehand?"

Again, I was unprepared for Finn's objections. I was talking to
him now. Isn't that what he wanted me to do?

"I *am* talking to you. The school is not open yet."

"But you've been thinking about it for some time and didn't
mention it."

He was correct, but I was not about to admit it. "You are seldom
home to mention it to," I said. "And you said I should discuss large
purchases. But I already have the money for this."

"Where did you get the money?"

I put a hand on my throat. If Finn knew me better, he would
know that I had a nervous habit of doing this when I was lying. "It
was money my mother gave me for my trip to America."

"Oh. I didn't realize. But you have to understand that things are different here. You haven't lived in Red Wing very long. And starting a dance school requires a good head for business."

Did he think I wasn't smart enough to open a business?

"I understand what is needed," I replied. I showed him the pile of papers, ones that contained the financial details of the business. "I believe it will succeed. Little girls everywhere love ballet. Why not here?"

He sat on the white sofa, his back straight. Finn didn't complain, but I noticed that he squirmed when he sat there, as if trying to find a comfortable position. There had been an indentation in the old sofa, a spot that marked where he usually sat.

"It isn't that I object," he finally said. "But I'm not sure it's a good investment of your money. Of course, I don't know much about ballet. Will it require a great deal of commitment?"

"If you mean will I have to spend time away from home, yes. It does require time and commitment. But I have much time now. The building I plan to rent is close enough that I can walk. And it may bring in more money for us. I will show you the building."

I hoped that appealing to his economic sense would help. Why didn't Finn encourage me the way Joe did? Joe was willing to take a chance on me. Why couldn't my own husband do the same?

"I'll take a look at the building. And if your plans are sound, well, I guess it's worth considering. If you feel strongly about it, I won't stand in your way."

I counted to ten before I said something spiteful. This was the best my husband could do? Why couldn't he support me?

"I feel strongly about it," I said. I turned and went to my room.

FINN CAME WITH ME TO THE OLD BUILDING, WHICH HE ADmitted looked structurally sound. He kicked at the pipes and rapped on the furnace with his knuckles, and I wondered if that was how one checked such things. I had my doubts.

"I remember coming here with my pop when it was a hardware store," he said. "The place is pretty old."

"In Europe this would be considered new," I countered.

Finn ran a finger across the thick grime on the large window that faced the front.

"It needs a good cleaning," I said, nervously twisting the straps of my handbag and tapping the floor with my shoe.

"What do you think?" I finally asked.

"I don't know much about running a business. I know even less about ballet. But the walls need painting. The wood floor could use refinishing. And I'm not around much to help," he said.

"We will paint the walls and polish the floors. It will look much nicer."

"We?"

"My friend, Nellie, and Etta and Sid Preston. They have volunteered to help."

Finn looked surprised that I had friends. "You're evidently doing more than just learning to cook," he said.

I just shrugged.

He pointed at the ceiling. "I'm not sure your students will be able to do one of those fancy ballet jumps in here. The ceiling isn't all that high."

"It is ten feet, plenty high enough for even the tallest child," I responded.

Finn shook his head. "Are you sure about that? What if you have a tall girl in your class?"

I set my handbag on the floor and took off my shoes.

"What are you doing?" Finn asked, then backed up as I proceeded to spring off one foot in a high leap with one leg in front and the other leg straight out in back, my toes pointed. My loose skirt lifted up, revealing my fit thighs.

I heard Finn gasp as I landed. His eyes were saucers.

"That is a grand jeté, and I can assure you no student will jump higher than me," I said, taking a breath, then putting my shoes back on and picking up my handbag.

Finn stuttered. "I . . . I've never seen anyone jump like that!"

My skirt was stuck above my knees and I noticed Finn staring at my legs as I patted it down. I waved off the compliment. "I could have jumped higher if I had stretched beforehand and wore my ballet shoes." It was sloppy. I was out of practice. Still, it felt good to know I could do a grand jeté when I needed to.

"I underestimated you," Finn said, apologizing.

"And what does that mean?" I had a smirk on my face. I was used to impressing those who questioned my abilities.

"It means I didn't understand how difficult ballet was. After watching that leap, I'm beginning to get it now."

"Thank you."

He let out a breath. "As far as this place is concerned, well, as my brother told you, I've always been conservative with my money, even when I was a kid. And this building has seen numerous businesses fail throughout the years, so maybe that's pushing bad luck. I never imagined when I was here as a kid in the hardware store that someday I'd be standing in the same spot imagining the space as a ballet studio. I don't understand much about ballet. But I can tell this means a lot to you. It's your money, and you're free to do with it as you please."

I instinctively reached a hand to my throat, my eyes darting away. I wished Finn were more enthusiastic. And I wished I hadn't lied to him. But it was too late to tell him the truth, and to do so would destroy my dream.

I finally looked back at him. "Then it is settled."

But my voice was unsteady.

CHAPTER THIRTY-SEVEN

❧❦❧

F INN CONTINUED TO FIGHT HIS WAR AT NIGHT. I DIDN'T knock on his door, but I paced the creaking floors of the hallway, listening to him yell for his men who were beyond saving now, hoping the sounds of my footsteps or the groaning of the walls would wake him.

"Did you sleep okay?" I would ask the next morning.

"I slept fine," he'd say, even though he had bags under his eyes.

Should I tell him I knew that all his men had died under his command? Should I try to get him to talk? To ask him what happened? His quiet demeanor convinced me that he didn't want any conversation.

One night as we were taking a walk downtown, Finn stopped to stare at a brick wall on the side of a building. His eyes held disbelief.

"Do you see that man?" he asked me.

"What man?"

"Is that you, Bucky?" he called out.

I looked around, glad no one else had heard, then took Finn's arm. "There is no one there, Finn."

He strained his neck forward. "I swear he was there a moment ago."

I shook my head. "I did not see him."

Finn's face reddened. "No, of course not. I'm sorry."

"Who is Bucky?"

Finn stared at the blank wall. "He was in my platoon overseas. Look, let's just forget I said anything . . ."

My voice grew soft. "You have called his name before. Many times, in your sleep."

Finn said nothing but nodded. His eyes were sad.

"He is dead, isn't he?"

He nodded again.

I thought of Lou. The next day I dialed Finn's mother.

"Finn is having nightmares from the war," I said. "I think he needs help."

"If he needs something to help him sleep, I can give him some of the sleeping pills they gave Jack."

"I am thinking he needs professional help," I explained.

"Earl experienced awful things in World War I. But he left them in the past. And Jack has done the same. That's what a *wife* is for," Bernice said. "To make him forget."

I hung up on her.

I thought of Joe then, of how handsome he was, of how he'd kissed my hand when I met him on the bluff. His mother couldn't possibly be this bad. I pushed the thought aside, feeling guilty; I shouldn't think of Joe, even though it made me happy to do so.

While Finn was gone for work, I spent every waking moment at Roza's Ballet Academy, which is what I would call my school. I painted the walls a sunny yellow to add light to the room, and Sid repaired and refinished the floor so that it shined with a rich texture I hadn't thought possible. I bought folding chairs for parents to sit on while watching their daughters, and ordered a tall mirror that spanned the length of an entire wall. Then I ordered two long barres to place at differing heights.

Etta and Nellie scrubbed windows and found a desk that a retired accountant wanted to sell. They helped design the sign for the ballet academy.

"You should call it *Countess* Roza's Ballet Academy," Alice said, her pigtails swishing with each push of the broom. She was helping to sweep the back room, which we would use as a changing room as well as for storage. "I can't wait to start lessons."

"I am happy you're excited," I said. "It will be fun, but also hard work. I see you do not mind working, though. You are an excellent helper."

Alice leaned against the broomstick, which was taller than her. "Maybe someday I will be a famous ballerina like you were."

"Perhaps. But remember that it must always be fun too."

"Was it always fun for you?"

"Most of the time it was. As you get older, it requires more commitment and sacrifice. That is when it becomes more difficult. But I always loved dancing, so I did not mind."

"I won't mind either."

I smiled. Alice reminded me of myself at that age; stubbornly determined to do well.

By the time Roza's Ballet Academy had opened, I had ten girls enrolled. Tammy, at five years old, was the youngest, and also the clumsiest. But her friend Judy was also enrolled, and Tammy followed her like an obedient puppy and tried hard to keep up with the older girls.

I counted them at each class; ten little dancers, some nervous, some clueless, all of them trying to copy their teacher's perfect form.

What I hadn't expected was the demanding mothers, one who whined that her daughter cried at night because she wasn't as good as Alice, who, as I predicted, excelled in class.

I had to use diplomacy in addressing the situation, when I would have loved to tell her that her daughter should work harder and cry less. I remembered the strictness of my own teachers and opted for a firm but casual style here in America.

"As more students enroll, I will be able to adjust the classes so there will be different levels," I said.

"Are you saying my daughter should be at a lower level?" she said, with her hands on her hips.

"No. But I must remind you that ballet is a serious business and I will not put up with fussy children," I told the mother, who then left in a huff.

After that, I decided to make the classes more playful so there would be less competition between the girls. This was America, after all, where ballet was still new and didn't suffer from the reputation of aristocratic influence.

News of the school spread quickly. Two weeks later, eight more girls signed up. Two weeks after that, the *Red Wing Republican Eagle* ran an article about the newest downtown business, and I gained ten more students. The youngest I accepted was six years old (five-year-old Tammy was the exception). Most were between seven and twelve. I even had a student whose mother was at Belinda's tea party.

"Your ballet teacher is a *countess*," the woman told her daughter before class started. Odd how the perception of my title changed according to the whimsy of convenience. Before, I had been made out to be the brunt of their joke. Etta had been right after all.

"That was in the past," I told her. "I prefer you not mention my aristocratic title. I am simply Mrs. Erickson now."

With the money I received from enrollments, I had enough to repay Joe half of the money he'd lent me. I wrote to him and arranged to meet at a coffee shop on the edge of town.

I arrived early and sat at a table where I could spot Joe when he arrived. Seeing him first gave me an edge that I needed. After his confession last time, I couldn't stop thinking about him. I still forged on with my new life, but thoughts of Joe were always there, like a recurring dream. And accepting his loan made me think about him even more. I wondered if that was his intention.

I told myself that Joe was part of the past, like the war and my aristocratic upbringing, that his loan was nothing more than retribution for the hurt he'd caused. But I found myself fantasizing about him, seeing us walking along the bluff again, only this time I'd let him kiss me. I tried not to think of him, but how could I not think of him when I would be seeing him again? I'd been overly excited about this simple meeting, even buying a new dress for the occasion.

His handsome form appeared in the doorway, and I fought the urge to pat my hair.

He was dressed in casual slacks and a plaid shirt, and he winked at the waitress, who smiled at him. I felt a flash of jealousy, but pushed it down.

"You must hold your hands stiff at your side so you don't draw attention to yourself," Mama used to tell me at important events. I remembered Mama's words now and kept them glued to my lap.

Joe's face lit up when he spotted me. He sat down across from me. "Have you ordered yet?"

"Just tea," I responded.

"I'll have coffee," he told the waitress. I had been there forever before being waited on and Joe only had to sit down to have someone appear at his side.

"You look remarkable," he said.

I held my chin up. "Thank you. You look well too."

He arched his eyebrows. "If you're going to keep being so formal all the time, I'm going to have to start dressing like a banker."

I remembered how we could barely keep our hands off each other after long absences.

"But you are a banker," I said. "At least you are my banker."

Joe let out an easy American laugh. "You're right."

How I missed that laugh!

He winked at the waitress, who set a steaming cup of coffee in front of him. She flashed a flirty smile at him. "Will there be anything else?"

"No, thank you," I said a bit coldly. She smiled at Joe before she left.

He took a sip of his coffee. "Tell me how your ballet school is coming along."

"It is better than I could have anticipated. We are holding our first dance recital in a few weeks. I am so nervous about it, more than when I performed myself. All the parents will be there, and I am not sure the girls are ready yet."

"I'm sure it will be great. I knew you'd succeed."

I took an envelope out of my handbag and slid it across the table. "This is half of what you lent me. I expect to have the other half when the next session begins."

"You're amazing," Joe said, shaking his head. "I mean, I didn't doubt you'd pay me back, but I never would have guessed it'd be this soon."

"I do not like owing people."

"I know," Joe said, his voice becoming serious. "You wouldn't even accept my offer to pay your way back to Europe. I'm so glad you didn't now."

His words held a danger I couldn't quite identify. It might just be the danger of my own affections. I realized how much I had looked forward to seeing Joe again, of how he was like an intoxicating habit I couldn't quit. Did Finn feel this way when he saw Pearl?

"How is your business? What do you sell?"

"I sell seed to farmers. Our company is doing very well. Our nation needs food more than ever now that the troops are home, and Europe is starving for food as well."

"I know that firsthand. You must work long hours," I said.

He shrugged. "I'm on the road a lot. Of course, that doesn't make it any easier when my wife complains all the time. It's not like she didn't know what she was getting into."

"My husband is an engineer for the railroad. He is gone for days at a time. That is a facet of certain occupations."

"See? You get it. I don't know why Lily is so difficult."

"I do not have much choice. It is not what most women would choose."

He twirled his finger around the rim of the coffee cup. "It's not just that. I admit that I still resent her writing me off while I was gone. Getting a Dear John letter while you're in combat isn't the best for morale. I'm not sure I'll ever forgive her for it."

I nodded. I suspected that Finn felt the same way, even more so. He always acted uncomfortable when he was around Pearl. He barely spoke to her.

"Is your new husband attending the dance recital?"

"I do not know. He said that he does not understand ballet. What is there to understand? I think it is an excuse to remain uncultured, to not support my dream."

I felt my cheeks heat up. It wasn't like me to complain about Finn, even when I felt he deserved it. I'd tried to include him in my business. I'd shown him the building to get his approval. I made sure Finn had a hot meal on the table when I had to be at the ballet school. I never complained after a difficult day, even when my feet ached or I had to deal with an unruly child. And yet Finn rarely asked about the academy, how things were going.

"He's missing out. If you'd like moral support, I'd be happy to . . ."

"No! I mean, I do not think it would be appropriate."

He flashed a hurt look, but nodded. "I understand."

"It is enough to know you care," I added. "I love ballet. It is what makes me feel most alive, and I have missed it so much. To be honest, this school has saved me, and I owe you deep gratitude."

I had my hands around the coffee cup, letting its warmth seep into them. Joe suddenly reached over and put his hands over mine. I didn't object. I only hoped no one noticed.

"I have to see you again, Roza. I'm only asking for a cup of coffee once in a while. Just to talk. You're the only person I can talk to, you know. You're the only one who really understands me."

I had to admit it was nice to have someone I could confide in, someone who understood.

"I cannot meet here in town," I said, sliding my hands out from his.

"There are other coffee shops in other towns," he offered.

I was silent a moment. Finally, I said, "Mariska had her baby last week. A little girl. I am thinking of visiting her next month."

Joe smiled. "There's a perfect little coffee joint in St. Paul. I think you could walk there from Mariska's apartment." He took a pen and wrote down the name of the shop. "You'll love it. They have delicious scones."

"That would be nice," I said. "I can tell you about the recital then."

"I look forward to it," Joe said. "I can't wait to hear a detailed report."

Yes. Coffee and scones. An opportunity to let him know about the recital, I told myself. Nothing more.

But my hands were shaking, because Joe's smile promised more than a meeting between friends. It promised much more than coffee and scones.

CHAPTER THIRTY-EIGHT

WHEN I OPENED THE FRONT DOOR, I KNEW IT WAS TROU-
ble. Two men in dark suits and fedoras stood on the doorstep. One man held an official-looking badge. Neither man was
smiling.

"Are you Roza Mészáros?" the man with the badge asked.

"I used to be. I am now Roza Erickson."

"We're with the U.S. State Department. May we ask you some
questions?"

My heart fluttered. I immediately thought of the hiding spot
where the Chopin manuscript was stored, and my eyes automatically went upward where it was hidden. Had Finn found it and
reported me? He wouldn't do that. Would he?

Finn came up behind me. "Who is it?"

"They say they are from the U.S. State Department," I said,
stepping aside. "They want to ask me questions."

Finn filled the doorway. "What's this about, gentlemen?"

One of them produced a photograph. I remembered when it was
taken. I had just finished performing in *The Nutcracker*. I was still in
my thick makeup and pink tutu, ecstatic after having completed my
first principal role. But in the photograph I am expressionless because I am standing next to Josef von Hauser, who was wearing his
newly attained Nazi uniform. I hadn't wanted to pose with him or
accept the bouquet of roses he'd handed me that I held in my arms.
Some members of the orchestra were Jewish and had already been

arrested. Another member of the ballet, who had been a good friend of mine, had quit and escaped to England because he was subject to "valid" rumors that he didn't have a girlfriend or wife.

Upon seeing the picture, Finn let the men inside and led them to the sitting room. I followed behind, but didn't sit down.

The men removed their hats. Both of them were older, with short, dark hair. One wore glasses, which he adjusted as he wrote something down on a note pad.

"Do you know this man?" the man with glasses asked me, pointing out Hauser.

I gave the man a contemptuous look. "Of course I knew him. We are in the same picture. He was Josef von Hauser, an Austrian Nazi. I heard he was killed by the Russians."

"That's correct. We're looking for something that Hauser stole during the war. A very valuable composition."

"Why are you asking me?" I knew I sounded defensive, but I could barely contain my emotions. How much did these men know? I held my hands together to keep them from shaking.

"Because we were told that Hauser had a great affinity for the ballet, particularly a certain ballerina."

I could not tell these men that Josef's family had been friends of my family, that they were trying to hold on to their fortune by changing their alliances, which my father condemned. It was the only time I ever heard Papa swear.

I also could not tell them that I found Josef boring and spoiled even when I was a child, that he used his newfound Nazi power in the same brutish way, and that I came close to being raped by him despite our family affiliation when he forced his way into my apartment in Vienna.

"He was a wolf who pursued *every* dancer in the corps de ballet," I said. "Particularly my roommate, Greta."

"Do you know where she is now?"

I shook my head, surprised by the emotion in my voice. "She disappeared one day during the war. I never heard from her again."

"We thought that since you were both members of the aristocracy, he might have confided in you. The Russians claim they never found the composition and said he may have given it to someone close to him."

"I was not close to him," I asserted. "I hated him. He betrayed his country."

"None of his family survived the war," the man said. "I guess that's what happens when you choose the wrong side."

What a stupid thing to say! "It made no difference which side you were on. People died regardless," I said.

"True. But they died as traitors."

Would that make me a traitor as well? I had danced for the Nazis. But what choice did I have? Did any of us have? I could have spit on this man. I folded my arms to keep from striking him.

The man stood and handed me a card. "If you hear of anything, or think of anything that might be helpful, give us a call."

I accepted the card but shook my head. "I do not know anything. I cannot help you."

"Thank you for your time, then." He tipped his hat at Finn, and the men showed themselves out.

I clutched the card in my hand. I felt Finn's eyes on me.

"I'm sorry," Finn said.

I looked at him. "What are *you* sorry for? This was not your doing."

"I shouldn't have allowed them in. They upset you."

"Of course I am upset. They were on a fishing expedition, and I was the bait."

I wished Finn would not be so weak. He should have stood up for me.

But mostly I wished that photograph had been destroyed. I worried that they knew more than they let on. If they ever found out that I had the Chopin composition, I would be quickly deported. Or worse. They would brand me as a traitor too.

CHAPTER THIRTY-NINE

PERHAPS IT WAS THE STATE DEPARTMENT VISIT THAT prompted Finn to plan a day of sightseeing around Red Wing. We packed a picnic lunch and drove to a park on the Mississippi River. As we sat on the blanket watching steamships and a riverboat make their way down the dark water, Finn reached over to kiss me. I was unprepared for it, and frankly, I was still upset about the men who had barged into our house with that picture.

I pulled back, making a fake coughing sound. "I am sorry. I may be catching a cold."

"You've been working too hard. You spend so much time at your ballet school."

"That is because the recital is next week. There is much work to do," I explained.

"Oh," he said, and I could see he didn't understand what was involved.

"I have music to arrange, and costumes, and food, and set designs. I have an interview with the newspaper, and I must make the place very clean to impress all those who attend."

"All that for a children's recital?"

"Yes. All that." I folded my arms.

"Then maybe you don't want to spend the day sightseeing since you have so much to do." He sounded hurt, as though I'd insulted him.

"I did not say that. I am just telling you what is involved."

A long silence followed. Was he sulking? He had no idea how hard I worked, and he didn't seem to care either.

We didn't stay much longer, but when Finn asked if I wanted to go home, I shook my head.

"I have heard much about the Red Wing Potteries. I would like to see it."

Finn's mood improved immediately. He took the long way around, pointing out landmarks as we drove past the post office, high school, library, and the county courthouse. We arrived at a yellow, flat-topped building with huge lettering on the front. RED WING POTTERIES SALESROOM. The parking lot was crowded.

"This is it," Finn said. "My mom has a few stoneware crocks. It's the oldest pottery maker in Minnesota. Started in the 1860s."

He opened my door and helped me out, holding my hand as we walked inside, as though our little spat was long forgotten.

We walked among the busy aisles, looking at the different designs, picking up stone jugs, flowerpots, and vases, and examining them. Their new dinnerware patterns were nice, but I couldn't help but compare them to the exquisite beauty of Hungarian porcelain pottery. My mother had a complete set of the Victoria pattern named after the queen, who was a symbol of royalty and wealth in Europe. Did Mama still have any of her dinnerware, or had that been confiscated as well?

I ended up selecting a small blue teapot to purchase. It was plain and simple, but that suited me. If I couldn't have a piece of Hungarian history, I would have a newer American one.

Finn stopped at the furniture store next. "I still want you to redecorate. Maybe we can pick out some furniture together this time?"

I doubted Finn was interested in furniture shopping. Was this an apology? I would gladly accept. We looked for a kitchen table to replace the heavy wooden one at home that was functional but had seen better days. Finn had few ideas other than to suggest that it be solid wood or sturdy Formica to match the breakfast nook in the corner. Our huge stove covered almost an entire wall, something we desperately needed to change, and our kitchen was a dark shade of gray. It needed fresh paint, something light. And there was a lot of open, empty space. Perhaps a rectangular table would fill out the middle?

I cringed at an enamel one, bright red. At its Americanness, which drew attention to itself. When I saw a wooden table the color of a blue robin's egg I knew I'd found what I wanted. It had an extended top so we selected three extra chairs with matching padded blue seats.

It wasn't until we were home that I brought up Finn's attendance at the recital. I had assumed he'd come, but from our previous conversation, it was evident my assumption may have been incorrect. But he seemed to be in a good mood now. Perhaps that was in my favor.

After pacing back and forth in front of Finn as he was reading the newspaper, trying to come up with the best way to ask, I finally blurted it out. "Are you coming to the ballet recital?"

He looked up from the newspaper. "I thought it was for your students."

I put my hands on my hips. "It is a public program for everyone. The recital is on Thursday, and you'll be home that evening. Perhaps if you attend, you will understand more about ballet, and my school."

It was more than that. This was the first recital of my school, my first attempt at business, and I would be judged by every mother and every business owner in Red Wing. Finn should understand how important this was to me. He should understand that I needed him to be there.

Finn sighed. "And be the only man there? It's for little girls. I'd probably be sitting with a bunch of mothers bragging about their *talented* daughters."

"And you can brag about your talented wife," I countered. "There will be other men there." I knew at least one who would attend: Sid.

"I'll think about it."

He looked back down at the newspaper. Think about it? That was all he could say?

"This is important to me. I have worked so hard! And my own husband doesn't even care? You think buying a new table excuses you from supporting your wife?"

"I thought this was just a hobby."

"Hobby? You think ballet is a hobby? My entire life has been one of sacrifice: rehearsals, classes, performances. All in pursuit of a career that you think is tiresome and boring? None of it was easy. All of it is gone! And now I have a chance to reclaim a tiny bit, and you do not care at all."

"I didn't mean . . ."

I waved my hands in the air, searching for something to throw. They finally landed on the white vase sitting on the coffee table. I flung it against the wall, where it shattered. Pieces flew across the wooden floor and the braided rug, landing near my feet.

Finn jumped. "Roza!"

"Finally, I have your attention! You say you do not understand ballet, but you do not try. You say this is for little girls. Well, I was a little girl once with dreams of ballet. And I worked so damn hard to make those dreams come true. My papa supported me. He saw me dance professionally one time on the stage of the Vienna Opera House. And soon after he was gone. Executed by the Germans.

"And I could not go back to Hungary then. I had only myself to rely on. Who could I trust? Half of the Opera House musicians were members of the Nazi Party! Those cheering the parades, was it because they supported the Germans or because they were afraid? Then I saw little boys in suspenders and shorts giving the Nazi salute! The Gestapo routinely sat in on our performances. I had to curtsy and have my picture taken with those pigs. Everything that belonged to us was confiscated, and Hungarian intelligentsia was to be killed. It was only ballet that saved me from that fate. Then the Opera House was bombed and I didn't even have ballet anymore. Every day there were air raids and bombings, buildings falling down around me, tanks rumbling through the streets, and people being hauled out of their apartments and never seen again. I didn't know if I would be alive from one day to the next."

I couldn't stop the angry tears that followed. Finn stood and moved to my side. "Roza, please don't cry . . ."

I pushed him away. I was being hysterical now, but I couldn't stop. A tidal wave of disappointment and anger swept over me. "After we were dismissed from the ballet, we were on our own. I dressed in shabby clothes and cut my hair short so I would not draw attention, so I would not be raped like many other women. I had no one to protect me and no money. I did not want to be like those women who sold their bodies for a cake of soap or a bar of chocolate. So I stood hours in line for little rations. Those people who came early, who broke the morning curfew, were shot by the Germans and left to rot in the street. The rats gnawed on their bodies as we stood in line. I often threw up the mealy bread I was given."

I gripped the edge of the fireplace mantel. "By the time the war ended, we were all starving. I saw people eat sawdust, and my friend's pet rabbit was stolen. I sold clothing and family heirlooms on the black market. I was ashamed, but at least I was not among those searching the gutters. And no matter how much I managed to sell, it was never enough, only a few shillings. I was barely surviving."

"I understand, Roza. War was hell for everyone."

"No. You do not understand. You may have been in the thick of the fighting, but you were not living under their thumbs like we were. You didn't see looters rummaging through unsteady buildings at night when they wouldn't be seen, and the beautiful parks filled with concrete barriers and flak towers, the Prater Ferris wheel lopsided, as though it might fall over at any moment. You did not have to walk by the white stone primary school used by the Nazis as an assembly camp for those waiting to be deported to concentration camps, and know that when someone went in there that they wouldn't return. And you did not spend an entire lifetime preparing to be a ballerina and have everything go wrong."

I was shouting, angry at fate, at a world that could produce such evil and such destruction when all I wanted was to make something beautiful: a perfect pirouette, to tell a story through dance. Ballet was my passion, and it was ripped away from me at my prime. And I felt ashamed, because I knew others suffered so much more. None of it was Finn's fault. But so much had been lost.

"After all that, after making it through the hellish war and the months following, I thought that I had finally found love. I hung on for two years after that, thinking only of my life in America. Do you know what it is to travel halfway across the world only to be humiliated by rejection? To face going back to a country that was worse off than before the war?"

I didn't wait for an answer. "And now I was the enemy in Hungary, because the Communists posted lists of all who went to capitalistic America. So instead I come to a strange town, to live a life that I do not understand and know nothing about. I have tried. You do not know how hard I have tried, even when your family did not like me. And what do I have to show for it all? I am even shunned by the neighbor women."

His arms were around me now. I raged against him at first, but my strength had vanished and I collapsed on his shoulder, letting the wetness stain his plaid shirt.

"All those years of hard work to make my dream come true. They were for nothing." I let out a sob.

"No," Finn said. "It made you strong and brave."

"And what use was that? I could not even make a damn pie."

"But you make delicious pies now. I can vouch for that. And as far as the neighbor ladies, in a small town like this you can't worry about what anyone thinks of you."

I sighed. "I do not care about those women. It may come as a surprise to you, but I do not want to be known for making a pie. I just want to feel that my life has been worth something. That there was a reason to survive the war, to come all this way . . ."

He wiped away a tear from my cheek. "I'm sorry for everything the war has taken from you. I'm sorry I didn't understand how important this school was to you. I do know how hard you've tried, though, and your life is worth everything to me."

I turned my face away. I could not confess feeling that way toward Finn, and I didn't want him to see it in my eyes. I looked at the painting above the fireplace. Daffodils fluttering in a silent breeze next to a small pond. I had chosen it because I wanted to live there, wherever that pond was located. Where there was no war or broken dreams and only yellow fluttering daffodils.

Finn turned my face back to him. His voice was soft. "I do understand dreams and loss. I know how hard it is to be brave."

Crying had exhausted me. I felt limp and defeated from holding it all in. I sniffed and let out a long breath. "I do not want to be brave anymore."

He held me close, patting my back. "You don't have to be, Roza. You're safe now."

In Finn's arms, I did feel safe. But was that enough?

CHAPTER FORTY

A LICE'S BLOND HAIR WAS IN RINGLETS, THE TOP PULLED back. Some girls had their hair in tight buns, others had theirs in short ponytails, depending on the length. Bobby pins fell like dust particles around the back room, where they waited for the performance to begin.

I had found a local woman to make the costumes, a task she'd taken to heart, and she was there helping with last-minute tucks of the shiny bodices and stiff tutus. The shoes, though, I would not skimp on. I insisted each child have a good pair of ballet shoes.

Nellie had made her famous ginger cookies for the event, and Ettie poured lemonade into miniature paper cups. I had borrowed chairs from other businesses nearby.

But I was unprepared for the crowd that came to see the first ballet recital of Red Wing, Minnesota. Most were women and daughters, of course. But there were a few men in the audience too. An announcement of the recital had been written up in the newspaper, noting how many girls were now pointing their toes around town and listening to Tchaikovsky, as if my little school was responsible for bringing class to a sleepy railroad town. And maybe it was!

"There aren't enough chairs," Etta said.

"They should have come earlier," Nellie said. "They can stand at the back."

Etta whispered to me, "Next time you should hold it in the school auditorium. The stage is nice and big."

I nodded. I'd wanted to hold it at the studio so people would become acquainted with my school. But I'd underestimated how many people would come. I'd assumed it would only be parents of the dancers.

Would Finn show up? I wanted to show him the fruits of my labor. I wanted him to be proud of me. He hadn't said anything since my breakdown last week.

I saw a man enter, his hat similar to Finn's, and my heart lifted. A different but familiar form filled the doorway instead. I rushed to greet him.

"Cecil, how did you hear about this?"

He gave me a warm hug. "I'm a newspaper man. When I read about a ballet school opening up here, I immediately thought of you."

"This time I give permission for you to write about this recital," I said. "In fact, I hope you do."

"I intend to. The headline will be 'Culture Comes to Red Wing.' I have a few other things to talk to you about, but I'll wait until you're not so busy."

I made sure he had a good seat, then went to the back room, where twenty-eight nervous dancers waited.

"Just remember," I told the little ballerinas, "before you go out to perform I want to see your smiling faces. That way, the audience will be happy and will smile too."

"I'm so nervous, Mrs. Erickson," Alice said, her arms fluttering about her.

I bent down so that I was even with her face. "But you have practiced very hard. Now is the time to share your gift. Be brave, my little dancers. All will go well. *Sok szerencsét.*"

The music started, Tchaikovsky's "Dance of the Little Swans," and I patted each girl on the shoulder as she stepped out to perform.

They did well, the two lines of girls somewhat even. I whispered at them when to hold hands and when to turn at the appropriate times, even as Tammy, the youngest one out there, kept looking at her parents and became confused and turned in the wrong direction. I held my breath when Tammy tripped while skipping around her partner and almost fell.

The older girls danced to Brahms "Hungarian Dance" while the little ones took a break. And then they all performed to "Dance of the Hours." They poured their hearts into it, even little Tammy, who pointed her toes with every step, and my own heart filled with pride.

I expected polite clapping but was not prepared for the rambunctious applause that came at the end. And even more surprised to see Finn standing in the back, clapping along with the rest. The entire troupe curtsied and tiptoed off stage. All of them had flushed faces and exuberant smiles.

I made an appearance onstage to a standing ovation, my face brimming with pride. "Thank you for coming," I said. "And thank you for supporting our first ballet recital."

Afterward, Sid, Etta, Nellie, and Finn helped to put away chairs and clean the building. There was much congratulating of the performers as well as me, who felt this night was the first time I truly fit in since coming to Red Wing.

"Please consider adding a class for four-year-olds," several parents implored. "The little sisters want to attend too."

I promised to think about it.

"You have a real knack for graciousness," Nellie said. She put a round hat with blue flowers over her gray hair as she prepared to leave. "Glad I only worry about food and not my service."

I laughed. "You're the only restaurant owner who could say that and mean it."

"I pity the man she yelled at who took two cookies," Sid said.

"Wasn't right. One cookie is enough for anyone," Nellie said.

I hoped that man wasn't Cecil.

I approached Finn, who was talking with Cecil. "This is a surprise."

"Thought I should see what the whole recital thing was about. And as someone recently reminded me, I have a lot to learn about ballet."

"And what did you think?" I asked, trying not to look too anxious.

He shrugged. "I've never been to a ballet or a recital before. The music was real nice. And the parents seemed happy."

"The kids were adorable," Cecil said. "And they worked very hard. As did you, I'm sure."

I sighed and sat down, removing one of my shoes and rubbing my foot. "Some people believe this is a little hobby, no big deal." I looked at Finn when I said that. His face flushed and he seemed appropriately embarrassed.

Cecil touched my shoulder. "How wrong they are. You're the talk of the town, Roza."

"Thank you."

"You deserve it. You've done a great deal in the short amount of time you've been here."

"It has not been easy, but I have made good friends."

"Is everything going okay otherwise between the newlyweds?" Cecil looked from me to Finn.

I answered before Finn had a chance. "Yes. Of course."

"Great to hear. I have a couple of offers to run by you two. *Look* magazine sent a representative to my office. They want to get your complete story from beginning to happy ending. Their rates for that sort of thing are very attractive too."

The last thing I wanted was to have my story written about, especially since the visit from the State Department.

"Do you want to talk it over?" Cecil asked.

I shook my head at Finn. "No," he said. "We decline the offer."

"You'll probably feel the same about the other offer, but I feel bound to tell you about it anyway. There's a radio program in New York called *We the People*. You may have heard of it. It's very popular. Seems they're extremely anxious to have you two appear on their program. It would include a honeymoon trip to New York, lavish entertainment, and a tidy sum for your bother."

I answered immediately. "No. As we said before, we are anxious to lead a normal life."

"I understand. And I respect your decision."

Cecil gave us a ride home after I'd turned off the lights and locked the door.

"It's a nice house," he said, when he parked in front. "I love the white porch railing and the Victorian style. I'm very glad you found happiness, Roza. I admit I was concerned, not because Finn isn't a decent guy," he said, nodding at my husband, "but marriage is a hard go-around, no matter who you pick."

"Would you like to come in?" I asked him.

"I would, but I have an early start tomorrow and a long drive back to the Cities. Maybe next time. Good to see you again, Finn."

We thanked him and got out of the car, then watched him drive away. I paused at the front door. "I would like to sit on the porch for a little while."

"Do you want me to sit with you?"

"No. I need some time alone."

"I'm sorry about what I said about the recital," Finn said. "I know it meant a great deal to you. I didn't mean to sound disparaging."

"That is okay. I know this is all new to you."

"Well, then . . . goodnight." He leaned over and kissed me, his lips lingering an extra beat.

"Finn?" I said, as he opened the door.

He stopped and looked at me, and I realized what he wanted

me to say, what he was hoping I'd say, but I wasn't ready. I'd sensed it in his kiss, the desire. How much longer would he be willing to wait?

"Thank you for coming to the recital," I said, and saw the disappointment in his eyes.

"Sure," he said, and went inside.

I sat on the chair, thinking about what Cecil had said, that marriage was hard in the best of circumstances. Finn was a nice man in many ways. I'd picked him because I thought I wanted this simple, small-town life. I was happy that the ballet school had taken off. It felt so good to be involved in ballet again, as though I'd reclaimed a part of myself.

The smell of chalk and crisp leather shoes had brought everything back: the rhythm of fast-beating hearts and moving arms and legs; the energy of struggle and determination. My happiest years had been spent in ballet.

I thought of my last curtain call, when bouquets of flowers were thrown onto the stage. Where were the flowers tonight? Finn had not brought any.

I sighed. If only I'd known that would be my last curtain call. I would have appreciated it so much more.

But at least I now had Roza's Ballet Academy. Without it, I'd be lost in this town. And if it weren't for Nellie and Etta and Sid, I'd have no friends at all.

But I wasn't sure this was the life I was meant to live. In my heart I had to admit that seeing Joe again gave me joy. He was everything that Finn wasn't. And he had enough faith in me to help make my dream come true. If it weren't for him, I wouldn't have the ballet school.

When Finn arranged that first date to hear the Minneapolis Symphony, he was thinking of me, of what I would like. But it wasn't because he was a fan of such music. He didn't even play the piano in his sitting room. And his family was uncultured as well. None of them showed the least bit of interest in my ballet school or in any area of the arts.

We had been married five months now. I felt as if Finn was waiting for me to make a romantic move. But I was afraid that if I did, I would think only of Joe. And I wondered if Finn still held a hidden desire for Pearl. He'd told me that first day that he didn't want a platonic relationship. The fact that Finn hadn't yet pressured me for sex was both a relief and a frustration. Another example that my husband was too restrained and weak, even though I was secretly thankful at the same time.

A breeze swept up onto the porch, and I felt a chill and went inside. Finn was already in bed. I went to my room, feeling more alone than ever.

I shook my head. This was not the romantic love story that *Look* magazine would be interested in.

MINNEAPOLIS STAR NEWSPAPER

August 29, 1948

IN THIS CORNER

CECIL ANDERS

HERE'S THE FINAL WINDUP on Llona, our Hungarian countess, and her search for a GI husband: She married a graduate of the University of Minnesota. He was a captain in the army, is now a railroad engineer, making good money. The two of them are now living quietly and very happily in one of our smaller cities.

STRONG INDEED IS their desire to keep out of the limelight. *Look* Magazine sent two representatives out to get the complete story from the beginning to the happy ending. *Look*'s rates for that sort of thing are very attractive, too. The pair turned down the offer. The radio program *We the People* was extremely anxious to have the two of them appear on their network. It could have meant a honeymoon trip to New York, lavish entertainment for them, and a tidy little sum. That was rejected also. They're very anxious to lead normal lives and they're going to do it—even if Hollywood beckoned.

CHAPTER FORTY-ONE

❧❦❧

"HOW OFTEN DO YOU HAVE RECITALS?" FINN ASKED BEtween bites of his pancakes.

Despite my exhaustion, I had gotten up early and made a hearty breakfast. I sipped my coffee, wondering if this was just polite talk, or if Finn was worried about having to attend more recitals. At least he'd shown up, although he hadn't seemed impressed.

"Not that often. Usually at the end of an instruction period. Perhaps two or three times a year." This first one had been more of an attempt to recruit new little ballerinas and a chance to show the town what my studio was like.

"That's good." He nodded his approval and, perhaps, relief?

Good? "We had a full house, you know," I said, sitting up straight. "And Cecil Anders drove all the way from Minneapolis."

"Yes, I know. Was he in town for something else? I wondered why he'd drive all that way."

"You make it sound unimportant." My voice was hard. Would Finn ever understand that this was more than just a ballet school? If offered so much: culture, artistic expression, and physical activity. It also was important to me—which should have been enough for him.

Finn looked offended. "I didn't mean it like that . . ."

"I wish to visit Mariska," I interrupted. "I have been wanting to see her baby, and I have a break between ballet classes." I paused, wondering if I sounded too bossy. "If that is all right with you."

"Sure," Finn said. "You can take the train. See where I spend all my time."

He didn't seem the least bit upset that I wanted to go. He was almost giddy about it, as though making small talk and having dinner and spending time with me was so difficult to navigate, and he'd been given a few days reprieve from this hardship.

"That would be nice," I said, feeling my voice catch, as though the guilt was bubbling up inside my throat. I had kept so many secrets from Finn already. And now I was taking my husband's train to meet my former fiancé.

But I am going to see Mariska and her baby, not only Joe.

I called Mariska to make plans. Jakab would pick me up from the train station and bring me to their new apartment.

Finn drove me to the train station for my departure. I was surprised to see Jack in a railroad cap and uniform. He was sweeping the floors of the depot, moving at a slow pace, with one arm slung over his crutch.

"You did not tell me Jack was working here," I said.

Finn shrugged. "I figured he needed a chance to prove himself. And it sounds like he and Pearl are getting serious."

"Does that bother you?"

Finn tilted his head. "It bothers me if she's taking him for a ride. I've been there. I know what she's like. But my brother seems happy for the first time since the war. I'm not going to ruin that."

"Besides," he added, "I have you now."

I felt another stab of guilt. Finn purchased a ticket for me.

"So you're the famous Mrs. Erickson we've been hearing about," said the man at the counter, who introduced himself as John Breene. "Finn talks about you all the time. He wasn't kidding when he said he got lucky."

I looked at Finn, whose ears had turned pink.

"I am the lucky one," I told Mr. Breene.

Another man in a porter's uniform approached us. "Sir," he said, addressing Finn. "Would you like me to take the lady's luggage?"

"Yes, thank you," Finn said. "Roza, this is Shell."

"Hello." I held out my hand, which Shell shook.

"It's a pleasure, Mrs. Erickson. Your husband is one of the best we have."

As men greeted us, I was impressed with the respect they showed my husband.

Finn accompanied me to the train and made sure my luggage was on board.

"Give Mariska and Jakab my best," he said. *"Vizslát, kedvesem."*

"What? You are speaking Hungarian?" It wasn't the best pronunciation, but it was good enough that I understood what he'd said. *Goodbye, my darling.*

"I've been learning Hungarian during layovers," he admitted. "I wanted to surprise you."

Surprise, indeed! I put a hand on my heart. "That is a very big surprise. Thank you."

He leaned down for a quick peck goodbye. I leaned into him, making the kiss last a long time. His hat fell off as he gave a passionate response, which left me feeling dizzy and hot.

"Goodbye," I said, as he helped me up the steps.

I sat down and watched him from the window, fanning myself.

He waved from the platform as the train left, and I sat back, wondering where that passion came from, and the sudden desire arching inside. I was struck by how reverential the men were toward Finn. How he'd gotten a job for his brother. How he was learning Hungarian for me. I hadn't realized any of it.

An hour later the train pulled into the St. Paul Depot. I departed and stood on the same platform as when I'd first arrived in Minnesota only months ago. So much had changed since then. This time Jakab was waiting for me, and I waved and hugged him.

"Congratulations," I said. "I am anxious to see your little girl. How is she doing? And Mariska?"

He laughed. "Mariska is very happy, but I am very tired. Our *baba* does not sleep at night."

"That is to be expected," I said.

He carried my bag to his rusty car, which I had envied when I'd first arrived. Now it seemed old compared to Finn's truck. Their new apartment was in a nicer complex of buildings. The porches didn't sag, and the outside had a brick facade instead of the faded wood of their previous apartment. Tall oak trees lined the street.

This apartment had its own bathroom instead of a shared one, a small living room and kitchen, and two bedrooms. Mariska was cooking with one hand while holding the baby, but she put down the spoon and gave me a hug and kiss on the cheek.

"I am so happy to see you," she said.

I gathered the baby in my arms. Mariska accepted the present I had brought her: a beautiful pink dress with lots of lacy frills, which made Mariska cry in gratitude.

"She's beautiful," I said. "She has your eyes and hair, Mariska. And she has Jakab's nose."

"Yes. Nádja is just what I imagined. We are so happy." She sat down on a kitchen chair while Jakab stirred the pot of soup on the stovetop. "And how are you doing? You must tell me everything."

I related how I didn't much care for Finn's family, how his brother was dating Finn's former fiancée, and how I didn't really fit in.

"Of course you do not fit in. You're a countess," Mariska said, as though it were common knowledge. "You are too dignified for a small town."

"I do not want to be known simply as a countess."

Mariska made a tsking sound. "There is nothing simple about it. You are unhappy there?"

"Not really. Finn has a very nice house, and a woman cleans once a week. I have a few friends, and I just opened Roza's Ballet Academy, and we are doing very well. Cecil Anders even came to see a recital and wrote something about it in the newspaper. Of course, he didn't mention that I was a Hungarian countess. He only wrote about culture coming to Red Wing as it now has a ballet school."

She shook her head and laughed. "Only in America could such a thing happen. How did you get money to open a school? From your tight-fisted spouse?"

Mariska still joked that Finn was either poor, or had a snake in his pocket, which is why he didn't reach for his cash to impress me on our first date.

"No," I said. "I got a loan."

"A bank!" Mariska exclaimed.

I opened my mouth to correct her, then closed it again. It was best Mariska didn't know where the loan came from.

"And Finn has taken me to very nice restaurants in Red Wing. One is called the St. James Hotel, and it reminds me a bit of the Griechenbeisl in Vienna, but of course not nearly as old, and it doesn't offer Viennese cuisine."

"And your love life is good, no? Will you soon have a playmate for my little Nádja?"

Only Mariska would ask such questions. I felt my cheeks heat up. I hadn't ever discussed my sex life with anyone, not even Greta. I wanted to confide in Mariska and tell her about Joe, but I was afraid she would reprimand me.

"I am not pregnant yet."

"You have been married months already. What are you waiting for?"

"I am still getting to know my husband," I said. "Don't forget that we were strangers when we married."

"And what better way to get to know one another?" Mariska said, twitching her eyebrows.

Jakab laughed, causing the hotness to spread from my cheeks to my neck.

"You have embarrassed her, Mariska," Jakab told his wife.

Mariska smiled. "After she holds little Nádja, she will want one just like her."

"That is true," I said, taking in the smell and warmth of the newborn. I had thought of children often when I was waiting to come to America. But those thoughts had disappeared when Joe married someone else. I was not ready for a child with Finn; could not even imagine it.

Péter arrived after school, and I gave him the candy I'd brought after remarking on how tall he'd gotten, and how handsome and tan he was from picking beans all summer.

It wasn't until I was in bed that I gave in to thoughts of meeting Joe the next day. I told Mariska I had to check out equipment for my ballet school. Not exactly a lie, as I would be visiting a local ballet studio later to speak with its owner about business growth.

I still felt a pang of guilt, especially after Finn's passionate kiss. But it didn't match the love that consumed me when I thought of Joe. What use was it to see him, to think of him? It only made me want him more. It added a layer of regret to any happiness I might find now. I would tell Joe I couldn't see him anymore. There was no other way.

THE COFFEE SHOP WAS ACTUALLY A BUSY RESTAURANT, WITH two rooms filled with patrons enjoying breakfast. I found Joe in the back room, which felt more private, even though many other tables were occupied. Joe had a cup of coffee in front of him, and he was studying the menu.

He stood when he saw me, and gave me a peck on the cheek. "Thank you for meeting me," he said, flashing a bright smile.

He held out my chair for me and whistled at a passing waitress. "A cup of tea, please. Do you want eggs, Roza?"

"Yes. That would be nice."

"She'll have the same as me."

I'd only known Joe three months before he proposed. And he still remembered that I liked my eggs over easy? Would Finn know this after five months of marriage?

Joe sat in the chair next to mine. "How was the recital?"

"Excellent. I have more students enrolled now. I will soon be able to pay you the rest of your money."

He waved a hand in the air. "Don't worry about that. I'm impressed you've done so well in so short a time."

"Thank you again, Joe. The ballet academy has made me very happy."

"I'm happy that I could be a small part of it."

The waitress delivered the tea, and I added a teaspoon of sugar. When I looked up at Joe, I noticed his smile had faded. He lit a cigarette and sighed.

"What is the matter, Joe?"

He looked away, letting out a puff of smoke. "I don't want to spoil our time together with my troubles."

"Please. I want to know."

Amid the clatter of dishes and chatter in the air, it was hard to talk. But Joe reached over and took my hands. He leaned forward so his face was close to mine. He smelled of aftershave and Camel cigarettes.

"It's over between me and Lily."

"What? When?"

"Last week. She's moved back to her parent's house."

"I am so sorry, Joe."

"I'm responsible, really. I couldn't offer her what I didn't have to give."

He looked me in the eyes. "My love was already promised to someone else."

I gulped back a sob. "Oh, Joe."

"I've missed you so much, Roza. I don't know how I could have let you get away."

What I'd longed to hear. What I'd secretly prayed for. I felt a tear roll down my cheek.

He wiped the tear with his finger. "We're meant to be together," he said in a low voice.

His touch felt like velvet. "That is what I always thought," I said, but I couldn't stop the tears.

"Don't cry, darling."

He looked around at the crowded restaurant. "We should get out of here. I have a place not far away."

My eyes widened. "I cannot."

"We need privacy. To talk."

The way Joe said it, he was not thinking of talking. I didn't trust myself alone with him. "But the food has not yet come. And it would not be proper."

He spoke in a low voice. "You've been improper with me before, Roza. Don't you remember?"

Couldn't he see the impropriety? Everything was different now. "That was before, when we were engaged. It is too late now, Joe."

"It's never too late. Don't you see? You're here for a reason."

I shook my head. I could barely speak. Didn't he realize how he made me feel? I wanted to be with him, wanted to get up from this table and go to his bed. To have *his* child. But that was not possible.

"I know I have no right to spring this on you, Roza. But please, think about it."

"How can I think of it? I am married to someone else."

"Then tell me you don't love me, that you don't think about me, and I'll leave right now."

Despite all that had happened, my heart still loved this man. I shook my head. "I cannot."

He smiled. "You do love me."

"I do," I confessed.

"I'm filing for a divorce," he said, and my breath hitched. "I'm not going to make you decide to do the same right this minute. That wouldn't be fair to you. But please, think about it, Roza. Think about our love, and the rest of your life. You could open a ballet school here instead, if you want. You'd make me the happiest man in the world, and I promise I'd make you happy in return. I'd take you to the opera and to fancy restaurants. I'd treat you the way you deserve to be treated. Have you ever visited Minnehaha Falls? You'd love it."

It all sounded wonderful. I reached over and put a hand on his cheek. I had mooned over him for so long, and now I had a chance to be with the man I loved. Everything that stood in my way seemed trivial at the moment, even though I knew it was far from simple.

He took my hand and kissed it. "I love you more than he does," he whispered.

I pulled my hand away as our plates were delivered to the table. As I put my hands in my lap, I looked down at the flattened fried eggs on my plate that matched Joe's.

Not over easy.

CHAPTER FORTY-TWO

ARRIVED AT THE TRAIN STATION WHILE FINN WAS AWAY AT work. I thought of him driving the train, of the responsibility he faced each day, driving thousands of miles, day in and out, summer and winter, while bearing the responsibility for the safety of every person on board. Each day he spent hours behind the wheel hearing the clacking of the tracks, the whistle blowing, and the steam spouting. And when he came home, he faced the nightmares of a war he left behind.

I'd thought of him as uncultured. But he worked so hard. How much time did he have for such things?

I still felt the desire for Joe, of being close to him, of feeling his touch. He was so charismatic, so delightful, while Finn was restrained and quiet. Finn only took me out to appease me; he'd rather spend his time at home. But Joe loved the nightlife; when I met him we'd spend half the night in American and British clubs in the Kärntner Strasse. I remembered how much in love we had been. Had I changed so much as to forget all of it? Could I deny that it was Joe who I was meant to be with?

The sun was setting, and the air was chilly. I took my bag, put on my coat, then decided to walk home. But I only made it to the parking lot when a black car stopped in front of me. I peeked in the window. Pearl was behind the wheel, her platinum hair pulled tight in a bun on her head.

"Finn asked me to pick you up. Sorry I'm late," Pearl said.

I opened the door and got in. "I could have walked. It is not that far."

"Nonsense. Finn wouldn't want you to walk. Jack would have picked you up, but he went to the Cities yesterday to get a new fake leg. He's determined to work his way onto a train as a porter. I know he says he's only half a man because of his leg, but he's getting better about not feeling so sorry for himself. Finn helping him get this job was a big step in the right direction, pardon the pun."

"How does he manage to drive a car? It cannot be easy with only one leg."

"He's creative that way. He uses the crutch to push on the gas, and his other foot for the clutch. He gets by, but I drive a lot too."

"I am going to learn how to drive," I said. Finn said he'd teach me.

"Good. Every woman should know how to. Jack's mother doesn't drive; most women don't. I'm kind of glad I learned how, though. Especially with Jack missing a leg."

I wasn't sure how I felt about Pearl giving me a ride home. I didn't trust her. But Pearl hadn't given up on Jack yet, and that was something. That man didn't make it easy to like him.

As Pearl drove downtown past the local bar, I recognized the man Finn had introduced me to at the church social. He was walking crookedly, stepping in front of cars, which honked at him as they tried to veer around him.

"Is that Lou?" I asked.

Pearl pulled up at the stop sign. "He's drunk again. Honestly, I don't know why Finn keeps giving him money. He just drinks it up."

Finn gives him money? "Let me out here," I said.

"Don't be silly. You shouldn't talk to him. He gets a little crazy sometimes."

"I will be fine," I said, grabbing my bag. "Thank you for the ride."

"You're nuts," Pearl said as I got out of the car. "Don't say I didn't warn you."

The car behind her honked its horn, and Pearl drove away.

I walked over to where Lou was standing, partly in the street.

"May I help you get home?" I asked him.

Lou tried to steady himself before answering. "You're not supposed to be here. They'll be advancing soon." He pointed at the bluff. "The Germans are just behind that hill."

"It is okay," I said softly. "We are safe. I will take you home."

"Home?" He looked around, dazed. "Are you Polish?"

"No. I am Hungarian."

"You know what they'll do to you, don't you?"

I put my arm out. "Not anymore, Lou. The war is over."

He leaned on me, suddenly deflated, as though the air had been forced out of him. "The war is over? Oh, yes."

"Finn has nightmares too," I said.

Lou shook his head. "It's a dark cloud I live under every day. It's too hard to live this way."

How did Finn manage to hold down such an important job when Lou couldn't work and could barely function?

"Tell me where you live, Lou."

I walked him home, holding my small suitcase in one arm and steadying Lou's uneasy gait with the other. He didn't weigh much; I wondered how often he had a meal to eat, or if he just drank his meals. He smelled of alcohol and sweat and clothes that hadn't been washed in too long a time.

"Drinking will not help erase the war," I told him as I helped him into his shabby apartment. It was what Finn would call a "hole in the wall." It stunk of dirty dishes and moldy food, urine, and other unrecognizable stenches.

Lou tried to speak, but he was half asleep, and he slurred the words, spittle coming out the sides of his mouth. "Nothing helps. They come for me all the time now."

I almost repeated what Finn's mother said, that keeping busy helped. But did it really? There was a Polish phrase I had heard often quoted: "*Nie wywołuj wilka z lasu.*"

Don't call a wolf out of the woods.

We were all supposed to forget, to pretend it never happened, to go on with life. My mantra for the last year and a half had been *the past is past*. But we all suffered nightmares. Finn ducked anytime a car backfired or he heard a loud noise, certain gunfire was nearby. And he saw a dead man on a dark street.

I made certain Lou was resting in a chair before I left. At least he wouldn't be hit by a car or have to spend the night on a bench outside. I hugged my coat against me and walked home.

I spent the next day at Etta's learning how to make stuffed peppers.

"You're awfully quiet," Etta remarked as she watched me chop onions. She was cooking the meat in a pan; the sound of sizzling hamburger competed with Bing Crosby crooning a love song on the radio.

I was thankful I could blame my tears on the onions. They seemed to come out of nowhere. Were they tears of guilt, or tears of regret? Or tears of indecision? I didn't know what to do about Joe, or how to feel about Finn. I thought my heart could only be happy with Joe. But how could I tell Finn? And did I want to? Would life be any easier with Joe?

"I am thinking that there is much I do not know about my husband," I said, wiping my eyes.

"Uh-oh. That doesn't sound good."

"It is better than it sounds." I remembered how safe I felt with my hand in his, how his kisses spurred me into wanting more, even as I was convinced I still loved Joe. What did it mean when you were attracted to another man when you professed your love to the first one?

"I've known Finn since he was a kid. He was a few years behind me in school. He was a respectful boy. Not the kind who ever got in trouble. Always kind to everyone else."

"I am learning this about him," I said. I didn't say how this made it harder for me to tell him about Joe. How it made me feel worse for thinking of leaving him.

"He was always so cheerful too."

"He is not so cheerful now," I said.

"He will find joy again. Give him time."

I split the peppers with Etta and then brought home the bounty of our cooking. Finn would be home soon, and I set the table and warmed up the food in the oven.

When Finn arrived, I heard a strange sound coming from his jacket.

"What is that noise?" I asked.

Finn opened his coat and produced a gray kitten with white markings on its face. It was lean and straggly, and it took all its energy to make a mewing sound.

"I found her down at the tracks. Didn't want her to get run over. I don't think she's eaten anything in a while."

I put my hands on my hips. "A kitten? What am I to do with her?"

Finn flashed a sheepish grin. "Maybe give her a bowl of milk?"

I smiled at the tall man in front of me cuddling a tiny kitten. He kept surprising me in good ways. There was much I didn't know about him still. "Okay." I filled a small bowl with milk and set it down on the floor. The kitten hungrily lapped it up, then licked her paws as she surveyed her new surroundings.

I tried to pick her up, then regretted it as the kitten stuck her sharp claws into my arms.

I put her down, then brushed the marks on my arms.

"Ouch! She didn't claw *you* up," I said.

Finn shrugged. "She was freezing when I picked her up. She must have liked the warmth."

"She is very independent," I said. "She should have a strong name."

"I'm not good at names," Finn said, petting the scrawny kitten between her ears. "What do you think we should call her?"

I thought for a moment. "Karola. It means strong. She must be so to survive among the railroad tracks and the dangerous river nearby."

Finn nodded. "I like it."

And just like that, we had a pet. Karola chose Finn's bed to curl up on, and for the first time in weeks I didn't hear Finn's nightmare screams through the door, but only a soft purring.

CHAPTER FORTY-THREE

I COULD TELL SOMETHING WAS WRONG THE MINUTE FINN arrived home. He didn't flash his usual smile or ask how my day had gone. When I greeted him at the door, he didn't even try to kiss me.

Was he just tired, or was there something else bothering him?

I went to the kitchen and stirred the stew I had made. I was becoming a decent cook thanks to Etta; and Mariska had written down several recipes from our Hungarian homeland. Karola skittered about the kitchen, watching me cook. She still didn't allow me to pick her up, but had a habit of rubbing up against my ankles, flicking her tail as she took in the aroma of cooked meat and potatoes and onions.

After scooping stew into a bowl, I set it on the table and went to get my coat.

"I have a new ballet class starting soon. There is a bowl of stew for you on the table."

"Can we talk about something first?" Finn asked. His voice sounded strange.

"I do not want to be late." I turned to leave.

He grabbed my arm. "I want to ask you something before you leave. But you have to be straight with me, Roza."

I scrunched up my eyebrows. "What is straight?"

"It means you have to be truthful."

"Oh. Of course."

Finn put his hands in his pockets and looked at me with earnest eyes. "Jack was up in St. Paul last week to get a new leg, and he saw you at a restaurant. You were holding hands with a man. He said you looked real 'cozy.'"

My throat tightened. This isn't how I wanted Finn to find out.

I sat down on the sofa. "I saw Joe, the man who was my fiancé."

"The one who jilted you?"

I was wringing my hands, wishing I had something to hold on to. "Yes. I must be honest with you. He is the one who loaned me the money for my ballet school."

Finn's mouth was set in a hard line. I could see his fists tightening in his pockets. I had never seen him angry before.

"I know I should have asked you first. I have paid half of the money back already. And will pay the rest soon," I said.

His voice turned oddly calm. "What about the cozy part? This isn't just about money, is it?"

My eyes filled with sudden wetness. "No."

"Do you still love him?"

I had conflicted feelings about both Finn and Joe. But I couldn't deny what I felt. I nodded.

"I took my marriage vows seriously, Roza."

"As did I. And I have not cheated on those vows, Finn. But that does not change how a person feels."

"And you don't care that he's married to someone else?"

"Of course. Just as I care that I am married. Joe said that he made a mistake. He is getting a divorce."

It was as though I'd punched Finn in the stomach. He looked completely stricken. "And that's what you want too?"

I broke down then and sobbed. "I do not know what I want."

Finn's voice was now frosty. "I guess since our vows were never fulfilled, it would be easy get an annulment, if that's what you want."

He turned to go upstairs, but stopped. He sounded tired. "I tried to make you happy, Roza. I'm sorry I wasn't what you wanted."

I heard his heavy steps as he went up to his room. I wanted to stop him. But what could I say? What *was* there to say?

THE CLASS WAS A BLUR AS MY MIND WAS MUDDLED WITH RE-grets. The only thoughts I had were how I'd ruined everything. Perhaps Mama was right. It might have been better if I'd simply returned to Budapest. At least I would have been with her and János.

That evening after class, I stayed late, filling out paperwork and sweeping the floor. Then I turned out the lights save a small one near the entrance. I was in no hurry to go home. Finn would most likely be in bed, his door closed. And if he was waiting up to talk to me, what could I say? I didn't want to face him right now.

Instead I put on my pink ballet shoes and my leotard and matching silk skirt. My body was long and thin; not as muscular as before, but still tight in the right places.

I found the record of my favorite song from the ballet *Esmeralda*, which I'd danced to at the Vienna Opera House, the only record I'd brought with me from Austria, a small remembrance of one of my finest performances. I plugged in the Admiral record player and turned on the switch. Then I fit the needle into the groove of the record and stood for a moment, listening to the beautiful, haunting music of Cesare Pugni.

Slowly I began to move, and although I couldn't dance as well as I had done years ago, I still could lift my chin just so as I did a plié, could feel transformed by the music and movement of my body. I felt my calf muscles straining, my hamstrings flexing. I loved feeling strong.

It was who I was and what I'd trained for so many years: a ballerina. And before that I was a countess. Who was I now that both of those things had been taken away?

I closed my eyes, thinking only of my performance and the way the music filled me inside, my feet and arms moving in perfect obedience, as if they remembered all these years later just what to do. The studio and the war and this small town disappeared, along with Joe and Finn and all my worries; only the music remained, and the remembrance of standing onstage, in thick makeup and stiff bun, my hand-stitched costume and the blinding lights that protected me from the audience, so that all that was left was the performance, and the rush of butterflies that came before it.

My muscles ached with the effort. How I missed that feeling! I relaxed into the trance of the music, and the work that had defined me for so many years. This was what I loved about dancing; this was what I missed the most. Letting myself be immersed in Esmeralda's story: the beautiful gypsy girl who marries a poet to save him from death. But the marriage is one of convenience. She falls in love with the handsome captain Phoebus, who is engaged to someone else. When he is stabbed, it is thought that Esmeralda is guilty, but as she's about to be hanged, it is the kind Quasimodo, the Pope of Fools, who saves her time and again. When Phoebus arrives, miraculously cured, he clears Esmeralda's name.

I was almost to the climax of the dance, when I opened my eyes and stopped. Finn was standing in the darkness, watching me.

We stood staring at each other for a long moment. I was panting from the effort of my dance, wondering what he was doing here at this hour. I hadn't heard him come in.

I opened my mouth to ask, but before I could speak Finn advanced and drew me into his arms. He smelled of soap and his freshly laundered shirt.

"You're the most beautiful, graceful woman I've ever seen," he said. "I'm sorry I didn't realize how important ballet is to you." And then he kissed me.

He'd never kissed me like this before, and I responded before I knew what I was doing. I took in his scent and his lips, hungry for more of him, my hands feeling the tautness of his back, the warmth of his tall body against mine.

Then he pulled back. The music was still playing, and Finn put his arm on my waist.

"Will you dance with me?"

I felt as though I was spinning under a spell. I nodded, and put my head on his shoulder, then closed my eyes to steady myself. It was the first time we'd ever danced together. This was the first time I'd ever felt this close to Finn.

"I thought about what I said back at the house," Finn said softly, into my ear. "I can't give you up without a fight, without telling you how much you mean to me. I'm in love with you, Roza."

I looked up into his eyes, wondering how he could possibly love me after all I'd kept from him. I'd been mooning over Joe for so long, and here was this man in front of me who'd offered his whole life. I hadn't noticed his quiet constraint before, how kind he was. I found out by accident that he helped his brother find work and gave money to Lou. Then he brought home a stray kitten. He was learning my native language. He was respectful at all times, just as he'd promised in his letter.

I'd thought of him as the poet, the marriage of convenience, but he was Quasimodo and Phoebus, rolled into one.

And how had I repaid him? By sneaking around with my former lover.

I stopped dancing and asked him the question that had been gnawing at me since we married. "Why did you really answer the newspaper article? Did I seem so pathetic that I looked as though I needed rescuing?"

Finn looked stricken. "Not in the least. I remember thinking that the way you held your chin on your hand, you looked formidable. And beautiful. But your eyes held sorrow. To be honest, after two years, I was lonely. I had figured maybe I wasn't meant to get married. And I didn't think I deserved to be happy. And then I saw your picture, and I thought, what was the point of going to war if I was going to return and live alone for the rest of my life? And what if I could take away that sorrow in your eyes?"

This man I thought was weak was actually a tower of strength, and his kindness overwhelmed me.

Did I love this man? I still wasn't sure, but I suddenly desired him with a hunger I'd never known before.

"Let's go home," I said, and kissed him again.

CHAPTER FORTY-FOUR

WHEN WE MADE LOVE, I DIDN'T HESITATE. I FOLLOWED Finn to his room, then slipped out of my leotard and bra and underwear and turned to face my husband. I put my arms out toward him, eager to share his bed. Finn had a look on his face I'd never seen before; one of longing and desire, and gratefulness. He reached out and kissed my breasts, then worked his way up my neck to my mouth.

He was gentle but forceful at the same time, and when I cried out during our lovemaking, it felt as though I had let go of the sadness I'd locked up inside for so long. Afterward, I only remembered that there was not the shame or regret I'd felt with Joe, no wondering if I would see him again. I wanted Finn with a passion I didn't expect and could never have anticipated.

My legs were woven across his as we slept on and off, never quite getting enough of each other, so that an hour or so later, the powerful urge returned to make love again, as if trying to make the night last forever, to beat away the sounds of birds chirping in the new day.

At last, exhausted, we slept late into the morning. When I opened my eyes, Finn was watching me.

"You are spying on me again, my husband. This is becoming a habit." But I smiled as I said it.

I reached out for him and he kissed my palm. "I should have told you about the nightmares before we married," he said.

I put my fingers on his mouth. "Shh. I understand. You do not have to tell me. I have enough war memories."

"I've heard you," he said. "I've seen you also react to loud noises."

I didn't think he'd noticed.

"Yes," I admitted. "As do you. But my nightmares are not like yours."

"I know." He looked away.

"You do not have to tell me," I repeated. When I first heard him scream, I didn't want to know. I didn't want to relive any of that horrible time. I wanted to pretend it didn't exist. But now, as I thought of Lou, I realized that if Finn continued to bottle up his memories, he would eventually erupt and lose his mind, or worse, he'd bury them so deep he'd lose completely the man he used to be.

I only hoped it wasn't too late, that he hadn't already lost too much.

"I ordered them into that field," he said, his voice cracking. "It was my decision. Every single man was hit."

"You were hit, too, weren't you?" I touched the faint scar that ran along his side.

He nodded. "I was shot twice and lost consciousness. By the time reinforcements arrived, it was all in vain. Not a single man had survived."

"That is not true. You survived."

He let out a sour laugh. "The only one who *shouldn't* have. How just is that?"

"Just? There is no justice in war. My mother still waits for my father to come home, even though I know he was killed with all the other men who had positions of power. She refuses to believe this, and now that the Communists have taken over, her life is no better than it was under the Germans. Everything that was taken from us will never be returned. My father is dead. Our lives have been ruined. None of that is just.

"Surviving is harder than dying. At the orphanage I saw girls as young as twelve who were raped and forced to give birth to Russian babies. And I saw other girls who killed themselves rather than have those babies."

I nuzzled into the crook of his arm. "There is only forgiveness." He started to speak and I shushed him. "Not from others. We must forgive ourselves for living."

"I'm not sure I can do that," he said. "Those men relied on me. When I woke up and found out what happened . . ."

"But you must have been following orders too."

"Yes. But I could have found a different route. I shouldn't have sent them out into that field. Those woods were swarming with German soldiers. I failed them. Every single man."

"You did not know the Germans were there. You were with your men, Finn, where you were supposed to be, doing what you were supposed to be doing. In Vienna, the apartment building next to mine was bombed. There was no warning ahead of time and many of the residents died. I remember asking why. Why did those people die, and we lived? I could not accept that it was part of some greater plan. I could not believe God chose those people to die and us to live.

"I still do not understand why we escaped death. But you were spared, Finn. And so was I. Think of all that we have been through, and how we have found each other. Perhaps that is enough for now."

It was odd for me to be saying this when just last night I had thought of leaving him, but I realized that I might actually love my husband, that perhaps I had for some time and hadn't allowed my-self to feel that way. I'd been too preoccupied with Joe.

I felt Finn's mouth on my neck. "Does that mean you're going to stay?"

Karola jumped up on the bed and stared at me, as if she resented me taking her place.

I pointed at the kitten. "If she will let me."

Finn kissed my earlobe. "I think she can learn to share."

I turned to him, feeling a renewed passion. "I will not share you, my husband. You are all mine now."

Half an hour later I got out of bed. I put on Finn's pajama top. "There is something I must show you."

"What is it?" he asked sleepily.

I didn't answer. I hurried toward the closet in the spare bedroom where I'd hidden the Chopin manuscript. After prying the board loose, I stuck my hand down and found the object where I'd left it, still in the Bible.

I checked the condition of the manuscript, which was still wrapped in newspaper and a towel. It appeared no worse for having spent months in the floorboard, and I said a prayer of thanks.

I brought it to Finn's room and set it on the bed between us, a symbol of my love and trust.

Finn cocked his head. "A Bible?"

"No." I took the manuscript delicately out of the towel and put it on the sheets. "Hauser killed my roommate, Greta, I've no doubt about it. And he tried to rape me. If the Russians hadn't invaded only a few days later, I'm certain he would have found me and killed me too."

Finn touched my cheek. "I'm so sorry."

I nodded. "I know. I should have told you about this, but I was afraid. I do not want there to be any secrets between us now."

"You lied to those men?"

"I had to."

He bent down and softly touched the manuscript. His voice held awe. "This is real, isn't it?"

"Yes. I stole it from him. He was a Nazi. I do not regret it. Are you going to report me to the authorities?"

Finn shook his head. "Of course not. I would never do that. But I do think you should call those men from the State Department and let them know you have it."

"Call them?" I looked at Finn with pouted lips. "Why can't we keep it?" I knew I sounded like a spoiled child, but I couldn't bear parting with the composition. The Nazis had stolen all the artwork from my parent's home. Mama had written how she'd cried for weeks when they removed the Van Gogh. For the last two years I had thought of this composition as my insurance policy, something that would provide for me in case the worst happened. It was retribution for all that the Nazis, and subsequently the Communists, had stolen from my family.

Who knew what the Communists would have done with it? Burn it?

"It's stolen property, Roza. I know a lot of guys who brought back German rifles, but this is different. This is priceless. Hauser stole it from someone too. It belongs in a museum."

"What if they deport me? Or put me in jail?"

"Roza, you're a hero. You saved a valuable composition that would have ended up in the hands of the Nazis. It could have been destroyed."

"What if they do not see it this way?"

"We'll make them see it that way."

I buried my head in the pillow. "I am scared."

Finn rubbed my back. "I won't let anything happen to you, Roza. I promise."

If I could not believe my husband, who could I believe? While I hated to part with the composition, it was also a dark cloud that followed me, constantly threatening to expose me. Now that Finn knew about it, the cloud lightened.

My stomach growled and I sat up. "I am going to fix us something to eat. But first I need a shower."

I kissed Finn, who was still studying the composition, and went to the bathroom. Now that I'd shown it to him, it was as though everything was brighter, even the dingy light that hung above the mirror, the one I wanted to replace with something nicer. I took a long, hot shower, then rubbed the mirror with the towel and smiled at myself, admiring my reflection. *Why do I feel so giddy? Is this happiness?*

But thoughts of Joe soon emerged. What would I tell him now? In Finn's arms last night, I felt truly happy. But when I was with Joe, would those old feelings return? I had thought I could only find happiness with Joe. Could I trust myself to see him again? Would Finn even allow it?

Afterward, as I was getting dressed, I heard the sound of piano music drifting up the stairs. I followed the lilting melody down the steps. It was unlike anything I'd ever heard before.

I stopped in the doorway to the sitting room. Finn was playing the piano; he sat on the bench in his T-shirt and pajama bottoms, but his lithe fingers moved like a maestro. He'd said he could play, but I didn't know he was this capable. Another thing I didn't know about him.

He didn't see me, as he was so engrossed in the music in front of him. As I walked into the room, I saw what he was playing. It was the Chopin composition.

I sat down next to Finn. He stopped playing; he had tears in his eyes. "We're the first people to hear this," he said. "It's never been published."

I choked up. I'd considered its material value, but not its intrinsic one. Under Nazi occupation, the penalty for playing Chopin's music was death.

"It is magnificent," I said. "Please. Keep playing."

And he continued. He struggled as it picked up speed, but the air filled with notes that rose and fell with romantic abandon. I had never heard such beautiful music. It spoke to my soul; a composition so powerful that it had the ability to provide refuge and healing to two survivors. We were both sobbing when the music finished.

CHAPTER FORTY-FIVE

※❋※

I WATCHED THROUGH THE WINDOW AS THE MEN WALKED UP onto the porch and knocked on the door. I could feel my heart pounding through my sweater. What if I didn't answer? Was it too late to change my mind?

Finn let them in.

One man looked familiar, the older man with dark hair. He had on the same fedora as before, and I thought he was wearing the same suit. The other man was younger, but he had an official air about him that made me believe he was in charge. He was also the first to speak, and said his name was Bob Schraan.

"We are very anxious to see this document you mentioned on the phone," Mr. Schraan said.

Finn looked at me before speaking. "You must understand that my wife is cooperating by turning it over to you. That she took it from the Nazis and brought it to the U.S. with the distinct purpose of protecting the composition."

The older one raised his eyebrows. "Did you declare ownership of this upon your entrance into the United States?"

"No, of course I didn't," I said.

"And may I ask why you didn't?"

I held my hands at my side so I wouldn't look nervous. What could I say? That I planned to sell it if I needed money?

Finn spoke up before I could answer. "She wasn't sure who to trust. My wife saved a very valuable composition. She risked her life by stealing it from a Nazi SS officer. To question her motives is unacceptable. And if you continue to do so, we will find someone else to speak to."

I stared at him open-mouthed. I couldn't help but marvel at my husband.

Finn continued. "Before we turn it over, we will need a written document that absolves Roza from any wrongdoing by bringing the composition into the country."

The younger man held up his hand. "Mr. Erickson, we have no plans to take any action against your wife. We know that this composition, regardless of its worth, could very easily have been destroyed by the Nazis if she hadn't saved it."

Finn continued. "We also want your help in getting Roza's mother and brother out of Hungary. As aristocrats, their safety is in question."

The men looked at each other for a long moment before they finally nodded. My heart filled with gratitude for Finn. I would convince Mama to leave, which would not be as hard now that she had experienced life under Communist rule.

Mr. Schraan turned to me. "You have accomplished a very heroic act by smuggling this manuscript away from Hauser, who was known for several murderous acts, without regard to your own well-being. And we appreciate your willingness now to turn it over to the U.S. State Department. We are happy to provide you any written document you want from us." He paused. "And we will help your family cross to the western border."

He wrote this down on official U.S. State Department paper and signed it before handing it to me.

"What are you going to do with the composition?" I couldn't imagine what would happen if the Communists got their hands on it.

"I'm not sure where it will go, but I can guarantee you this won't end up in Communist hands," he said.

Finn looked at me. I reluctantly nodded okay.

I let out a breath as Finn left to get the manuscript. "May I offer you some tea?"

Both men nodded. "That would be great, Mrs. Erickson," Mr. Schraan said.

As I left, the older man bent down to pet Karola, who hissed at him and bit his hand.

"Good kitty," I said.

A FEW DAYS LATER, JACK KNOCKED ON OUR DOOR. I LET HIM in. "Finn is upstairs getting ready for work," I told him.

Jack had on his work uniform from the depot, a pair of denim overalls over a long-sleeved shirt. He held his cap in his hands, and was using a cane today instead of the crutch that usually accompanied him. I wondered if he had his new artificial leg, but it felt rude to ask him about it.

"I need to speak with him," Jack said.

"Please sit down. I will get him."

I returned a moment later. "He is dressing. He will be down in a minute. Is something wrong?"

I noticed now that Jack's eyes wouldn't meet mine.

"I'm sorry if I caused you a hard time, but blood is thicker than water, you know," he said, and when he looked at me, he seemed embarrassed. "I was only looking out for my brother."

I nodded. He'd ratted me out, but I couldn't be as angry with him as I wanted to be. If he hadn't told Finn, the last few days wouldn't have happened, and I'd still be planning to leave. I still didn't like Jack, but he would always be Finn's brother, someone I'd have to put up with.

"How is work?" I asked him, wondering if that's why he was here.

"It's not what I want," he muttered. "But it pays the bills. Pearl got a job as a bank teller. She makes as much as I do. You ever hear of such a thing? A woman getting paid as much as a man?"

"I have heard of many women who earn more money than men," I said. "If they are capable, why shouldn't they?"

"It's not right, that's why. Don't get me wrong. I know Finn was trying to help me, but he could have pushed for a porter's job for someone who gave a leg for the war. I'm cleaning out toilets and sweeping the floor and emptying garbage all day."

Finn walked into the room just then. "I already told you. You have to work your way up. That's the way it is there. Is that what you wanted to see me about?"

"No," Jack said standing. "It's about Lou."

"What about him?"

Jack fidgeted with his hat. "There's no easy way to tell you this so I'm just gonna come out with it. Lou killed himself last night."

Finn's face blanched. "Killed himself?"

"He hung himself. Poor bastard. I guess he couldn't take it any longer."

Finn sat down, visibly shaken. I sat next to him and took his arm. "That is awful," I said. "Does he have any family?"

Jack shook his head. "None that we know of. Or none that wanted to have anything to do with him."

"Why? Because he fought bravely for his country? Is that how heroes are treated here? He needed help with his drinking. He lost his mind serving in the war. You lose a limb and think the whole world owes you."

Jack looked taken aback. "Listen here . . ."

"Roza," Finn said. "Please don't say . . ."

I stood up. "I must say something. You two are brothers. You have both suffered from the war. It is time to acknowledge that neither suffering is worse than the other."

Jack sniffed. Finn stared at the coffee table.

"I will leave now," I said, wondering if I'd spoken out of turn. Before I left the room, I stopped. "If Lou had family who cared for him, would he be dead now?"

THE FUNERAL WAS A GRAVESIDE SERVICE ON A CEMETERY hill with a few men in attendance, mostly former military men. A chilly wind blew across the leaf-strewn ground. But Lou garnered a full military escort and honors. Jack and Finn wore their uniforms. Finn stood rigidly beside the flag-draped casket attended to by members of the American Legion. I held his arm tightly, as though keeping him from getting too close. As though the desperation that had driven Lou to take his life would spread to Finn, and I was the only tether from that despair.

The night after Jack broke the news about Lou had been the worst. Finn had thrashed about the bed, screaming for his men to take cover, trying to ward off the Germans in his dreams.

I had put my arms around him, wiped his forehead, and coaxed him out of it, until at last he registered my presence, red-faced and embarrassed at having almost knocked me off the bed.

"I'm so sorry," he'd said, holding me close.

"Do not be sorry," I'd reprimanded him. "The demons of war are responsible."

But at the funeral I worried my life would become one of care-taking. I'd spent my whole life in pursuit of my own dreams; could I now spend the rest of it keeping my husband from the brink of hopelessness? What if I failed? What would my life be like then?

Pearl stood at Jack's side during the funeral. My mother had owned several fur coats; I could tell immediately that the brown fur Pearl was wearing was fake by the blunt tips of the strands, and because I knew Pearl couldn't afford a real one.

Afterward, as Finn spoke with other men in uniform, Pearl approached me. She had a lit cigarette in her hands. The smoke curled up into the cold air.

"Jack told me you read him the riot act."

"What is riot act?" I asked, confused.

"You bawled him out. Not that he didn't deserve it. I guess it made him think about things more. About Finn, and his nightmares. He said he still has them?"

"Yes," I admitted.

"He used to sleep like a baby when I knew him before the war." Her cheeks turned pink. "Not that he ever slept over or anything like that."

I remembered why I didn't like this woman.

"Finn was different when he came back. He didn't smile anymore. He barely talked. And I know Jack can be mean sometimes," Pearl continued. "He says things to make other people feel bad, but it's just because he feels bad about himself."

"You really care about Jack, don't you?"

Pearl flicked the ashes of her cigarette on the ground. "Well, I ought to since we're going to get married."

"Congratulations." I wasn't sure if I was happy about this news. I doubted that Pearl was marrying Jack to get close to Finn, but I still didn't trust her. Was she a woman who latched on to whoever was available, or easiest? First Finn, whom she left because she didn't want to wait for him; then another man she didn't get along with; and now Jack, who wasn't easy to get along with. Would she leave Jack for another man? Pearl wasn't exactly ugly, although her eyes were too narrow and her mouth too small and her hips too wide. And now I would have to deal with her at family functions.

"Thanks. I'm going to have Jack's baby."

"Oh. Well, congratulations on that too."

She nodded. "I just wanted to tell you that Jack apologized to

Finn. He understands that shell-shock can be just as bad as losing a leg. Especially after what happened to Lou."

I nodded. I appreciated that Jack made the first move toward peace with his brother.

"It's good to see Finn looking more like himself again," Pearl said. "He looks happy when he's with you."

And that's when I decided I would make peace with Pearl too.

"Perhaps you and Jack could come to dinner next week," I offered. I still hadn't invited Finn's parents. That would have to wait.

"Yeah, that would be nice," Pearl replied. She looked over at the gravesite. "I should have come with you when you stopped to help Lou. I feel bad about it. But Lou's always been kind of crazy, in case you're thinking Finn will end up like him. They're not the same. You don't have to worry about that happening to Finn."

I nodded my thanks. That was the nicest thing Pearl had ever said to me.

CHAPTER FORTY-SIX

PERHAPS THIS WAS A MISTAKE. IT WAS NOVEMBER, THREE months since I'd last seen Joe. So much had happened.

I fussed with my dark, wavy hair, which had grown several inches since my arrival in the U.S. I was nervous about seeing Joe again. My stomach twisted, and the toast and coffee I'd had that morning threatened to come up. But Finn had trusted me to go by myself, even as he'd offered to come along, hoping perhaps that I'd say yes?

"This I must do alone," I said.

He'd accompanied me to the train and kissed me long and hard before I left, as though he worried I'd forget him during the short trip to St. Paul.

"I almost let you go before," he said in a worried voice. "I didn't think I deserved to be married to someone as wonderful as you."

I had assured him he had no reason to worry. But now as I sat on a park bench outside the domed conservatory in St. Paul, I wondered if I was wrong. For one thing, I should have met Joe at a restaurant, where it would be easier to keep my feelings in check. And two, it was freezing out; my toes felt like icicles and my nose kept running.

I almost went inside to wait for him, but then I saw him approaching. He carried a bouquet of roses in his hands, and for an instant I remembered that day on the train platform, when I'd waited an interminable amount of time for him to come and imagined him just like this. I was tempted to fall into his arms as if these past months had never happened.

Perhaps this was a mistake, I thought again, for how could I separate that person who had spent almost two years fantasizing about her life with this man from the woman I was now?

And before I had a chance to stop him, Joe sat the flowers on the bench and leaned down and kissed me. It took me back to that first night I'd met him, when he had walked me home and kissed me in the early hours of dawn. His kiss had held promise then, and I felt it again on his lips. But I wasn't certain what it promised this time.

"Darling," he said, and I pulled away before I fell under his spell again. How could I allow myself to feel this way after all that had passed between me and Finn? I felt like a yo-yo being pulled back and forth. I had to put a stop to it.

"I'm cold," I said. "Could we go inside?"

"Yes, of course." He picked up the bouquet and took my arm.

Inside the Conservatory, the aroma of fresh flowers overpowered the roses in Joe's arms. I was thankful for the warmth. We followed the rocky path through the glass-domed Victorian garden, taking in the scent and sights.

"Do you remember when you took me on a tour of the Belvedere Gardens in Vienna?" Joe said.

I nodded. During the war the exquisitely manicured shrubbery had fallen into disrepair, but it was still magnificent to see. I remembered pointing out windows in the damaged Schönbrunn Palace, where I'd once dined and danced with royalty.

"You danced with royalty?" Joe had made a whistling sound.

I hadn't told him that to brag, but to understand how it was before, how much things had changed during the war. We'd only spent three months together, but it had been three intense months in which we'd clung to one another, and now, years later, it was easy to think we could slip back into that same closeness.

"It seems so long ago, doesn't it?" I said, thinking of all that had happened since then.

"There's a sunken garden you have to see," Joe said, guiding me along the path. "It's the most romantic place here."

Mariska had said that anyone could find romance among the delicate and sweet-smelling flowers of the Conservatory. I should not have come here.

It was hard not to get caught up in Joe's charismatic charm. He had rescued me from the horrors of war. He had sent life-saving food and money after the war. He was forever my handsome prince.

But I reminded myself that he betrayed me when I needed him most. That Finn was at home waiting for me.

"Are you okay?" Joe asked, for I was walking unsteadily down the stairs.

"Just a bit queasy," I said, and leaned on him for support.

It was humid inside, and I sat down on a bench hidden deep in the ferns, listening to the gurgling of water from a miniature waterfall nearby. It was early, and we were alone. The bench was set back, away from the path.

I took an envelope out of my handbag and handed it to Joe.

He looked inside. "You paid me back in full already?"

I nodded, but didn't mention that Finn had added to the amount from my business, that he didn't want me owing Joe money.

"You're amazing," Joe said and put his arm around me.

My heart fluttered. He still made me feel that way, as if I were melting in his arms like a shapeless piece of wax that only his caresses could mold into the woman I was meant to be.

Was it possible to love two men at the same time?

"I told you about my divorce," he reminded me. "It will be final in a few weeks."

I caught my breath at those words. At our last meeting I had professed my love to him.

"I'll be a free man," Joe said.

"Joe," I said, forcing out the words, "I have decided that I must honor my marriage."

He put the bouquet down on the ground and took both of my hands in his. "But you belong with me, you said so yourself."

"I know I said that. I thought so at the time. But things have changed."

"Are you saying you no longer love me? Is that what you're saying?"

I wondered how it became so hot so suddenly. I started to fan myself with my handbag. My eyes were filling despite my determination not to cry.

"You know that I have always loved you, Joe. You will always have a special place in my heart. But I must not see you again."

"Roza, I got a divorce so that I could marry you."

"I did not ask you to get a divorce."

"You said you loved me. You can come with me now. Do what your heart tells you, not some formal dictates of morality. Forget everything that happened and remember why you came to America in the first place."

The room was spinning now. My head felt light and dizzy, and my stomach cramped. What made me think I was strong enough to do this on my own?

"I came to America to marry you," I said.

He touched my cheek with his hand. "You did. And now you can. It's easier than you think, darling. It's just you and me here. No one telling us what to do."

I shook my head as if to rid it of his words, his sway. "No. You betrayed me once, Joe. Now you want to interfere with my marriage."

"No," he insisted, "I made a mistake that I'm trying to correct.

You gave yourself to me before I left Vienna. You gave me your heart and soul. You said so yourself."

"I cannot trust you."

"You can trust me, Roza." He was pleading now, on his knees in front of me. "I won't leave you again. Believe me."

"It is too late."

I stood then, wanting to get away from him, from his charm and sensuousness, and his persuasive words that he turned against me. I had Finn now. He was my rock, my safe place. I concentrated on my hand in his, on how it made me feel. I remembered our lovemaking, how Finn had stood up for me in front of the State Department. I couldn't leave him.

I only knew that the room was spinning, that I had to get away.

"Roza. Don't leave."

Joe's words lacked shape and sounded strange. I took a step, but the spinning became whirling, and then I couldn't hear the gurgling water anymore, and then I couldn't see Joe. Everything went dark.

CHAPTER FORTY-SEVEN

I AWOKE TO BRIGHT LIGHTS AND A STERILE SMELL. I WAS IN A hospital bed in a small room with whitewashed walls. A window looked out upon tree branches that were almost bare, except for a few clinging yellow leaves.

I had on a white gown, not my dress, and a blanket was drawn up just below my neck. I attempted to sit up, but felt cramping and a rush of liquid between my legs, and lay back down.

Voices floated into the room. Women's voices.

A nurse approached, an older no-nonsense-looking woman with tight gray curls who tucked my blanket in on the sides with precision strokes of her hands. "Mrs. Erickson, how are you feeling?" Her voice sounded singsong, as though this was simply a greeting rather than a question that held real meaning.

"Silly," I replied.

"There's no need to feel that way, but you have to lie still. The doctor will be in shortly."

"But I only passed out . . ."

"Don't attempt to get up," the nurse reprimanded me.

"Is my . . . husband here?" Had Joe brought me here? Was he waiting outside the room?

"We've called him. He'll be here shortly."

"That is good," I said, feeling relieved.

The doctor entered just then, an elderly man who matched the nurse in age. He was kinder than the nurse, though. He uncovered my arm from beneath the blanket and took my pulse. "Mrs. Erickson, you put a scare in us. You lost a lot of blood."

"I . . . did?"

"Yes. I'm afraid you've had a miscarriage. But not to worry. You're in fine shape to have children, and you can try again as soon as you're able."

I didn't even know I was pregnant! "But I have not missed my time of the month," I said, remembering that my last menstruation had been very light and lasted only two days, and I hadn't had one yet this month.

"You were very early along, so that's why we were surprised by the amount of blood. You should be fine to go home tomorrow, though. Just take it easy awhile. Strictly bedrest for the next week."

"Thank you," I said.

He patted my hand. "Now don't feel too depressed about this. It's common to have a miscarriage and doesn't mean you won't have a house full of children in a few years. I recommend that you and your husband keep trying."

After he left, I stared at the tiled ceiling, wondering what I would say to Finn. I hadn't expected to become pregnant so quickly. The last three months Finn and I had been making up for the early months of our marriage. Our lovemaking helped lessen the nightmares for us both. Now, I couldn't wait for him to return from his trips.

And knowing I had been carrying Finn's child, a different face took shape in my mind than the ones I'd fantasized about for two years. This child would have had my dark curly hair and Finn's reassuring hands and kind eyes. This child that no longer was.

"There's a 'family' friend waiting to see you," the nurse said, and her voice dripped with judgment. "Shall I show him in?"

"Yes. Please."

Joe entered a moment later, his hat in his hands, his eyes full of concern. He came over and took my hand. "I'm sorry, Roza. I didn't know. Are you okay?"

"Yes, I am fine. I did not know either, Joe. It was a complete surprise to me." I felt a sudden urge to cry; my eyes filled with the loss of a baby I didn't even have a chance to acknowledge. I remembered how I'd worried after Joe left Vienna that I would be pregnant and have to deliver a child whose fate would be precarious at best. After the Russians came, abortions in Vienna were as common as the cold. And now, when I least expected it, when I wasn't even considering the possibility, a new life had taken root inside me.

"I'll bring you back to my flat and take care of you, darling."

I squeezed Joe's hand. "You must realize I cannot leave my husband now."

"Don't say that . . ."

"I must. You will always be special to me, Joe. I will always love you because you were my handsome rescuer, my prince. Remember how we used to say, 'the past is past' as a way to get through the horrors we read about and saw? Those emaciated people who came back from the camps by the truckloads? We only wanted to live in the present, to start a new life and forget the past.

"But who are we, if we forget everything that came before? What have we discovered about ourselves if we don't acknowledge our mistakes or learn from the past? We must remember the good as well as the bad. Perhaps, especially, we must remember the horrors of the war. So that it never happens again.

"I loved you, Joe. I will remember our love. But I will also remember that you abandoned me when I needed you. I can forgive you now because I have a new life and a new husband. And I love my husband. I love Finn."

Until I said those words out loud, I wasn't sure they were true. But our child! I had lost our child! We had created a life together and I was overcome with deep sorrow. I wanted nothing more than my husband by my side now.

Joe removed his hand. He looked visibly shaken, this confident man who rarely had anyone say no to him. Was he so sure that I would come with him? Didn't he ever give thought to the idea that I might say no?

"You belong to me, Roza."

I lifted my head up. "Belong to you? You think because I agreed to marry you first that you have any say in my life now? I have always made my own way in life; first as a ballerina, and then in surviving the war without my family to help. I do not belong to you, Joe. I belong to no one."

"You sound sure of your decision," he said, "but you didn't speak that way when we met before. Are you sure this is what you want, Roza? Do you need more time? Because if I walk out that door, I'll be out of your life forever."

I started crying. "This is what I want, Joe. I do not need time. I need you to leave." It came out raggedly between my tears.

He looked defeated. "Fine," he said in an unkind voice. "But you'll regret it, Roza."

He turned to walk out, but he stopped when he saw Finn, who was standing in the doorway. Finn's arms were folded, and he glared at Joe, not letting him pass.

"I won't ever let her regret it," Finn said, daring Joe to contradict him. "I'll make her the happiest woman in the world."

"Can you?" Joe asked, smirking. "Can you make her love you the way she loves me?"

Finn's hands curled into fists.

"Yes, he can," I said in a defiant voice, and both men turned toward me. "I do love him, Joe. I thought I loved you, but you let me down. Finn will never do that."

Joe sniffed. "So you're throwing *me* over? For him?"

"Yes. I am. It is my choice to make. And I choose Finn. I want you out of my life forever." I knew it wasn't easy for Joe to accept. His charm and good looks had usually gotten him what he wanted. It felt good to say it, not in a vengeful way, but as a weight off my shoulders, because I had finally proclaimed my love for my husband out loud. I was done with Joe.

He looked at Finn, who still blocked the doorway. Joe stuck out his hand. "Then I guess the better man won." But his voice held contempt.

Finn stared at him a long moment. I wasn't sure if he was going to shake Joe's hand or slug him. But he relented and shook his hand.

"Don't ever contact my wife again," he said, before he let him pass.

Then Finn rushed to my bedside and smothered me with kisses.

CHAPTER FORTY-EIGHT

ONE YEAR LATER

I TROMPED DOWN THE COLD SIDEWALK, SNOW CRUNCHING beneath my boots. The air was brisk, and gray clouds overhead held a promise of more snow to add to the mounting piles that lined the streets.

I walked carefully, watching my steps so I didn't slip as I made my way downtown. I passed Belinda's Tudor-style house and briefly remembered the invitation I'd received last month to a social gathering, one on which I'd hastily scribbled an apology. It seemed Roza's Ballet Academy had made me a prominent member of the community, and thus a desired guest.

I felt a certain smugness in sending my regrets. Should I feel this way? Perhaps not, but I couldn't help but enjoy snubbing the women who'd once snubbed me. What was that saying? A leopard can't change its spots? I had accepted lately that I was still an aristocrat at heart no matter how much my circumstances had changed. I didn't expect deferential treatment, but I did expect good manners. And those women had none.

When I finally reached Nellie's café, I went inside and sat down on the same stool I always sat on but found that my bulging coat didn't allow for as much room as before.

"You're going to need two stools pretty soon," Nellie said.

"Ugh. That is not funny."

Etta sat down next to me. "You're carrying high just like I carried Alice. That means it's a girl."

That was what Mariska had told me too. And Mariska was always right about these things.

"By the way, Alice is so excited. She's never performed on a real stage before. I think the entire town will be in attendance."

"*The Nutcracker* is a favorite of many people," I said, rubbing my stomach. The fact that tickets had sold out made me proud. I was responsible for bringing ballet to this town, a bit of culture to a place that traditionally focused more on stone cutting and lumber than the arts. "I am grateful for all the help too. I could not do this alone in my condition."

Not only had several high school students volunteered to help with everything from costumes to scenery design, but I had "borrowed" a few ballerinas from the Twin Cities Ballet Company to add depth to the production. Finn had constructed some of the sets, and he would be at the performance. And of course, my friends were there to help as always.

"They only show up for your cookies," I told Nellie, who denied it, but secretly looked pleased.

It would be hard to watch others dance the roles I had once performed, especially when I could barely move with any grace, let alone do a plié. There would be other performances. I would dance again, perhaps not professionally, but I planned to participate in recitals. It would always be a part of me, just as my countess title would be part of me. For what if I completely ignored the past? What good came of forgetting my heritage? To forget Papa and Mama and János and Greta? And all the people I'd danced with? They made me who I was.

Mama and János had escaped to Austria, with the help of the

State Department. They were still awaiting their visas to travel to the U.S. I hoped they would arrive before the baby's birth. The Chopin manuscript had helped me, after all.

Finn had to learn to live with his past as well. He talked more about his war experiences, opening up a little at a time, like a slow-blooming flower. He might always struggle, but I would be there to support him and stand by him. He would honor his men by living life to the fullest.

Speak of the devil! Finn entered just then, his collar turned up against the wind, his cheeks pink from the cold. Flakes of snow dotted his brown hair, and he shook his head. Finn had an easy smile lately; I thought it was due to my expanding stomach.

I felt the baby kick and smiled. *This daughter of mine* was already practicing her dance moves.

I greeted Finn with a kiss. "*This daughter of yours* is driving me crazy. She won't stop kicking."

"Takes after her mother, I see. But what if it's a boy?"

"If it's a boy, we'll name him after you."

"Did I tell you my real name was Finlay Erickson?"

My eyes widened. "I did not know. But now that I think of it, Finlay is the perfect name for a male ballet dancer. He will be the best in America."

"Then he will have gotten only his name from me," Finn said with a carefree laugh.

"If he is handsome and kind, he will get much more from his father," I reassured him, and for only the second time since I'd met Finn, I saw his boyish grin return.

"And he or she will inherit some class from a countess mother," Finn added.

"You have a lot of dreams for this child, don't you?" Nellie said.

"Of course I do," I replied. "After all, America is the land of dreams. And I found mine. His name is Finn Erickson."

And this American countess hugged her American husband.

MINNEAPOLIS STAR NEWSPAPER

September 17, 1950

IN THIS CORNER

CECIL ANDERS

REMEMBER THE HUNGARIAN countess for whom This Corner landed a husband after several thousand proposals were sent in for her? Llona and her husband stopped in Minneapolis the other day. They're still very happily married. With them they had their first child—a son, eight months old. That was one project that worked out pretty well, it would seem . . .

AUTHOR'S NOTE

THE JILTED COUNTESS IS INSPIRED by a true story, one I first read about in 2015 in Curt Brown's history corner of *The Minneapolis Star Tribune*. (It's also included in his book *Frozen History: Amazing Tales from Minnesota's Past*.) A mysterious countess, who ended up in Minnesota, jilted by her fiancé two weeks before her visa was due to expire, appeared desperate for a spouse. To add to the mystery, when reporter Cedric Adams (or Cecil Anders as I call him in the novel) first shared her story, she used a fake name. I was immediately drawn to the idea of this bachelorette the newspaper named Llona, who ended up with 1,786 offers of marriage, perhaps a world record, and who chose to settle in a small Minnesota town, with a stranger no less, rather than go back to her home country.

No one knew what became of her, or what her real name was, despite offers by magazines and radio shows who wanted to cover this amazing woman's story. As a writer, I was intrigued by a cultured countess trying to fit into life in a small Minnesota community. Did she ever cross paths with the GI who swept her off her feet in Austria, and later married someone else just months before she arrived in Minnesota? Did she find happiness with the husband she chose, one she'd had just one date with before they married? This is the fairy dust of fiction, and my imagination was ignited.

Although much of the story is fictional (after all, I only had part of the story), I did use Cedric Adams's actual articles from *The Minneapolis Star* newspaper (with permission). The real countess did go on three dates and settle in a Minnesota town. And as far as I know, she did find happiness in the U.S.

After I'd written my fictional story of the countess, I decided I wanted to find the real version, if just to see how she'd fared, and whether she was even still alive. Would she want to tell her story now, after all these years? Or did she still want to protect her privacy, to remain anonymous these many years later?

The only thing I had to go on was the picture that was used and a vague description—that she was born in Vienna and lived in Hungary, where her father served as a minister to Austria before World War II. They lost everything in the war.

I spent a great deal of time at the Minnesota History Center Library looking for clues to her real identity, hoping that she might still be living in the Midwest or have family here. I searched marriage licenses, looking for a name that sounded like a countess.

I found out through Cedric Adams's articles that her husband was an Army captain, that he became a mechanical engineer, and that they moved to northern Minnesota. Later, they moved to Illinois and had a baby boy sometime during the second year of marriage. They received numerous offers from *Look* magazine, radio networks, and others, but turned them all down to protect their privacy (a fact that seems unlikely today with all the reality TV shows).

I'm still searching for her and will continue to do so, but, of course, will protect her privacy if that's still her wish. I'm hoping that these many years later, if she's still alive, she might want to share her incredible true story.

And in the meantime, I hope you enjoy my rendition of *The Jilted Countess*.

ACKNOWLEDGMENTS

IT TOOK TEN YEARS TO BRING THIS NOVEL TO LIFE, BUT RO-za's story never left my mind. I'm so glad I'm finally able to share it with you. And I owe many people for their help along the way. My friend Janet Graber, to whom this book is dedicated, sent me Curt Brown's article in *The Minneapolis Star Tribune* in 2015 and said that I should write this story. It took me several years to do so, but I never wavered, as this story was too great a gift. My agent, Marly Rusoff, is the best person to have in my corner—I'm so grateful for her. My editor, Sara Nelson, saw the potential of this "first bachelorette" story, and I'm thrilled she connected with it. Thank you to Edie Astley and Yelena Nesbit, as well as Suzette Lam, Jane Cavolina, Joanne O'Neill, and Megan Looney. Thank you also to Megan Beatie at Megan Beatie Communications.

My gratitude goes out to Alexandra Shelley, who helped me revise portions of this book when it was a terrible draft. And to my writing group members: Janet Graber, Nolan Zavoral, Pat Schafer, Ricki Thompson, Jane O'Reilly, Susan Latta, Carol Iverson, and Aimee Bissonette, who have given me feedback on this story for ten years—that's what you call generous!

A special thank you to Emese Drew, a Hungarian who lives in Minnesota, who graciously read my novel. And thanks most of all to my family, who gave me space and time to write, and cheered me on through it all.

ABOUT THE AUTHOR

LORETTA ELLSWORTH IS THE AUTHOR OF THE HISTORICAL novels *The French Winemaker's Daughter* and *Stars Over Clear Lake*, and five novels for younger readers—*The Shrouding Woman, In Search of Mockingbird, In a Heartbeat, Unforgettable,* and *Tangle-Knot.* Her books have received many accolades, including ALA Teens' Top Ten, the Midwest Booksellers Choice Award, *Kirkus Reviews* Critic's Pick, the International Literacy Association Notable Book Award, the Bulletin of the Center for Children's Books Choice Award, the Northeastern Minnesota Book Award, and the Charlotte Award.

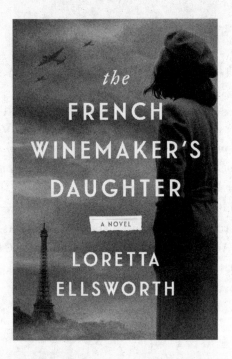